JUST BEFORE TOO LATE

by
Mel Currie

(of Channing Memorial UU)

Just before too Late © 2019
By Mel Currie
ISBN: 978-1-7341911-0-3

I dedicate this book to my family, including my ancestors - those known and those unknown to me.

CONTENTS

A FEVER OF UNKNOWN ORIGIN

I *guess it's too late. You got me started.*

One hundred and fifty centuries ago my ancestors crossed the Bering Land Bridge and established a receiving line in North America. Then they waited for my European ancestors to conquer the Atlantic and drag my African ancestors to the Big Bang. And now who are our allies? The Indians aren't. The whites aren't. The new immigrants from Africa sure as hell are not. Putting all the posturing and sloganeering aside, we don't even embrace ourselves most days. We're fallout from the collision, post-Contact detritus. We're stuck in history's oven and that's ugly business: the ultimate mongrels - drunken Indian, cowed African, two-faced white man, what one-drop-rule Plecker called one of the most undesirable racial intermixtures known. The latest news flash from academia is that race is a social construct. In our case, the construct's foundation is empty pride and a deluxe cell-phone plan (pot-to-piss-in not included). It's the stuff holy books are made of.

I don't spend much time wondering if there is a god or gods. It's too big a question. I do mathematics instead. But if I were to consider one of the blueprints offered by a major religion, my conclusion would have to be that god is not worried about efficiency. He's quite willing to take several million people and grind them together for five hundred years to produce a few prophets, or whatever you want to call them, to herald a new age. Besides, efficiency would rob the story of biblical majesty. So, maybe Plecker in Virginia and his cronies elsewhere were simply divine border collies, policing the color line until all the arrangements were made. In the meantime, the rest of the world gets a whiff of the herd – the smell of things to come. They watch us through the window, their noses pressed hideously against the glass. God softens them up for a hundred years with Jazz because he has to get the civilizations of the world accustomed to listening. English becomes the world language and his new human concoction gives it flavor, generation after generation. He lets the universe get used to seeing us as spokespersons, Aunt Jemima, Uncle Ben. And when they're leaning forward to hear more, he gives them Miles Davis, who turns his back on them and blows his horn. Relenting somewhat, he offers *the likes of James Earl Jones. Then back with Uncle Ben and Aunt Jemima, except that he calls them Colin Powell and Condoleezza Rice. And then we have to think about what messiah will be heralded and if that messiah has already been here. Clearly, it wasn't Martin Luther King. He's morphed into a federal holiday.*

Then a high-pitched voice said, "Tell 'em how you feel!" And Paul McCarahan woke up.

What he felt was the fever. It was still there, along with the T-shirt soaked through. You might call it night sweat, but it was daytime. Paul had taken his first dose of antibiotic two hours earlier. His doctor, after pronouncing the letters FUO in apparent frustration, prescribed a shotgun blast against any infection that might be lurking and causing the Fever of Unknown Origin. Paul could either go into the hospital for further tests or try the antibiotic. And if he had been a cowardly man, he would have chosen the hospital, given all that had transpired in the past week.

First, there was the phone call from a Pittsburgh Post-Gazette reporter who wanted to talk. He thought that after twenty years it was time to revisit the so-called "Geometry Killing." Was Paul up for an interview? "Sorry," Paul had said. "Sorry, but I might be dead myself in a few days." The reporter tried to persuade Paul that the story would be better if he provided some input. An article would be written, one way or the other. Paul said he would get back to him if he survived the fever.

Paul's doctor emanated good cheer, even though it had been seven days and he still didn't have a diagnosis. He made some lame joke about the West Nile virus running rampant on the Allegheny. "You're basically healthy, Paul. Healthier than any fifty-eight-year-old man I've ever seen. This thing's going to lift." It had lifted on day five and come back on day six. Now here he was on day eight with a sweet glaze of sweat covering the bald portion of his head and kinking up what was left of his hair.

Paul rolled across the bed and then stood. He felt less zombie-like than he had earlier in the day. In the bathroom he searched his face and it provided a sense of comfort. It was not a matter of vanity, just assurance that he was still intact. Besides, his face was not among the more sympathetic. Wiry eyebrows arched over large, dark eyes that even in innocent situations caused many people a degree of anxiety; that perhaps not everything met with the gentleman's approval. But the face was seamless and it could be granted that he looked no older than his fifty-eight years. Even with the long-established male-pattern baldness and the crisp, gray hairs in his close-cropped beard, the casual observer would not have necessarily guessed that he came of age at the height of the Vietnam War. McCarahan had skin the color of an autumn leaf, one that still clung to the tree just before the onset of winter, no longer the brilliant hues of October. Just one fading flush away from plain brown and somber.

Paul accepted that his doctor was stumped when he changed the subject and revealed that he had always thought that Paul had gotten a bum rap from the news media. "You know that Geometry Killing business, just because you're a mathematician. Paul said, Yeah." He hadn't said a whole lot more twenty years earlier when a gang of reporters had tried to capture his emotional state after what McCarahan said was an accident. His response was, "I guess it's always a bad thing when anyone dies this way." Of course, implicit was "... even a white cop who was just acquitted a week ago of murdering a black teenager." Paul said "Yeah" again to whatever the doctor had said.

Three days after the accident, Paul somewhat callously told a reporter that he didn't think that it was possible for the State of Pennsylvania to indict him, given that he hadn't even received a traffic ticket. Paul added that the lady who knocked his car into the cop, like an expert pool player, might be a candidate. She was the one who made the left turn through the intersection after the light turned red. "Besides, I don't know a whole lot about angles. I'm not a geometer. I'm a topologist." That's how the Geometry Killing was born. The catchy name was Paul's fault. But he was right about the legal system. There was no indictment.

In fact, some sort of intuition had been in play, a rare moment of extreme clarity. Everything worked and it was conceived so quickly that, though purposeful, it would be hard to call it premeditated. This was beyond calculation. Paul had experienced maybe a half-dozen moments like this in his life. One was when he suddenly saw through to the foundation of a theorem that would become the crown jewel of his doctoral dissertation.

Paul had spotted Stan Yaros, unmistakably Yaros, crossing the street and knew he was going to kill him. He crushed him against a building at the corner of Grant and Fifth during rush hour. People ran screaming like animals from the spot, some of them nearly getting run over in the traffic, which continued unabated. For a few seconds, Paul looked through the windshield at Yaros, Yaros with the question mark on his face. Paul's eyes said, "I am the answer, mother fucker." Yaros died on the spot and a lot of stories got written about the cold Pitt mathematics prof from the East End.

Paul was at the scene for a couple of hours. When they let him go, he walked into an alley and relieved himself. That's what happens after the excitement dies down. You realize that you have to pee. And at that moment his piss smelled to him like fresh flowers.

***

Paul took his temperature for the sixth time that day. He had taken it three times before he went to the doctor's office. The thermometer read 99.9, down from the high of 100.8 that morning. So maybe the fever was on its way out, 'lifting' as the doctor had said before he prescribed an antibiotic. It was still two degrees above his baseline temperature. Paul muttered, "I'm going to die in this house someday, by myself." The only question was whether or not he killed someone else before that happened.

The bedroom-study held minimal comforts, a box-spring and mattress on the floor. There was also a large wooden desk with a folding chair and a bookshelf. An air conditioner had been jammed clumsily into the window, one of four that he installed shortly after he bought the house. His alarm clock and telephone sat on a 1995 telephone book next to the bed.

The rest of the rooms in the four-bedroom house were furnished after a similar fashion, if they were furnished at all. One of the bedrooms was given over to his genealogy work: boxes with census records, photographs, death certificates, twenty years of record sleuthing, with the oral history that was largely supplied by his paternal grandmother serving as the foundation. There was another folding chair and a card table with a pile of papers detailing the results of DNA analysis that he had persuaded more than a dozen leery relatives to undergo.

Another bedroom was littered with memorabilia from the places he had lived, Germany, Alabama, Connecticut. He had a small box of medals won on the track during his sprinting career at Peabody High School and Yale. There was a plastic bag with newspaper clippings and a certificate that would never be framed, naming him an All-Ivy Selection. Batons from the Penn Relays, Florida Relays, and the 1969 NCAA championships lay side by side. He had a plaque that the National Association of African-American Mathematicians presented him to commemorate a talk he gave in Providence, Rhode Island for the Mathematics Association of America.

Only one room hinted at the amount of money he had been able to squirrel away over the years. His Steinway grand piano stood starkly in the living room. It was the only object in the house that got dusted. It was the one material luxury that Paul had allowed himself. As a teenager, he had sworn that he would master the work of the great pianists from his East End neighborhood: Billy Strayhorn, Erroll Garner, Mary Lou Williams and Ahmad Jamal. By the time he reached twenty-five, he would know that he could not do it. His father once tried to annoy his sister Loretta, Paul's aunt, by saying that he had gone out on a date with Ahmad Jamal's sister. "Just think how well Paul would play if I had spent more time with her." She shot back, "I went out with Ahmad Jamal once. I don't think it rubs off."

Paul bought the house from an Italian woman, who had been late to join the white flight from the East End. And she took a terrible beating on the price. When Paul came back from Alabama to take the job at Pitt, he wanted to buy the frame house a bit further down the street, the house where Ahmad Jamal grew up. But it wasn't available. Instead, he bought the brick house and put a Steinway in it. A few years later the Jamal house was abandoned and falling apart. Most of the houses were simple frame constructions, dating to before World War I. He used to know everyone on the street. Now he knew none of his neighbors.

The street sloped steeply to a dead end and a brush-covered hillside that fell to the railroad tracks. Beyond the tracks was another descent through woods to Washington Boulevard. The tracks followed the boulevard for a mile to the banks of the Allegheny. Paul had grown up in the next block, further up the hill. But when he played on this block as a kid, he could occasionally hear the lions roar in Highland Park Zoo, which was far beyond Washington Boulevard and high on a far hillside, at least a mile away as the crow flies. When he was very young, before his mother left, he and his father would stand above the railroad tracks after dark and fire pellets with a slingshot in the direction of Highland Park. His father made him believe that they were actually hunting big game. He felt an excitement. By the time he was ten years old he rarely spent time with his father. Paul and his friends would sail flat rocks at the trains as they passed. Back then there were commuter trains as well as freight trains. Now the tracks were only used sporadically. In those days, he and his friends would call out to the conductor, pleading, "Throw a flare! Throw a flare! Throw a dirty rotten flare!" And sometimes they did.

On day two of the fever, Paul had received a large manila envelope. Its contents were now on the floor next to the piano, preprints of a paper recently published in the Transactions of the American Mathematical Society. The title was "Topological Avenues in Analytic Number Theory." The author was Paul Edward McCarahan. He always used his middle name on publications, not just the initial. Whenever Paul was asked about the origins of his mathematical ideas, he would always respond that he didn't know. He would say that he was willing to give credit to a muse and he thought that the mathematical muse and the musical muse were the same. After the muse started the ball rolling, Paul worked with the devil on the details. But he hadn't heard from the muse on this paper. He didn't write it and he didn't know who had. On the other hand, here were the preprints, mailed to him, complete with his middle name.

"I am beleaguered." He said this aloud too. A few more shots like this and he could lose his nerve. In celebration of the fever, Paul sat at the piano and played his most recent composition. It was a somber piece and he had given it a Lakota title, Hókhahé, a manly cry meaning something like 'onward.' "I am beleaguered," he said again. "But, so what."

***

The first two times it had been animals. He was twelve years old and he killed a bird in the middle of winter, shot it out of a tree with a BB gun. It hadn't been killed outright. It just lay there in the snow with blood running from its beak. Paul was forced to shoot it again. Days later a dog left the bird, by then headless, next to the curb in front of his house. It wasn't many years after that when he found a rabbit lying by the railroad tracks. The hind legs had been partially severed by a train and its body was encrusted with flies and yellow jackets. Paul had walked further and then come back, knowing that although this was not his doing, he was obligated to finish it. He couldn't let it wait in the heat for the sun to go down. As he lifted a piece of railroad tie above his head, the rabbit tried to lift what was left of his hind leg to ward off the impending blow. Its eyes had bulged. Shaken, Paul missed, had to lift and slam once more.

He felt shame over the bird and sorrow for the rabbit. But Paul would say that killing the cop Yaros did not weigh heavily on him, no more than that other man, nameless to Paul, who had also gone out with a question mark on his face. But these events did have scope. He was only nineteen when the first one happened, the year of the Tet Offensive. Paul was not in Vietnam. He was in Germany, the summer between his sophomore and junior years at Yale. Young men from his neighborhood drifted home from Vietnam in the late sixties and some of them had been initiated into killing too. But for most of them, it had been at a distance, not like Paul's sweaty, grappling dance on a train in the Rhineland. It was the perfect crime, if not being detected is the measure. Paul had not even seen any mention of it in the Düsseldorf paper, *Die Rheinische Post*.

He had never set out to kill either of these men. The German thing could hardly be called a murder. Viewed legally, some might come to the conclusion that he had gone too far. But there were mitigating circumstances. The Geometry Killing was an opportunity that had presented itself, with justice and the law on opposite sides of the fence. In Paul's view, justice had prevailed. Yes, the killings had scope. One was deeply hidden, unshared. One had turned him into a media sensation for months.

Paul felt that the Geometry Killing may have been what made the difference between his getting tenure at Pitt and not getting it. Being a black man decried in the local press had not hurt him in academic circles and it happened while the deliberations for tenure were taking place. This is not to say that Paul's research program had been lackluster. He was the master of creating mathematical baubles, isolated gems of originality. On the other hand, some questioned whether his string of baubles amounted to anything more than a tour de force that ultimately did not advance the state of the art. When the university granted him tenure, he made the front page of the Post-Gazette again.

***

By the time the reporter called back, his temperature had dipped to 99.0 and he felt his strength returning. "I won't do an interview over the telephone. If you want to do an interview, come to my house. And no photos. Seeing my picture in the paper is upsetting for people close to me."

The part about "people close to me" raised a question. There were few people who could be described as close to Paul. One was his sprite-like, seventy-five-year-old lover, and it wouldn't bother Ruth. At any rate, after twenty years there were only a few people who still connected his face with Yaros and Paul preferred that the communal memory not be refreshed.

Ruth would shrug it off. Their relationship was in its fifth year and they had talked about the Yaros matter very little. Once Ruth had joked about it after they had made love. "I'm going to die in your arms and you'll be in the paper again. 'The Geometry Killer finds a new angle and rams old white woman to death in her bed.' Well, these days maybe they won't say 'white.'" Even this was more about her age than it was about Yaros.

He had met Ruth at a bus stop. Most days he didn't drive. He would walk the four miles to campus or use public transportation. It was good for his fitness level. She had been first to speak. "My name's Ruth Gable. My granddaughter had you for calculus." Paul didn't bother to go through the routine about how she happened to know who he was. When she told him her granddaughter's name, he didn't recognize it. "She said you were demanding but fair. She got a B." Paul had been falling under the sway of older women since young adulthood. She was seventy when they met and he was fifty-three.

The first time he visited her, she tried to teach him how to dance. She had been a widow for twenty-two years and she had not danced since long before her husband died. Ruth told him not to worry about precision, just follow the music. She skittered about like a water bug, bouncing around Paul and off him when he failed to follow the music. Ruth had nice legs and small breasts. Her gray hair and summer dress swirled together. Ruth Gable got his attention.

***

God is a useful device if you can talk yourself into it. Paul leaned towards ancestor worship instead, even though he felt slighted by the rather meager pantheon of ancestors he knew to call on. He only researched his paternal line. His mother's genealogy had proven to be beyond his grasp. She was Afro-German, born in Ghana in the twenties. Her maternal grandfather, who was German, had brought her to Germany when she was two years old, a few years before the rise of the Third Reich. As far as Paul could tell, he may have been conceived in his mother's country, but he was not born there.

On his father's side, he knew the surnames of his 2nd great-grandfathers, but the maiden names of two 2nd great-grandmothers had been lost to time or at least to the records of North Carolina and Virginia. The lights went out on most of the branches in the early 1800s. He knew the names of only two ancestors who were actually born in the 1700s. One was a white man born in 1798, a 3rd great-grandfather. The other was an emancipated man, probably of Native American and African descent, who died in Free Town, Brunswick County, Virginia in 1811. From the emancipation papers, Paul concluded that he was sixty-one years old at his death. A listing by the state of his belongings included one gallon of rum and a cowhide.

Paul turned to DNA testing soon after it became available. The existence of a god is questionable, but there certainly is a double helix. Most of this work was complete, the tracking down of cousins and cajoling. He had never met some of the cousins until he asked them to open their mouths and swab. To complete his great-grandparent survey, he still needed to locate a maternal-line descendant of a North Carolina great-grandmother

Paul would have been embarrassed to admit that he had been spurred on by seeing Henry Louis Gates host a PBS show that covered the subject with celebrity subjects Oprah Winfrey, Quincy Jones, Whoopi Goldberg, Ben Carson, and some other names he didn't recognize due to his hit-or-miss relationship with popular culture. Gates was a freshman at Yale when Paul was a senior. So was Carson. Paul loved genealogy and it was as if he had caught these unworthy freshmen flirting with his girlfriend.

Paul pushed it as far as it would go with biogeographical analysis. His father and his younger brother had died by the time the technology was available, but he could test himself, his half-sister Thelma, and a few paternal cousins.

His own analysis read 18% northwestern European, 4% Native American, and 78% sub-Saharan African. No East Asian contribution was found and none had been expected. The Piedmont Siouan bands of Virginia and North Carolina had left their traces. The obligatory contribution from northwestern Europe was in plain view. They all met up with the Bantu speakers. He was fallout from the Big Bang, "one of the most undesirable racial intermixtures known," an intermixture that the census records veiled by labeling a few of his ancestors with the word "mulatto." Paul himself would not be called a mulatto. His looks were suitable for selling insurance in a TV commercial. The oxymoron "unambiguously African American" applied.

His Y-chromosome signature was unusual. It was E1a, making him a descendant on his strict male line from a man who lived perhaps 40000 years ago; a man who was likely one of the aboriginal North Africans. His Y-chromosome had been passed over millennia from father to son with the unmistakable collection of mutations that define the signature. E1a failed to thrive and became a rarity, with a small number of these men, a remnant really, found mainly in Mali and northern Sudan in modern times. A number made their way to the Americas due to the transatlantic slave trade. A few Ashkenazi Jews carried the signature too, a likely legacy of trading settlements in the southern Sahara, pre-Diaspora. Then there were the men with roots in the southeastern United States. They identified as white and had a story about an Anglo-Saxon male line, which the biological examination disputed. E1a was the McCarahan line. A few of Paul's McCarahan cousins had sons, so the

McCarahan version of the signature would be in North America for another generation at least.

The story of his mitochondrial DNA was his mother's strict maternal line. It was a signature found throughout western Africa and not at all surprising, given the little he knew about his mother's origins.

Paul had only one surviving sibling, his sister Thelma, and they were estranged. She was older by four years and his father's daughter by a woman that Paul had met only a few times when he was a child. As was the case for him and his younger brother Fritzi, their father's sister Loretta was effectively Thelma's mother.

Thelma had gotten on Paul's case one too many times. The last time they argued, it was about her accusing him of running around with "decrepit women." Thelma had no Y-chromosome to pass on and Paul continued to pour his legacy into barren vessels. Fritzi had lost his battle with the streets when he was in his early twenties, another E1a man gone.

Paul told Ruth that his Y-chromosome was a dictator, that his Y-chromosome called the shots. He was simply carrying out the agenda of 40,000-year-old mutations. "My prehistoric father is stalking you through me. My Y-chromosome is a divining rod." Ruth had gone quiet for a while. Then she said, "I think my granddaughter was attracted to you. She's been on the west coast a long time now, still no husband. You talk about your family tree all the time..."

He let her off the hook. "I think I'm going to remain a terminal node on the tree." At this point, he felt that nothing could happen for him sexually with a woman young enough to be fertile. Years of false starts were convincing. Out of the blocks too fast or not out of the blocks at all – frozen as the starter's pistol sounded. As time passed, he determined that he liked a woman's hormones to be delicately distributed, spread thin. Otherwise, the woman was too slippery. With Ruth, he could find sexual toeholds and make love to her imperfections. "That's right, Ruth. I'm a terminal node."

She shrugged. "Have it your way."

Paul was actually in a terminating frame of mind, twenty years after the Geometry Killing and forty years after the choreography on the train. He was feeling a twenty-year schedule in his bones, with his divining rod active and guiding him to his next opportunity, some man who needed killing. His Y-chromosome was not about baby-making. It was about fatal couplings, magic moments. Paul amused himself with the thought that someday DNA signatures would replace the zodiac in popularity with Haplogroup E1a as the signature of the grim reaper.

***

If credence is to be given to the words of Paul's father, Robert McCarahan, Ursula Kowalzik didn't know what end was up when he met her. "Just a frizzy-haired, brown-skin gal, who couldn't speak English and thought she was German. Well, she knew she was a nigger when I got done with her."

Robert McCarahan met her during one of his 'rampages.' On this occasion, he had stolen a truck and been away from his unit for more than a week. "I don't think she owned but one pair of drawers, hair all over her arms and legs. Just like the rest of those women over there, never heard of shaving.

"Hardheaded too. Wouldn't let me for a couple of months and me sneaking down there every chance I got. Then I come to find out no one had been in those raggedy drawers before.

"You had to feel sorry for her. She had had no family. She believes that her grandfather brought her there from Africa when she was a baby. There's some story about his being with an African woman in one of those countries, maybe Ghana, and living there for a long time. The two of them had a daughter and the daughter had Ursula. Grandfather got enough of Africa and split with Ursula for Germany. That's her whole known family history and I'm not sure that I even believe that this story is the truth.

"It was a little out-of-the-way village. The place might as well have been called Naziville. Mostly women and old men, but the hardest looking people I've ever seen. I took a rifle with me. Always.

"What beats me is how she ever made it through the war. Old Hitler wasn't partial to Negroes. Must not have had a rule to cover her. Or no camp..."

And it was usually about here that he would call for Paul to come out onto the porch. "Look at this boy." And he rolled up the bottom of Paul's T-shirt. "Twelve years old and hair all over his chest and belly. The woman was a werewolf. Go on back in the house, Paul. You know how black little Fritzi is. He had tiny blind hairs all over his back when he was a baby. A damn shame."

Robert McCarahan would drink his wine and Paul would wait for his leave to end, for him to return to wherever the army had stationed him. His father was short and dark. And, in contrast to his son, had a pleasant, even warm appearance. He made everyone laugh. Everyone except Paul. Paul feared that he would be like his father one day, a clown sitting around drinking wine.

But the elder McCarahan had not been a clown with Ursula. From the start, it had actually been serious in every way. He brought her food, clothing. He gave her the few luxuries she had ever had. And when she locked her legs around him, he felt that he could even drive out the meanness that had been her life up to then.

When he first met her, she was about to turn twenty. They were married on her twenty-first birthday by the village's one clergyman, a man for whom Ursula had done occasional housework. It was a solemn occasion in an unheated church, attended by most of the adults in the village. They had come to witness an end to the responsibility they had borne since her grandfather's death, an end to the obligation to clutch her to their cold, impoverished breasts.

The Prussian Kowalzik had drifted into town with his granddaughter Ursula in tow. He had dirt under his fingernails and was probably consumptive even then. He was a man who neither spoke their dialect nor shared their perspective. To earn a living, he had taken any and every dirty job, but remained an outsider. Günther Kowalzik wasted away while they watched out of the corners of their eyes, wasted away and drifted out of town to the graveyard.

The innkeeper's wife took Ursula in. At first, it was simply fun, a brown baby doll. And then, as these things go, the attachment became maternal. During the war, she feared the authorities would take Ursula away. It would have been too much to bear. When Robert McCarahan took her away, she did not flinch. It was their lot. Of the twenty-three men they presented the Reich, only four had returned. The men had gone to heaven. Ursula was going to a decent life in America.

Robert McCarahan's sister Loretta had mailed the dress that Ursula wore at the wedding. She had never worn a dress that was form-fitting. For the first time, she felt material stretched tautly over her buttocks, could hear the nylon stockings rub together as she walked. And when they returned to her room over the tavern, she had made him understand that she did not want to take them off. They had made love with the dress and the stockings and the black pumps, the dress rolled up above her hips, Ursula McCarahan in a frenzy, coaxing him on in vulgar Teutonic idiom.

"When I brought her over, she may have already been carrying Paul. I brought her right home to Loretta and my mother. There was no sense dragging her from army base to army base. Anyhow, there would have been no life for my boys in that, so I brought her here. We had the whole third floor and my mother was doing all the housework.

You know my mother. She hardly let Uschi lift a finger, especially after she found out that Uschi was pregnant.

"Now I'm saving all my money, all I can make and all I can steal. I was in Supply. Unless you're a damn idiot you could make an extra hundred dollars a month just moving stuff from one spot on the base to another. You didn't even have to take it to a fence yourself. Things went pretty well until a little after Fritzi was born.

"I would get leave to come home and see my family and all I got was bitch and more bitch. As soon as I walked in the door, she'd act like she hadn't learned any English. She'd go after me in German at the dinner table in front of my mother and sister. I came home three or four times to this.

"Now I'm trying to buy this woman a house and she's got her jaws tight because I wouldn't get us an apartment near where I was stationed. Or because she didn't have anyone to speak German to. Or she didn't like Loretta's friends from church. Like where she grew up she had a whole lot of company or something. She had Loretta and my mother. Plus, they helped her with Thelma and the boys.

"So, I told her I was going to do my job and she was going to do hers. Mine was in the army a few more years and hers was taking care of the boys and learning how to be an American. She comes back at me with this 'Well, I'm a German too' bullshit. I let her know what she was. What did she think I was? Fuckin' Irishman because my name is McCarahan? Start thinking that way and there wouldn't be a nigger left in the country. We know that ain't right. And I do mean 'ain't.'

25

"Anyway, I ask her how German she could be with a name like Kowalzik. It was time to set the record straight. I've been around enough to know that's no real German name. And the woman raises her voice to me, saying I'm stupid and that her grandfather was Prussian. Sounds like a Polack name to me. Shit, Prussia's in Germany, but it's sitting over there next to Poland. But now she's screaming and crying. Just carrying on like a wild woman. Hysterical. Loretta had to come up and put her to bed."

Robert McCarahan had been back on the base two weeks when he received Loretta's telegram. Ursula had left. Loretta and his mother could not stop her. She had taken the money in the shoebox and withdrawn eight hundred dollars from the account. It came to sixteen hundred dollars, almost one-half of their savings. A week later her letter arrived saying that she would be back for her children. In reply, he wrote: "If you come back, I'll kill you. You should be killed for what you've done." He turned the bankbook over to Loretta and never saved a penny again.

Robert McCarahan's father died when Robert was on his first tour of duty and a younger brother quickly ran the family's wallpapering business aground. Then, as a final act of meanness, he ran Robert's car into a pole, killing himself and thereby escaping his brother's wrath. McCarahan was left in Europe with Ursula Kowalzik. He sat beside Uschi on her bed and recalled what his father said to him before he left for the service. "Be sensible. Save as much as you can. Because when you come home all these folks will have to offer you is a cold black hand." At the time Robert had thought it funny and laughed. His father simply repeated his warning. "That's right. A cold black hand."

***

Dear Paul,
I hope that you will understand and eventually forgive me. I would be very pleased to speak with you, if you are amenable to that.
Ernest Robinson

There was also a telephone number with a Philadelphia area code scribbled as an apparent afterthought. Paul had not seen Ernest Robinson since Ernest dropped out of Yale nearly forty years earlier. In the fall of 1966, Pittsburgh's East Side had delivered two black teenagers from rival high schools to Yale's freshman class. Both majored in mathematics. Ernest disappeared sometime in 1969 during their senior year, at a time when it appeared that the campus would not survive its student body's nervous breakdown. Deferments for graduate school had been curtailed and Vietnam War protests threatened the university. Bobby Seale's trial was in New Haven across the Green from the Old Campus. Man had set foot on the moon that summer for the first time. It was the year that the first women were admitted to Yale College.

If Paul had taken a minute and turned to the references when he got the preprints, he would have seen "Robinson, Ernest: Unpublished Manuscript." But he hadn't and the two-sentence note took him by surprise. It always seemed impressive to him that the Yale alumni magazine found its way to his decaying neighborhood. Now here came Ernest Robinson, stealthy at first with the preprints and then ten days later a handwritten message of contrition.

Paul and Ernest had moved in different circles in New Haven. Paul helped cover the difference between his costs and his scholarship support by doing odd jobs for the secretary in the German department. Beyond that, most of his spare time was spent shuttling back and forth between the campus and West Haven for track practice. In Paul's view, Ernest had gone off the deep end when he joined the God Squad, a group of a dozen or more Yalies who squatted on campus corners with assorted musical instruments and proselytized. And when the campus began to seethe their senior year, Ernest vanished and, like Jesus, began his hidden years.

Paul was bound and determined not to drop out. He knew that if he did, he would never be able to drop back in. The white boys were acting out, talking shit about revolution, growing their hair. Paul was convinced that in a few years they would cut their hair and get back in step, so he ignored the student strike in the spring and went to class. His senior essay on topological groups was submitted on time.

Three weeks before graduation, Paul reported for his induction physical. Believing in the miracles that resided in his own psyche, he manipulated his blood pressure upwards by imagining himself sprinting through the curve of the 220, making up the stagger on an opponent. When they took his pressure again, fifteen minutes later, he dredged up the mechanics of stabbing to death that hapless German two years earlier. He finessed the draft.

Less than three months after graduation, his Aunt Loretta died. Paul took his one-third share of the insurance money, the rest going to Fritzi and Thelma. Then he flew to Germany and found a part-time job teaching algebra at the Kaufmännische Schule IV in Düsseldorf. During those six years, when he thought of him at all, Paul imagined that Ernest had given Caesar his due, died in Vietnam, and gone on to his reward in heaven.

***

Paul's fever was gone. Three measurements in a row were at 97.5.

***

The reporter showed up with a photographer. He received them in the piano room. The photographer was close to being sexy, a lot of character in her face, but, as it was with most young women, she lacked seasoning. She had a way to go yet.

Paul set up a couple of folding chairs and seated himself on the piano bench with his back turned to the piano. He said, "Nothing good can come of this. You must know that."

The reporter came off as sincere and sincerity was a quality that Paul valued, even when it was misplaced. "No, Dr. McCarahan, I don't know that. I've thought about this story off and on since I was in high school. Yaros is the most interesting traffic fatality in Pennsylvania state history." He was going to continue, but Paul cut him off.

"So, who's the second most interesting traffic fatality, John?" Paul looked at John as if he expected an answer. John got a little red in the face.

"By the way, I thought we had agreed over the telephone that we were not going to have a photoshoot. And you've brought Cindy..." Paul looked at the photographer. "That is your name, isn't it?" She nodded. "You've brought Cindy into this ugly neighborhood and exposed her to me for no good reason."

John waved his hand. "I was hoping you would change your mind."

Paul looked at the pull-up bar that he had mounted in the door frame of the piano room and then he eyed John. John was pudgy. "If you do three pull-ups, I'll agree to Cindy taking my picture and putting it in the Post-Gazette."

John shook his head and tried to laugh. "I've never been able to do a pull-up."

"Okay, just hang from the bar. Look like you're trying really hard and let Cindy take a shot of that for me, then I'll pose for you."

John stiffened. "No, I'm not going to do that."

"You're a good man, John. You know where to draw the line."

The reporter breathed in and started over again. "Look, believe it or not, I grew up in a mostly black neighborhood on the North Side. I was just starting high school when this geometry thing happened. Most of the black people on my street... They came close to celebrating."

Paul leaned back casually against the piano. "Yaros shot a black teenager in the neck and then dragged him half a block to his squad car like the kid was something with antlers. He put handcuffs on him and then took his time calling for an ambulance. The boy bled to death in the street. A lot of black people think that this sort of thing happens too often. When something like a balance is restored, even temporarily, they celebrate."

Cindy had her legs crossed and was jiggling the top one.

"So, are you telling me that this wasn't an accident?" John seemed to think that he had broken new ground.

"No, I am not. I'm telling you that some people, including the ones in your neighborhood, got excited because they believed justice had been served. Look, Yaros claimed that he felt threatened by the boy. He saw him climbing out the window of an abandoned house. The street light was out. Blah, blah, blah, blah, blah. Part of what a policeman gets paid to do is handle his feelings. Yaros didn't. Then he dragged him down the street and joked with the cops who had just pulled up instead of getting the kid some medical attention right away. Your paper sold ads for weeks by promoting the Geometry Killing."

John objected. "It was about more than selling advertising. That was a real story. You went to high school with Yaros. Plus, I guess most people were thinking about the letter decrying Yaros' acquittal that you wrote to the Post-Gazette two days before the accident."

"Are you saying that I engineered Yaros' death to enhance my chances of getting my letter printed by the Post-Gazette?"

"No, I'm saying that the letter made what happened look suspicious. I mean what are the chances of something like that happening?"

"Everything that happens is improbable, John. Everything."

And that was pretty much where they left it. John asked him a few background questions about his life as a mathematics professor. He had done his homework and knew that Paul had run track at Peabody High School and then at Yale. "I don't run these days. I walk. But I walk quite a bit.

"I think it's a good thing that you're writing this article about me. All those guys from my era at Yale have been in the newspaper these days and it was sort of like I had become a has-been. John Kerry, Howard Dean, John Bolton, George Bush, Scooter Libby... They've all been making news. They're lucky that I didn't own a car when I was in New Haven. Cheney is a Yale dropout. But he wasn't from my era anyway, so he doesn't count.

"There's another one of them who's been lying low. Pell Dobbins. If you want a scoop, write an article on him. That would be good." Paul was warming to this. "I hear the rumor that Pell is on a shortlist for the next Supreme Court vacancy. The man was in my class at Yale. In fact, he and I were in the same senior society, Berzelius. 'BZ man Dobbins on Fast Track to the Supreme Court'. Write it, John." At this point, Paul was talking to himself and there was no response.

Cindy asked if she could try out his piano. He relinquished the bench and she played part of Clare de Lune. It sounded good. Paul was partial to the Impressionists.

When Cindy asked him to favor them with something, Paul's response was, "Dr. McCarahan does not deign to play today."

***

Paul knew that he should call Ernest Robinson, but he went for a walk instead. It was pleasantly cool for a June evening and he wanted to clear his head of John and Cindy. He walked to the bottom of the hill and then threaded his way through the brush down to the railroad tracks. Then he did what he had done for years. He mounted a rail and began balancing his way northward to the Allegheny River. Soon there were woods on both sides of the railroad bed. His street was the last one on that edge of the city. Paul looked toward the ridgeline that formed the horizon in the west. He could make out a few houses, but Ruth's house was not visible from the tracks. Lions had not been heard roaring from the zoo in decades, at least not by Paul.

He tried to remember the name of the boy that Yaros shot. After a few steps, he usually was not aware that he was balancing. Paul had done many miles on these rails when he was a graduate student at Pitt, preparing for his preliminary exams and, near the end, working to find what he termed the poetry needed to complete his dissertation. He finished up and took a position at Auburn. Within three years civil war broke out in Auburn's mathematics department and it was formally split along political lines. Pitt offered him a job. It smacked of incest, but Pitt needed more black faculty. So they went after their own PhD. Paul left Alabama and came home. A few years later he was involved in the most noted traffic fatality in the history of the state.

Paul had taken one class with Yaros. It was metal shop his freshman year at Peabody. He remembered watching Yaros and another guy bloody a kid and tear his shirt to shreds right in the middle of class because the kid was annoying. And because the kid was Jewish. The teacher was out of the room at the time. There were no repercussions.

Then he remembered. The name of the boy Yaros shot was Bobby Coleman, a ne'er-do-well. That's how the paper described him. There was also some line about "a troubled youth, who perished at age sixteen." At the funeral, the minister took the opportunity to sound off on the state of the black race in America. Paul didn't believe that there was a black race in America. He once told Ruth that black people in America did not constitute a race. "We are a phenomenon. That's precisely what we are, a phenomenon."

Paul moved swiftly over the rail, closing in on the Allegheny River. He saw the Phenomenon spreading out from the Big Bang, mostly zombies after the collision, but truly something to behold. And the Yaroses of the world had to be made to keep their hands off.

***

Giegengack found him where he was sitting in the infield of the Yale track and told Paul that he wanted him to run the anchor on the mile relay. Paul was in the middle of a daydream. He had run a pretty good 220, finishing second to his teammate earlier in the meet and thought he was done. Now here was Gieg telling him that Thompson was hurt and there wasn't anyone else fresh enough to run it. Paul protested. He made excuses. He hadn't run the quarter since high school and hardly ever, even back then. Thompson was the second-best quarter-miler on the team and usually ran the first leg.

Giegengack walked him away from the rest of the team. "Just run relaxed," he said. "Feel your legs under you. When you get the baton, you'll have ten yards. Don't squander it."

Giegengack had been head coach of the U.S. Track and Field team in the 1964 Olympics. He talked to Paul matter-of-factly. This wasn't the Tokyo Olympics. It was the Harvard meet. "Just make the bastard work, Paul. He won't catch you from ten yards back."

When Paul got the baton, the bastard had four yards on him. His teammates had botched their hand-offs. Yale already had the meet won. They didn't need the points from this event. Paul didn't need them either. He relaxed and felt his legs under him for the first 220 yards and cut it down to a three-yard deficit. Paul imagined himself getting close enough to smack the crimson-clad rear end with his baton, count coup. They went into the second curve. Paul was the best curve runner in the Ivy League. When they came out of the curve and onto the straightaway, the deficit was only one step. Now Paul wanted to see the guy's face. He was going to walk the bastard down and count coup. Paul actually glared at him when he blew by with seven yards left, feeling his legs under him. He had run the first furlong in a trance of mechanical indifference and the second in grinding, irrational fury.

On Monday morning, the Yale Daily News had a picture of Paul McCarahan still glaring after he crossed the finish line. The reporter tied the names of the two anchormen together to get the caption "Paul robs Peter" and he highlighted Paul's 440 yards of madness in the last event of the meet.

...Sophomore Paul McCarahan, a 220 specialist who was tapped at the last minute to fill in for the injured Carter Thompson, ran an electrifying anchor. After bad stick handling by his Eli teammates, the race was apparently lost. But McCarahan displayed the mettle for which Giegengack-coached runners have come to be known over the past three decades. He reeled in his Crimson adversary and then ran an absolutely scorching final 100 yards to put the race away and leave this reporter gasping as if he had just run 440 yards at breakneck speed himself...

Paul was not aware of the sneer on his face as he read the article. He was wondering what the reporter would have thought if he had heard Paul whining when Giegengack made his request. In fact, Paul did find out. He and the reporter Jim Gerhardt were both tapped into the senior society Berzelius. In a moment of candor, Gerhardt told him. "Yeah, I overheard you trying to weasel out. That made it even more amazing to me. There was nothing at stake. The meet was already won. You didn't want any part of that quarter mile. And then you ran like a man possessed."

Paul could have told him that he was possessed. From time to time he was that way. Three months after the Harvard meet, he was possessed and killed a man on an early morning train that ran between Düsseldorf and Cologne. From time to time he was that way.

In college, Paul was 5' 11" and 144 pounds of gristle. Giegengack suggested that the quarter-mile was a natural distance for him. "I saw something rise up in you on that relay leg." But Paul dug in his heels. "I'm telling you, Gieg. It hurts too much. That rising up stuff." Paul garnered All-Ivy honors his junior and senior years running the 220. He never ran the 440 again.

Paul saw Ernest Robinson the week after the meet. Ernest was on the Old Campus with his God Squad. Drumming up business for the Lord is the way Ernest would put it. He broke ranks to come over and shake Paul's hand. "Man, I was there Saturday. It was unbelievable. Shades of Orin Richburg!"

Richburg had been a Westinghouse High School athlete, Ernest's school. He was undoubtedly one of the finest schoolboy sprinters Pennsylvania had ever produced. Richburg was a couple of years older than Paul and he had seen him run many times. The last Paul heard, Richburg was representing the U.S in international meets.

Paul knew where Ernest was headed with this Richburg business. Ernest went there all the time. Paul had not gone to Westinghouse, even though his grade school was in the Westinghouse district. Paul went to Peabody; the other school on the east side of town. Ernest had a silly, almost romantic notion that he and Paul would have had four years of mathematical camaraderie together at Westinghouse. As it was, they didn't even meet until Yale. Paul had turned his back on Westinghouse. By the early sixties, it was on its way to being a hell hole. So, he had not gone where Thelma had gone before him and where Fritzi eventually went. And he had not followed in the footsteps of Strayhorn, Garner, and Jamal, who attended when the school was in its heyday. He had not followed Richburg. Paul went to Peabody and learned German, which Westinghouse did not offer, the German his father learned during World War II, the German that would land Paul a job in Düsseldorf the summer of 1968. Paul stopped Ernest before he could even get started. "I don't know how you even survived Westinghouse, Ernest. You must have done nothing but pray."

***

He dialed the number scribbled on the note from Ernest.

"So, what are you telling me, Ernest? You published your work under my name because your name isn't known? That doesn't make any sense. How's your name going to get known? By the way, 'Paul McCarahan' doesn't have great marquee value. At least not outside Pittsburgh." Paul paused for a moment and Ernest said nothing. Maybe Ernest didn't even know about Yaros. He should not have pointed in that direction. "I could get into hot water, Ernest. Plagiarism comes to mind."

Ernest was completely logical. "You haven't plagiarized. And you should value your work more. I've read most of it. Every one of your papers is a surprise. They're mathematical ambushes."

"Where do we go from here, Ernest? There's a guy in my department who works in analytic number theory. This paper won't go unnoticed. It's in Transactions, for God's sake. You expect me to go out and give talks on these results?"

Ernest remained steady. "I hope that you'll eventually present the material at a few conferences. I'm not in a position to do it."

"Why can't you present it yourself? There are universities all over Philadelphia. Liven them up. You'll just have to explain that using my name was a practical joke."

"Paul, I make my living as a doorman. There are days when I'm not even up to that and I've never given a real talk in my life. I can't do it. Not now. I want you to know that I view what I've put under your name as my life's work. I need your help."

"Ernest, I don't think so. It would take me at least a month to even understand the paper." But Paul knew that he would do it. There was something pathetic in Ernest's voice.

Apparently, Ernest knew that Paul would do it too. "Paul, there's one more favor I'm going to ask of you."

Paul said nothing.

"Can you find the time to come see me this summer, so that we can talk about this face to face?"

"Alright."

Obviously, this wasn't the first time Paul had shaken hands with the devil. Actually, this was more of a nod or a wink. At any rate, the summer was destroyed. He had committed himself to reading "Topological Avenues in

Analytic Number Theory." It would be the first summer in more than six years that he had made anything like a substantial mathematical effort. Summers were for playing the piano and visiting the Virginia and North Carolina haunts of his father's ancestors. Now he had to read Ernest's paper and he had to read it well enough to make it his own. Ernest told him it would be helpful to look at the last chapter of Daniel Berman's book, *Complex Analysis – Applications to Number Theory*. Ernest had gushed over Berman. "Berman had a gift." He was Berman's doorman. At least he had been until Berman died two years earlier.

Ten days of fever followed by Ernest Robinson. The summer was in the toilet. He had a commitment to go to New Haven for a meeting of Berzelius alumni. It would be his first trip back to Yale in years. He expected his nemesis Pell Dobbins to be there. And he was committed to taking Ruth Gable on his sacred trip through the Virginia and North Carolina Piedmont to visit cemeteries and ancient relatives, the dead and the near dead. Ruth had jumped up and down like a child when he relented and agreed to take her along. Paul hadn't made a trip with anyone since he was a boy. He could feel himself falling back on all fronts in this summer of commitment. But he also felt coiled, the stirring of his Y-chromosome, a premonition that a new harvest would soon be ready for reaping.

***

I learned German as if it were a language that I had spoken in another life, a life seeping into the one I have now.

I knew within weeks that my father did not really speak German. He knew German words and sentences, how to ask a girl out for a movie, but he had no intuition for the language, no sense of right and wrong. He wasn't one with the language. The muse had not favored him. I believe that language, mathematics, and music are the province of one muse. For me, there is no difference between the art of theorem proving and the art of musical composition. Mathematics, music, and language are all derived from an aesthetic sense. There are times when the muse shows me a thread and I follow it to some truth, and when I am done there is always the sense of inevitability: I've always known this theorem. I've always played this piece.

When the question mark is on a man's face and it is the last question that he will ever ask, the same muse is at work, the same aesthetic imperative. I was meant to usher him out. Everything fits. A father must look at his child and see the inevitability of that child's existence. I look at my two corpses that way and I don't believe that my fertility is at an end. It has been a while since the muse has guided me to that place, but I am now mature enough in this art to recognize a period of gestation. And when it happens, I will pass out cigars and say, "It's a Joy."

***

Pell Dobbins and Paul McCarahan became enemies during their senior year. They met for the first time at the end of their junior year when they both accepted the tap for the senior society Berzelius. Bickering began when Pell overhead Paul playing the piano in the cavernous Berzelius dining room. Pell approached the piano to listen and then made some remark about it being a shame that black musicians buried themselves in jazz and did not aspire to loftier heights. While Pell talked, Paul continued to play and closed with a pearly run up the keyboard. He looked at Pell and said, "That's as lofty as music gets."

It was the beginning of what the other thirteen members of that year's delegation eventually dubbed the Paul-Pell wars. During their year in the hall, which they called the "Tomb" due to its Mausoleum-like appearance, there was rarely a Thursday or Sunday evening dinner that the two did not entertain with an exchange. Everyone knew that once the two of them entered the conversation, an on-ramp to the subject of Race in America would be found. The topic was delicate. Paul and Pell were not. At one point in the early fall, Pell pushed back from the dinner table and said, "When it comes right down to it, I'm a segregationist. But this is all just in principle for me. I'm not militant about it." Then looking at Paul, "Here I am breaking bread with you and I'm completely civil."

This was about the time that the black cook and his wife were clearing the table getting ready to bring on dessert. Paul could feel them looking at him with expectation. "You're right, Pell, and I thank the gods that you grew up in Montana."

"That's right. I'm from Montana."

"And there were about two thousand Jewish guys available right down I-95 in New York City, all smarter than you on their dumbest day. But, instead, the Admissions

Board in its infinite wisdom shipped you all the way from Montana so that the black guy from Pittsburgh could get a real education."

"You can kiss my ass, McCarahan."

"No, I cannot." He delivered the words with an ample measure of certainty. It had been a little more than a year since Paul had killed his first man. "No, I cannot."

Paul was amazed by how venomous their exchanges became. It was as if he were just a spectator himself. Twenty years earlier the fabled Levi Jackson had accepted the tap from Berzelius, chosen it over Skull and Bones. Jackson was the first black student in the Ivy League to be elected captain of a team. His election in 1949 by the football team to be its captain made headlines in the New York Times. Jackson had been a Yale hero. Paul fell short of that. At any rate, Paul accepted the tap on his shoulder, which had come as a surprise. He received a key for the heavy metal doors and the sequence for the combination lock on the interior door. Every Thursday and Sunday evening he made the trek across campus from his residential college Jonathan Edwards, which was nestled next to Skull and Bones. Paul passed Scroll and Key and Book and Snake on his way to do battle with Pell at Berzelius. The ongoing feud made him feel small.

It became increasingly grim as the year wore on. Half of the delegation members were preoccupied with the low numbers that they had drawn in the December draft lottery, which essentially guaranteed that they would receive a letter from their draft board to report. The mood on campus was anti-establishment, and senior societies were clearly a manifestation of the establishment. Three members dropped out of Berzelius altogether.

One by one, the BZ men did their Thursday night audits, a baring of the soul before the other members of the delegation. Pell and Paul were doing this constantly anyway, revealing various layers of their psyche in verbal skirmishes. By the time they did their audits, it was anticlimactic.

The suggestion was made more than once that the two bury the hatchet. But Paul would not. And Pell would not. And eventually their predictable collisions became a diversion for the others from the looming pressures of Vietnam and the general uneasiness that beset the campus. Pell skewered Paul with the simple question about the two-hundred-dollar Berzelius scholarship that Paul had received. "What do you think the criteria were, Paul?" Paul didn't know. But from that point on it might as well have been a welfare check.

For his part, Paul methodically reduced Montana to a slur. He would appear to grant Pell everything and then take it away with a wave of his hand. "Let's assume that the average black guy is not as intelligent as the average white guy. Sometimes I look around and think it might be true. But what does that have to do with me?"

Of course, Pell had no counter to this. And Paul continued, "I'm not interested in the average of groups. Take the people in Montana, for example. Would anyone be shocked if their average IQ is lower than the average IQ of the people in Iowa? Probably not. But what does that have to do with Pell?"

It was a war that Pell had started. Paul was determined to finish it and then finish it again.

By late January they were into their 'reversals.' The reversals were designed to complement the audit. Every member was assigned a role that was in some respect counter to what they had divulged about themselves in the audit. Over his objections, Paul was assigned "White Supremacist." Pell was to throw himself into the role of a gay woman, the first woman to be accepted into the Whiffenpoofs. Pell had been opposed to the admission of women to Yale College and he was the Whiffenpoof pitch pipe. That fall women were admitted to the freshman class along with transfers into the sophomore and junior classes. Their class would be the last all-male class to graduate from Yale College.

Paul insisted that he give his reversal presentation in the ceremonial meeting room on the second floor with its straight-back chairs, instead of downstairs in the social area with its more comfortably upholstered furnishings.

That Thursday evening after a dinner that for some reason lacked a confrontation between Pell and him, Paul stood out on a small balcony that projected from the meeting room and overlooked the dining area. He looked down through the banners and chandeliers at the heavy wooden tables below him and could make out the letter 'B' ornately carved on their surfaces. The ceiling skylight was still some feet above. The fireplace in the far wall was large enough to allow one particularly short member of the delegation to enter it without stooping. He left the balcony and entered the meeting room where the men of Berzelius faced him assembled. Paul took his handwritten speech from the desk and delivered.

Shall America Remain White? This question may be answered in the affirmative today, but if delayed for several generations it may be forever too late.

"Taxation without representation" was the slogan that fired the colonists of 1776; "states' rights" was the cry that called forth the determined resistance of the South in 1861; and "making the world safe for democracy" was the thought that mobilized the resources of our land and hurried millions of our young men to arms when the rights of mankind were trampled upon.

As momentous as these questions were, in neither instance did losing to our foes mean absolute and irretrievable disaster. In each case, our conquerors were, or would have been, of our own blood and kind.

The change of rulers and the downfall of our government would not mean the change of ideals and the destruction of white civilization. The South rose in majesty and strength after defeat by her Northern brethren. As horrible as may be the thought, even domination by the Central Powers, people of our own race, would not have meant absolute and hopeless ruin.

These dangers were apparent to all and were met by armed and united resistance, but few realize that for 300 years the white race of America has been subjected to a process which, though more destructive than war, has aroused no popular fear, and has called forth only the most feeble and ineffective resistance.

Paul looked out at Pell Dobbins, who didn't make eye contact.

In 1620, thirteen years after the first landing of English colonists at Jamestown, there came to them a temptation from the Evil One, in which the alluring thought of cheap and controllable labor was held out to them. They fell and permitted a Dutch trader to land as a start twenty negro slaves. They quickly realized the possibility of utilizing this form of labor in the difficult work of felling the forests and breaking the new ground. They became willing partners in this nefarious traffic and then was produced the great American problem. Slave trade became immensely profitable and thousands of black savages were poured in upon our shores. This continued for nearly 200 years, when, in 1808, the further importation of negroes was forbidden.

Jefferson, Madison, Webster and Lincoln, all in their time, realized the danger and raised their voices against it. They went deeper into the problem than did the clamorous abolitionists who fanned the flames that broke forth into civil war. They realized that the problem was not slavery, but the presence of the negro in this, a white man's land.

Still, there was no eye contact with Pell.

Lincoln, in particular, repeatedly called public attention to the danger, and at the time of his death, a most unfortunate event for the South, was formulating plans for gradually returning the negro to his home in Africa.

The negro as a laborer is valuable, and if it were possible to preserve the race in purity with him in our midst, he would be a great asset. Because this cannot be done, and because the mixed breeds are a menace and not an asset, we have them as the greatest problem and most destructive force which confronts the white race and American civilization.

Both remote and recent history of many nations shows that in none of them have white and colored races lived together without ultimate amalgamation, and without the final deterioration or complete destruction of the white or higher civilization.

We behold with awe the evidences which we now find in Egypt of the wonderful civilization of the past when that country was white. The Pharaohs extended their conquest south and brought back as captives large numbers of negro men and women. Intermixture of the races began and progressed to such a point that one of the Pharaohs took as wife a negro woman whose son succeeded to the throne. This was about the time Jeremiah the Prophet warned Israel to break with Egypt and affiliate with Babylon. His warning was disregarded, Egypt was as a broken staff upon which to lean. The fall of Jerusalem and the Babylonian captivity resulted.

Egypt, then a mongrel nation, soon went down before Assyria and is today a feeble and helpless nation of brown people devoid of initiative and dependent upon white leadership and protection. Four thousand years ago, India *was ruled by Aryan conquerors, who instituted an elaborate caste system to prevent intermixture of the races.*

This system failed and the few survivors who might be called white are now looked upon as curiosities.

South America and Mexico were subdued by Spanish and Portuguese adventurers, who began at once to raise up a mixed breed.

Indians would not make docile slaves, and negroes in large numbers were brought in.

Much of South America and Mexico is today inhabited by a mongrel race white-black-red mixture, one of the most undesirable racial intermixtures known, as I can testify from my own observation of similar groups in Virginia.

None of our Southern States permits the intermarriage of whites and pure blacks, but all except Virginia and perhaps two others allow the intermarriage of whites with those of one-sixteenth or one-eighth negro blood.

This serious situation calls for the speedy enactment of laws based upon that of Virginia, which defines a white person as one with no trace whatsoever of any blood other than Caucasian, and forbids the intermarriage of whites with those with the slightest trace of negro blood.

Paul was now smiling and starting to feel it.

One community of about 500 of the triple intermixture in one county on the eastern side of the Blue Ridge Mountains, with a branch colony perhaps half as large across the mountain in another county, has been carefully studied by Professor Ivan McDougle, then of Sweetbriar, now of

Goucher College, and Dr. Arthur Estabrook, of the Carnegie Foundation; their report soon to be published. They find these people of low moral standard, as evidenced by the fact that twenty-one percent of their births are illegitimate. The army draft enlistment mental tests showed them very low, about D or D minus. A capable school teacher has never developed from these people, in contrast with the true negro. They differ from the true negro in the further fact that they show little disposition to attempt to build a church or maintain a religious worship, depending entirely upon mission work by white people. Their ambition seems to be limited to securing recognition as white, and if that fails as Indians.

In the United States Census of 1920, 304 succeeded in being listed as Indians, while in 1900 there were none such, and in 1910 only seven.

Another group of considerable size, making vociferous claims to being Indians, is being shown to be chiefly of negro and white composition and will be forbidden further intermarriage with whites. A number of cases has already been called to my attention of reversion under Mendel's law when children of marked negro characteristics were born when both parents were supposed to be white, investigation revealing that one of the parents was of mixed blood.

Can a more humiliating occurrence be imagined for a white woman of refined sensibilities?

The first eighteen months of our experience with the new Virginia Racial Integrity Act reveals a degree of racial intermixture previously unknown and shows that our State has already made a decided start in race amalgamation. The situation is certainly as bad in all of the Southern States, and worse in some.

The only positive remedy for the situation is that advocated by Lincoln and other far-seeing statesmen, the absolute separation of the races.

This will meet with opposition on the part of those who are willing to sacrifice the future salvation of the white race for the temporary and selfish gain to be derived from the use of cheap negro labor.

Unless this can be done we have little to hope for, but may expect the future decline or complete destruction of our present civilization, as has already been brought about in Egypt, India, South Africa, South America and the portions of Southern Europe which have been supplying us with the larger part of our immigrants.

Under the new act of Congress, much of this immigration and that of Mongolians will be stopped, but people of all grades of mixture from South America, Mexico, and the West Indies still have free access to our country.

In the attempt to solve this problem, the best that we have to hope for is to attempt, as we have done in Virginia, to hold off the evil day until the American people see the danger and are ready to adopt radical methods of cure.

The first thing to do, and in that members of this audience can take a leading part, is to arouse a more healthy public sentiment against racial intermixture, whether it be legally by marriage, or by illegitimate births.

The second effort must be to secure rigorous laws in all the States preventing the intermarriage of white persons and those with even a trace of negro blood.

The third measure and the most difficult embraces both of the others and will be aimed at preventing the greatest amount of intermixture which is of illegitimate origin.

This can be best accomplished by the public instruction of young men and schoolboys as to the crime against society and the white race of being a party to illegitimate mixture.

Along with this, adequate laws should be enacted to prevent illegitimate births by making the father responsible for the expense to the mother during her confinement and for the maintenance of the child afterward.

This would tend to make men more cautious and prevent many cases of illegitimacy now frequently considered by them as a joke.

Aside from its deterring effects in the prevention of racial intermixture, it is but a matter of common justice that the man should share with the woman the odium and burden of such misdeeds.

Finally, Paul and Pell locked eyes. Paul thought Pell was about to ask a question, but he didn't.

The future of the white race and its civilization in America, and the welfare of our children are in the keeping of this generation. Shall we arise to the situation and save our country from the terrible calamity which awaits us if we are indifferent? Shall we meet the situation with courage and determination, and secure our land forever for the unmixed descendants of those who have made it what we find it today?

Since this is our only course, let us stand shoulder to shoulder, with unyielding front, determined to preserve our racial integrity at all costs.

Let us turn a deaf ear to those who would interpret Christian brotherhood to mean racial equality.

Those who would have America perform her full part in the evangelization of the world must not lose sight of the fact that this will be done by us only as a white nation.

The colored race of the South has shown commendable zeal in providing for its own religious needs, but who can point to an example of any great concerted effort on their part to provide for the religious or physical needs of those afar off?

The mongrel groups of Virginia, which have descended lowest, unlike the true negro, are lacking in the initiative and zeal to provide for their own religious, educational, and even physical needs, but depend upon the white people to build their houses of worship and supply them with the Gospel and old clothes, under the guise of "Indian Missions."

These groups point clearly to the condition when our whole population is mongrelized. In that day, we will be a helpless mass of mental weaklings, incapable of strong government, and effective resistance to any nation of pure race which chooses to exploit us.

In the back row, Pell had begun picking his nose, as was his habit. He piped up, "What the hell was that flowery shit, McCarahan? I think you failed your assignment. That was really overdone. It sounded like 'Martin Luther King Has a Change of Heart' or some such nonsense."

It was in truth excerpted from a speech by Walter Ashby Plecker, which was read in 1924 before the Section of Public Health of the Southern Medical Association in New Orleans. It also appeared as part of the "The New Family and Race Improvement" booklet that was issued in 1925 by the Virginia Bureau of Vital Statistics. Paul found it quaint when he first read it. The speech reminded him of the general tone in his grade-school hygiene texts. Paul revealed all of this after taking ten minutes of criticism from the men of BZ for crafting a ludicrous caricature. Pell was furious and accused Paul of acting in bad faith. And then he said that because of Paul's mischief, he felt no obligation to do the lesbian portrayal, which he was slated to do the following week. And he didn't.

Paul first started reading Plecker's writings while he was taking a German literature course. He was planning to read Mein Kampf for the term paper and then stumbled across material on eugenics that pointed him back to America and Plecker. Paul eventually read Mein Kampf in the original German and was fascinated. But he was just as fascinated by Plecker.

Plecker was born less than two weeks before the outbreak of the Civil War. He became a physician and headed the Virginia Bureau of Vital statistics from 1912 until 1946, the zealous enforcement arm of the Virginia's Racial Integrity Act of 1924. He saw himself as the finger in the breached dike. Paul had said, on more than one occasion, that what he and his cohort really accomplished was the preservation of the Big Bang remnants as they aged in the bottle a few more generations. He would also readily concede that the result was more dregs than wine. So what.

Plecker was a man who had real power, plus a willingness to bluff when he didn't. Paul had a grudging admiration for that. He knew where to draw the line and he did it for thirty-four years without the benefit of any DNA analysis. Plecker thought he was safeguarding the purity of the white race, when in fact he and his allies were keeping the lid on the mongrel pot, helping to assure that a century after the end of the Civil War ended the Phenomenon would explode with full force. They were a bunch of kids shaking Coca-Cola bottles to make it fizzy and about to find out that the coke had mysteriously become nitroglycerin. Plecker's crowd guaranteed that there would be no "true negro" left in America. By the middle of the 20th century, there was a spectrum of mongrels instead, ready to take on the world, a world that could already hear the front edge of the tsunami.

In America, the Phenomenon had a long history of inadequate labels, but the label choice was beside the point. Plecker was a member of the Anglo-Saxon Club. Mongrels do not have clubs because they are one-offs, and Paul was proud of that. Paul saw clearly that one-offs were in ascendancy, at least a select subset was. The rest might be taking a bit of a beating.

He recognized a kinship with Plecker. They were both guard dogs of a sort. Plecker never managed to have any children either. He was a terminal node on his tree. Paul would be willing to pay a large sum of money to exhume

Plecker. He would take a chunk out of him for haplogroup determination, analyze his Y-chromosome signature.

***

As Paul had discerned, the reporter from the Post-Gazette also knew where to draw the line and he drew it beyond Ruth Gable. Ruth had made no protestations about photographs. She spoke clearly and candidly to John, sometimes jabbing at the air with her forefinger. Cindy captured Ruth's image. There was no mention of a pull-up bar, no demand that John exert himself. And when it was done, Ruth called Paul to warn him. "A reporter came to the house and I gave him a piece of my mind. I guess I lost my temper."

If Paul had not been feverish the days leading up to the interview, he might have thought to warn Ruth. He had not. So he checked his annoyance and said, "Well, now you're going to be famous too."

Paul and Ruth left for their Virginia and North Carolina trip on the day the story appeared in the paper. There was a picture of pixie Ruth pointing her finger, mouth pursed, legs crossed.

Twenty years earlier, the Geometry Killing may have helped him get tenure. But this rehashing of the deed would only get him furtive glances in the department. Paul would have to supply a fresh killing if he wanted career impact.

There were a couple of good lines in the article. Ruth had one of them. "If Yaros were still alive, would you be interviewing him about that kid he shot? You wouldn't. Because what he did was par for the course." The other was from the pull-up-challenged reporter. "The mathematics professor waxed philosophical about probability and the Geometry Killing." Paul figured that if he lived long enough, Yaros' death would eventually get every branch of mathematics mentioned in the Post-Gazette.

DANCE ON A TRAIN

After Paul's sophomore year, in the summer of 1968, and two days before his first trip to Germany, Paul's father had taken him to the bank. It was the strangest behavior Paul had ever observed in the man. From the house to the bank and back again, his father had never touched the bankbook and had avoided looking at it. He signed the withdrawal slip and stood beside Paul at the teller's window. The teller's request that she be allowed to enter the interest earned that year was not granted. His father said that there was no time. Loretta would take care of it. They left with seven hundred and fifty dollars in travelers checks. Paul returned the book to Loretta's desk drawer.

"That little bit of change you got from Yale isn't enough. I'm not having a son of mine going over there like a pauper. Not around those people. They're quick to look down their noses. Not to mention treacherous."

There was no discussion of the savings account. Paul hadn't known that his father had a cent. Except for some jitney work and his army pension, he had no income. Despite the good fortune of having his mother's house for shelter, he was barely able to support himself and Fritzi. It was a good thing that Thelma was married and on her own. Paul relied entirely on grants in aid, a small scholarship, and summer jobs. Loretta worked as an operating room technician and would occasionally send spending money to New Haven. But for the most part, her largesse was directed to Fritzi, who remembered only her as mother.

Paul and his father shook hands the day he left. "I don't know where she is, Paul. I really don't. If that's why you're going."

"I'm going because I spent six years learning the language. I'm not looking for her."

That was all. Between the two of them, Ursula McCarahan had never been much more than a pronoun.

In fact, the elder McCarahan had tried to find his wife. Two years after she ran off, he was reassigned to Germany. He spent a year looking for her, searching high and low throughout the region where she had lived. He said he was doing it for his boys. They needed their natural mother. Their grandmother's health was deteriorating and Loretta was devoting more time to her job. It was for the boys.

After combing through what seemed to him to be half of Germany, he found not a trace. Robert McCarahan grew frustrated and angry. The people in the village claimed to know nothing of her whereabouts. "She has two boys. They need their mother." But all he received were shrugs. All he saw were expressions of ignorance in their poor, worn faces.

A week before he was to return to the States, he went to the man who helped raise Ursula after her grandfather died, the man over whose tavern their marriage had begun. He promised this man that he would kill Ursula. The innkeeper turned his back and retreated into his house. From the doorway, he looked at McCarahan standing on the pavement in the summer sun. "Whatever you do is between you and Ursula," he said. "Es geht mich nichts an." And so, when Paul left for Germany fourteen years later, all Robert McCarahan was able to tell him was that he didn't know where she was.

There was a job waiting for Paul in Düsseldorf, courtesy of a summer work program. Paul had been able to get his residential college to pay for the flight. He had made the formal decision to major in mathematics and not in German. The summer would in effect be his final course in the language. It was all arranged, from mid-June to late August. He flew from New York to Paris on a Yale chartered flight and then caught a train for Munich.

He ate poorly the first five days. In Munich, he discovered that he was not fond of the Bavarian dialect and that he was not confident of his German, his previous conversations with native speakers, except maybe his mother, having been limited. He had only vague memories of her, much less of conversations. She left soon after his fourth birthday.

On the evening before he was to make the rail trip northwest to Düsseldorf, he had dinner in the hotel. Paul ate what they brought him, ate the cold pork and potato salad, then stayed at his table because he had nowhere else to go but back to his room.

After midnight, the restaurant cleared. Only the owner, his wife, and another couple remained. Paul would have left too if they had not invited him to join them. He explained that he did not drink, but they pleaded. The women were pretty and he was tired of his isolation, so he gave in. One of the women fed him bits of fruit from the bottom of her wine glass. She fed him with a dainty fork and Paul was forced to laugh. "I'm not used to the alcohol," he told them. He laughed and could not stop. It felt as if he had never laughed before.

The next day, he soberly undertook the trip from Munich to Düsseldorf. Each bend of the railroad tracks seemed to present the view of a fortress brooding on a hilltop, or a vineyard, or a tiny village. And in his sobriety, he said to himself, "This is where they speak the language that I forgot a lifetime ago." A thunderstorm hit, sent black clouds streaming over the hilltop fortresses, torrents of rain into the vineyards, pointed lightning bolts down into the villages. But Paul felt safe. After all, it was his mother's country.

He took up his job at the Commerzbank in the Letters-of-Credit office, took up the pink and white sheets, transactions. First register, then total. He was comfortable.

The section was dominated by women. The supervisor was a woman. He felt at home.

Paul grew more confident of his German and held lectures on professional wrestling, baseball, the richness of American ice cream. There was not much work that summer and his co-workers formed a willing audience. Sometimes he would lie prone on one of the tables and hold forth, his officemates clucking in mock dismay. He made up dummy documents and sent them off to nonexistent branch offices: Moscow, Indianapolis.

On the floors of crowded little bars on the bank of the Rhine, he had even ventured out to dance. He remained tentative, but he was out there. Once he was out there with a typist from the office. She was short with wavy blond hair that fell into her eyes, the first girl he had ever asked for a date. They had eaten hamburgers, barhopped, and spat into the Rhine. The mixing of holy waters, Paul explained, and she went along with it.

He wandered through Düsseldorf unsuspecting. That is, without suspicion that this was the essential staging ground for the rest of his life. Paul watched the whores on parade in the courtyard of his neighborhood brothel, nipples erect in negligee. He watched them beckon from the red light, women of every race, young and old, the question repeated as they moved from man to man, "Kommst du mit?"

At nineteen he was still a virgin. Sometimes he would talk to the other men standing there with their backs to the railroad embankment, men who had told their wives they were going bowling. "Get yourself a shot," they would say.

"You could be dead tomorrow." But he hadn't bought, unwilling to give himself up to these unknown arms and legs.

Instead he went his way, usually finding himself on the Königsallee in the center of the city. Lights shown on swans as they slept on the canal. The reflected rays gleamed green in the lower branches of trees that stood mute guard on either side of the waterway. There were sidewalk cafes, story-book bridges, and opulent store windows. There were tulip beds and lawns like golfing greens in the Hofgarten.

***

Paul felt at home. It was summer in the Rhineland. And it was night. He was on his way to Bonn by train because he thought that before the summer ended he should visit the West German capital. And he would have left earlier if he hadn't spent most of the evening drinking beer with the men from the office. But it hadn't seemed to matter.

The late-night locals were never crowded as they bumped down the line from one Rhineland town to the next. Paul occupied a compartment alone. He sat feeling the beer in his head and a slight pressure in his bladder. The train made the whistle stops between Düsseldorf and Cologne, where he would change trains for Bonn.

A man opened the door to the compartment and asked Paul if he minded company. Paul lied and said that he didn't. He was about Paul's height, but stout with dark disheveled hair. Each of the many wrinkles in his face was filled with dirt, dirt that appeared to have taken its time settling in.

"Where are you from? Are you an African?" The man spoke with the cadence of the Rhine, a cadence Paul had lately begun to discern in his own speech.

"I'm an American."

"Soldat?"

"Student. I came over for the summer." It was an explanation that Paul had given many times since his arrival and he was prepared to launch into the reasons why he had come. But the man did not ask.

"You're not a soldier?" His eyes moved over Paul's body. "You look very soldierly. Very trim."

"I'm a runner. A sprinter."

He continued as if he had not heard Paul's response. "I was once a soldier. I was once young like you and a soldier. Do you believe that?"

Paul nodded. "That's easy enough to believe."

"You should believe. Himmelfahrtskommando. We went against Russian tanks on the eastern front. Himmelfahrts-kommando. Do you understand?" Paul had never heard the expression before but took it to be a kind of death-or-glory squad. "I was personally responsible for the destruction of seven Russian tanks. Seven Russian tanks were mine. Do you follow me?" And Paul, not minding the story at all, said that he followed perfectly.

A smile revealed broken teeth. The wrinkles looked filthier. "I thought you would understand." He leaned forward and tapped Paul on the knee. "I was sure you would understand. You are very trim. Very fit. Like a soldier. I'm no longer young but I still have a fighting spirit." He reached into a worn leather briefcase and pulled out an instrument, which, but for the finely finished wooden handle, resembled an ordinary ice pick.

"I used this back in those days. There were always a couple who didn't want to stay in the tank when it got hot. It was like target practice. And then I would stick this in their throats to make sure they were finished."

Paul began to fidget. The pressure in his bladder had increased, but the alcohol in his head provided enough inertia to keep him from leaving the compartment to go to the toilet.

"I'm no longer young, but I can do almost anything that I could do then. Do you believe me?"

Paul went along. "Sure, I believe you."

"Let me show you." He extended his left hand toward Paul, palm up. His palm and the inside of his wrist were thick with scars. Taking the ice pick, he held it over his palm like a pencil. "Himmelfahrtskommando. Shall I write it?"

Before Paul had a chance to reply or even comprehend, the man had carved a small capital *H* in the meat of his hand, the blood trickling out to mix with the dirt. He handed over the ice pick. "You write the *i*."

In the stupor induced by shock and alcohol, Paul had actually leaned over the man's hand to begin, leaned over the scar tissue and the fresh wound. Then he caught himself and handed the ice pick back feeling disoriented. "We've both probably drunk too much." And he added, as if it were pertinent, "I'll be changing trains in Cologne."

The man slammed the ice pick into the seat next to him. "You look like a soldier, but you're not one! You are soft. You are not equipped with a soldier's spirit. What you need is a soldier's protection. I like colored boys." The man leaned forward and quickly kissed Paul on the lips. Paul tried to push him away, but he would not be pushed away. His right arm was wrapped around Paul's head and the bloodied left hand reached into his fly. "Komm'. Blas' mir einen!" And he tried to force Paul's head into his lap, onto the now exposed and erect member. "Blas' mir einen!" Paul felt that the vertebrae in his neck were about to explode. His hand found the ice pick and in the face of degradation, he gathered himself and drove it into the man's rib cage. Paul heard the air escaping through the man's mouth, then he felt the grip on his head release.

The man had fallen back into the seat on his side of the compartment. Paul stood to leave, but the man's legs were between Paul and the door. Shaking, trying to threaten, Paul, said, "Aus meinem Weg." Then abandoning German, "Get out of my way or I'll put this in your gut."

The man stood as if to leave the compartment but didn't. He had heard these foreign tongues before. He had seen the same desperation in the eyes of Russian tankers and in teenagers in the back streets of the industrial Ruhrgebiet. He was back to his theme, a soldier, to be one or not to be. "Ich bin Soldat. Du bist kein soldat."

Paul could not allow him to take a step. One step and he would be all over him. The ice pick would no longer be a threat. So when the man's hand jerked forward, Paul began his swing, roundhouse and wild. And all the angles were right. The swing ended as smoothly as it had begun, with the ice pick buried in the man's stomach. And at first, Paul thought that nothing had happened because the man did not make a sound. He just stood there, staring at Paul, motionless, as if poised to ask a question. Then Paul pulled the ice pick away and the stain spread across the shirt. He swung again hitting him in the neck this time and the blood squirted past and onto the window. Now the man was falling, but Paul pulled back and swung once more hitting him in the eye, snapping his head backward, retarding the fall. Paul left the ice pick embedded in the man's head as he fell. It was a capeless bullfight, a macabre dance, the man brushed against Paul as he met the floor facedown. The handle of the ice pick rested between the floor and the eye socket.

He looked at the man lying there and at that moment felt as satisfied as he ever had. Paul urinated on the body. Sliding open the compartment door, he took his suitcase, walked into the aisle and left the car. His perfect summer was over, ended by a swing for which all the angles were right, a deft pivot, a body bounding on its face. This was all that could be asked of perfection, a perfect ending.

In Cologne he never left the platform. He waited for a train back to Düsseldorf. There was a teenage couple kissing at the far end of the platform. Something he had never done, kiss a woman. A man had kissed him. He had killed a man. The hand on the platform clock jumped. Another minute passed. German trains were punctual. The local to Düsseldorf would come. Of this he was confident. If the couple would only stop kissing, maybe he could convince himself that there was something beyond the timely arrival that he could confidently predict. One kiss, followed by the choreography of the ice pick. He was sure he would never dance again.

Over the next week, Paul searched the paper in vain for mention of the body in the train. A few days after his train ride, the Soviets, with the help of the rest of the Warsaw Pact, occupied Czechoslovakia. There was nothing else on the German airwaves, no other event. Paul watched the news in the lounge of the residence for single men. Russian armor rolled through the streets of Prague meeting no resistance. No Himmelfahrtskommando.

Fear had its jaws very near the throat of the West German populace. It was a fear that radically altered relationships. In the Letters-of-Credit office, no one paid heed when Frau Bernhard invited Frau Özbek to lunch. This, despite the fact that a month earlier Özbek, a Turk and naturalized German, had screamed at Bernhard, screamed at her that the one thing the Jews should have learned during World War II was to keep their mouths shut. Frau Bernhard had wept openly then. Now no one paid heed. Bernhard's husband was in Czechoslovakia on business when the border was closed. She would take her comfort wherever she could find it, even from this ill-tempered Turkish woman. And no one paid heed when Paul suddenly had very little to say. Russian panzer was in Prague, within easy striking distance of the Rhineland.

Paul spent one more evening with Gudrun, the typist from the office. They went wherever she wanted to go, drank whatever she wanted to drink. But he could not bring himself to dance, to be in all that wild swinging of arms.

He bought her roses. When he left her that evening, he kissed her three times, kissed her three times to make sure that he had done it. Then he went to the neighborhood brothel Hinter dem Bahndamm. Paul gave a woman twenty marks and then got his shot because the bowlers had been right. He could be dead tomorrow.

Paul had been eyeing her ever since he found the place at the beginning of the summer. She was probably in her mid-fifties and she always stood indifferently in her window with an expression that was a few degrees on the sour side of passive. He had even seen her a few times at the grocery store. Paul asked her to keep her glasses on while they did it.

It was August 1968, only three months since Paul flew by the Harvard anchor and his coach had seen something rise up in him.

When he returned to Pittsburgh, his father asked him only one question. "Did you find her?" Paul answered, "I never looked for her." He wished he had.

INTO THE ANCESTRAL LANDS

In 1676, the year of Bacon's Rebellion, Paul had ancestors awaiting cultural extinction in the Virginia Piedmont. Their language was related to the Lakota spoken many hundreds of miles to the west. But they had long been isolated, surrounded by tribes of the Algonquian and Iroquois language families, constantly under threat of attack from multiple directions, the Tidewater, the north, the southwest. Then Nathaniel Bacon and his rabble applied the coup de grace, putting the white man's boot to their rear ends, breaking the Saponi and pushing them down to the North Carolina border. No later than the

Revolutionary War, Paul's Saponi ancestor was the son of a white man. The native Y-chromosome signature Q3, which had held the line for more than ten thousand years in North America, was replaced by western Europe's haplogroup R1b. In less than two hundred years the torch was passed again when the daughter of Paul's R1b great-grandfather was sought out by the E1a divining rod. And so, Paul, a Saponi remnant, carried haplogroup E1a, the signature of men who dawdled in the Sahara forty thousand years ago, the aboriginal North Africans. The white man was the middleman.

***

Except for a short nap just after they crossed into Maryland, Ruth had been running her mouth since they left Pittsburgh. Paul actually found himself enjoying her company. By midday, it was ninety degrees but Ruth was wearing his Yale letter sweater, a heavy pullover with the big blue letter *Y* that she found one day while rummaging through Paul's bedroom closet. This was around the time that Paul started mucking around with DNA and he said that some people wore their hearts on their sleeves, but all Ruth wanted to do was wear his Y-chromosome on her breast, to go along with the occasional vaginal infusion. Ruth didn't care for his remark. He let her add the sweater to her wardrobe and she had it dry cleaned. Her excuse for wearing it on the trip was that she had trouble sitting in a car for long periods with the air conditioner on. She was wearing a short skirt, giving Paul reason to doubt her reason, but he didn't challenge it.

"It's sort of like praying," Ruth said. She first broached this subject somewhere between Hagerstown and Frederick. Now they were creeping around the Washington beltway. "Any bad thing that I imagine happening, won't. That's what I believe. I spend a lot of time imagining how I might die."

Paul kept his eyes on the car in front of him. "How often do you find yourself imagining that I've killed you?"

"Lots. Stabbing, sexually transmitted disease, suffocating me with a pillow. It's a long list." She said this with gusto. "If I haven't heard from my daughter or granddaughter for a while, I run through a bunch of things that might happen to them."

"I have a problem with this, Ruth."

"What?"

"Suppose what you're doing really works. Given that you're going to die, wouldn't that mean that you're making it more likely that you'll die of something unimaginable? And that's not good. You can't even imagine how bad that could be."

"Paul, you're not a funny man."

"Not true. I make people laugh sometimes."

"When? When have you ever made anyone laugh? I think I've smiled once, maybe twice."

"Okay, here's a true story. One year while I was down in Alabama, at Auburn, I taught set theory. When I introduced them to the Axiom of Choice..."

"This isn't going to be funny."

"Give me one minute, ma'am. I told them that most mathematicians think that it's a good idea to make it an axiom, but some don't. And there are really heated arguments on the issue, believe you me. So, I asked, 'How many of you think the Axiom of Choice is a reasonable assumption.' Then I lied. I couldn't help it. I lied. I said that I had given a talk on the subject one summer in Seattle and a shouting match broke out between the two factions. One was screaming, 'Pro-Choice.' The other one was yelling 'Get a life.'

"Guess what happened then. The kids in my class started shouting the same thing back and forth and laughing like crazy."

"Now you're lying to me."

"No, I'm not."

***

In his years of researching the family history, Paul had visited Susie and Stephen, his father's maternal first cousins, a dozen times. Stephen was eighty-nine and his sister Susie was eighty-seven. Their spouses had died before Paul first met them and they owned houses on the same street in north Richmond, two blocks off the main north-south thoroughfare Chamberlayne.

Paul was the only member of the Pittsburgh branch who had ever met the Virginia relatives, the ones that had stayed behind when Paul's Hale grandmother and most of her siblings moved north after World War I. By the time Paul went south to find them, his grandparents were dead.

He was forced to turn to the records in the Virginia State Archives. It took him only one day to find the name of the man in Lunenburg County who owned his great-grandfather Hale. As the story went, his great-grandfather had seen the Union troops come into Lunenburg County in 1865 when he was a boy. A birth record in 1856 tied his great-grandfather to the owner Wadsworth. In the column that requested the relationship of the informant to 'child born' was the word 'owner.' Paul knew that this was an unusual find. Most black people would never be able to find a document to prove that any of their ancestors had been slaves. They could not prove that they were owed forty acres and a mule. The Birth Register in Virginia did not start until 1853. His great-grandfather was born in the window framed by that year and the Civil War.

After three weeks, he had traced the Wadsworths forward in time and found the last owner's great-granddaughter Ann in Lunenburg County. And it was through Ann that he got telephone numbers of his Richmond relatives. Now Ann was dead and most of the relatives she had pointed him to had also passed on. He was down to Susie and Stephen.

The siblings were waiting for him on Susie's side porch when Paul and Ruth arrived, two works of art warmly crafted in copper, leaning toward the street in expectation. Paul introduced Ruth and Susie hugged her saying, "You young people finally got here. My stomach's been growling for an hour."

Stephen did not eat. Paul had never seen Stephen eat. Susie said that her brother was picky, and also mentioned that at family gatherings he had been known to take his plate to his room to read a book and eat in solitude.

Susie was saying, "I baked some wings because I wasn't sure that everyone would like tuna salad." And that was the way it went with tuna, beets, chicken and some pound cake to seal it off. By the end of the meal, Ruth was calling them Cousin Susie and Cousin Stephen. Susie told the story about her hard-drinking, murderous, half-Indian uncle. "He had mean little eyes. I couldn't look at them." Uncle Will had left Susie a small fortune when he died in Chattanooga. But she had been forced to make a solemn promise not to share it with anyone, not even her brother Stephen.

"That's your father's side of the family, Cousin Susie. He wasn't a Hales"

Susie laughed. "You're an upstanding man, Paul. But the Hales men were as bad as Uncle Will. Drank like fish. Fight you as soon as look at you. But you're different. You're refined and educated." Susie looked at Ruth and winked.

"I will say this for Uncle Will. He never killed a man who didn't need it, and he usually got away with it. Uncle Will had a white lawyer. I don't think he ever spent more than a few months in jail for anything. And he drank, but he could hold his liquor pretty good."

Susie reached over and patted Paul on the top of his bald head. "You're my good cousin." She looked at Ruth and laughed. Stephen sipped his iced tea and eyed the food on the table with suspicion.

Before they left, Ruth persuaded the man who was cutting Susie's lawn to take a picture of the four of them with her camera. The man took two. Ruth believed that

Paul's expression in the first shot was unpleasant. There they were on a bright summer afternoon, three the color of red autumn and one the color of crystalline winter, crystalline winter in a white, varsity letter sweater with a large blue *Y*.

Stephen said, "So, you're headed down to Kenbridge." There were embraces all around. Paul even hugged Ruth, disoriented by it all.

It is seventy-five miles from Richmond to Kenbridge in Lunenburg County, Virginia, where his grandmother's Hales family had lived since before the Revolutionary War. The next point of interest would be in Orange County, North Carolina, where his father's paternal grandparents were born and the McCarahan line stretched back to the late 1700s at least. Then they would bounce north back into Virginia to Pittsylvania County, where Paul had a few dozen steers on a farm that belonged to second cousins. For tax purposes, this was a business trip. The automobile mileage and hotel expenses were deductible. Paul owned land in Lunenburg County and Orange County that he rented to local farmers. These were all tracts of land that had been owned by his great-grandfathers or, in one case, by the man Wadsworth, who also owned his Hales great-grandfather until he was nine years old and the Civil War ended. Now Paul owned the owner's grave. Paul had acquired a total of 110 acres in two counties for sentimental reasons.

The only money that Paul had ever borrowed in his life was to cover what his scholarship to Yale had not covered. His house, the land, his cars, his Steinway piano were all cash transactions. Not counting these possessions, Paul had managed to accumulate over two million dollars. He had made sound investments. Two years after Yaros, he sold the car that was so notably involved in an accident to a well-to-do black attorney at twice the Kelley Blue Book value. If he had not repaired the Geometry Killing's body damage, it would have gone for even more.

"I really like your folks, Paul." They had gone south on Chamberlayne and then taken the ramp onto I-95. These were the only members of Paul's family she had ever met, except for Thelma very briefly.

Paul ignored Ruth's remark. "One day I'm going to take some time to find the spot where Plecker was run over. The guy was eighty-six years old and still never looked when he walked into traffic. He was a real arrogant son of a bitch. I would be tempted to stay over tonight and try to find it, but I don't know Richmond very well."

"I think you actually like Plecker."

"Fascinated is what I am. It's people like him who made black people what they are today."

"What are they today?"

"People united in their non-whiteness. There should be plaque on Chamberlayne Avenue where he was flattened. 'Plecker's Last Stand.'"

Ruth laughed.

"I thought you said I never..."

"Well, occasionally you do. Paul, what I was talking about was your cousins. They're the salt of the earth."

"I didn't meet them or really even know anything about them until I was an adult. Now it feels like I've known them all my life."

In Petersburg, they picked up I-85 and headed southwest. By the time they took the exit for 460, the car was running low on gas. Paul pulled into a gas station. While he pumped, he had an insight, which led to rummaging through a shopping bag in the trunk, which is where Ruth saw him when she emerged from the restroom. Paul was muttering, "It's all clear to me now." The shopping bag was full of trail mix and other snacks. There was also a DNA kit, just in case he found a suitable cousin in North Carolina for a descendant of the ancestor that had eluded his DNA survey. Underneath the kit he had Marianne Mithun's weighty tome, *The Languages of Native North America*. At the very bottom was what he was looking for, Ernest Robinson's paper with Paul's name on it and Berman's book on complex analysis and analytic number theory. He opened the book and the paper on the hood of his Honda CRV. But it really wasn't necessary. He already knew.

"Why didn't you just say it this way in the first place?" Robinson was nowhere to be seen, but Paul was talking right to him. Then he closed both the paper and the book and jammed them back into the shopping bag. Paul looked blankly at Ruth. "It's always good when you finally understand."

Ruth said, "I guess so."

What Paul finally understood was how Ernest had transported the whole analysis to a "natural" topological space, transforming with great finesse the usually daunting mechanisms into a rather charming set of statements about a convergent sequence of convergent sequences.

"Ruth, we probably don't want to get into it." She had seen him do this a couple of times in the five years that they had been together and that sentence was enough to satisfy her. And Paul was satisfied that when he went to Philadelphia in two weeks, he and Ernest could now have a substantive discussion of the paper. In fact, he had observed something that he suspected Ernest had not. Paul had noticed an interesting relationship to the Twin Prime Conjecture, not quite the holy grail that the Riemann Hypothesis represented, but nonetheless one of the great unscaled peaks in number theory.

***

They were passing through Blackstone and only ten miles from Kenbridge when Ruth cleared her throat and then said nothing.

Paul finally asked the question. "What is it?"

"I want you to make a commitment."

"What?"

"You know that I'm not going to live forever."

"Well?" Paul could hear her choking up.

"Giselle is my heart."

Paul had not seen Giselle since she was in his calculus class many years earlier and he would only recognize her on the basis of pictures in Ruth's home, if that. He pulled over into a parking lot on Blackstone's Main Street.

Ruth said, "When I die, I want you to take an interest in her."

"Giselle's a grown woman. She must be in her thirties. She has a mother."

Ruth spat it out. "You've met Barbara. Barbara couldn't take care of a goldfish. She doesn't even know who Giselle's father is for sure. I'm not talking about money. I'll leave her plenty of that. I just don't want her to end up like her mother. Right now, she's working jobs that are beneath her. But at least she's working. I don't know where she's going, but I know where I'm going. It's inevitable."

And then she said very firmly, "I want you to agree in principle to take an interest in my granddaughter's welfare. You're a brilliant man. I'll let you figure out how to do it. Just let me hear you say you will."

Paul took quite a while to respond.

"In some sense, she's practically family now. I'll do what I can. You never know. You might outlive me."

"The odds are against it. I'm going to thank you now for all you're going to do. There's one more favor. I don't want us to broach this subject again. I can't stand to talk about it." Paul nodded at the steering wheel.

"Here's something that I won't insist on, but you might consider. Don't kill anyone else and land your ass in jail."

"I won't land in jail, Ruth. My Y-chromosome is unerring in its choices."

"Where it points, you do not have to go."

It was nearly dark when they got onto the motel parking lot in Kenbridge. Paul knew right away that he had made a mistake. Either it was a mistake to have brought Ruth or it was a mistake to have decided on this motel. At any rate, the two actions taken together were wrong. He had stayed in this motel once before and should have known better. Except for their car, the parking lot was empty.

Once in the room, Paul began his apology. "It's only one night. If you imagine we're camping out, it'll work a lot better. This is like a deluxe tent." He batted at a fly and the apology continued. "The whole county only has thirteen thousand people. Not enough to support a decent hotel. It's just forty-five dollars."

Ruth started to laugh. "I'll tell you one thing. I'm not taking a shower here. There are enough flies in the bathroom to constitute a plague. You're right. As long as I think of it as a campsite, I'm fine." Then Ruth did the honors and pulled back the covers to expose the sheets. No stains.

Paul dug out the trail mix and unrefrigerated bottles of water and they got into bed with *The Languages of Native North America* between them. They had spent six months working through it together and now they were going back over points of interest. Before she inadvertently married into money, Ruth taught high school Spanish and Latin. She had a knack for exotic grammars. They lay there together looking at the section on inverse number in the Kiowa-Tanoan language family. It was Ruth's turn to teach and she had prepared the section carefully. She began, "Nouns have a default number that depends on the class to which they belong. There are four classes, but there's only one number suffix '-sh' for all classes and when you use it, the default number gets inverted..."

Paul said, "Remind me what the four classes are."

After some back and forth on the concept of inverse number, the two fell asleep with Mithun's tome lying between them, Ruth's delicate rump exposed. Paul woke up at some point and turned off the light.

In his dream, Paul and Ruth were trying to locate their children. Of course, they were desperate. They had done so much work each time to conceive. Ruth said that they were being cared for by a woman she trusted, but she could not or would not reveal the woman's name. She led Paul through Pittsburgh neighborhoods that were maddening in their subtle differences from what he had known them to be. For a while they were on foot and then, magically, they were in a car. They drove incessantly through the city. Every turn yielded a logic-defying surprise. Their children remained with the unnamed woman and Paul knew that they were running out of time. He yelled out, "Ruth, what's the bitch's name?" and woke up to morning in Kenbridge, Virginia.

They had breakfast at Mildred's Meals, the only restaurant in town that Paul was aware of. It was at the corner of Church and Broad Street. Five blocks of Broad Street made up the commercial district of the town. They were relieved to have survived the night in the motel and to find themselves sitting in this homey place, with the luggage stowed in the car. The dining area was about the size of a large living room, which it may have been at one time. A trickle of customers came and went, nodding a genteel good morning. It was 9:00 and they had missed whatever breakfast rush there might have been.

"What were you screaming about in your sleep? All I could make out was 'bitch.'"

"A dream. Actually, a nightmare. Someone had our kids and we were going to pick them up. I couldn't follow your directions."

"I wouldn't lose my kids, Paul. Let me tell you. I never used a baby-sitter with Bobbi. Not once. And I was the babysitter for Giselle whenever Bobbi went out, which was every other night."

"Well, last night you let some woman have our kids. Driving in Pittsburgh was something out of Alice in Wonderland."

An elderly woman crossed the restaurant and smiled in their direction. "That's Mildred."

Paul first met Mildred when he had lunch with Ann Page, the great-granddaughter of Walker Wadsworth, whose grave Paul now owned. Ann had been in the process of showing Paul her Daughters of the American Revolution papers when Mildred stopped at the table and Ann made the introduction. "This is Dr. McCarahan. He's visiting Kenbridge for the first time. His grandmother was born here in Lunenburg County."

That was a couple of years before Ann facilitated Paul's purchase of a fifty-acre section of the old Wadsworth farm, which included graves and the ruins of the house that her 5th great-grandfather Thomas Wadsworth had built before he went off to the Revolutionary War to meet a musket ball in New Jersey at the Battle of Monmouth Courthouse. He survived his wound. Paul suspected that his great-grandfather Hales was related to the Wadsworths, but he did not know this for sure. He and Ann had danced around the subject. Now he tried to remember how long Ann had been dead. A decade?

"That's Mildred," Paul said. Then Mildred came to their table and Paul introduced Ruth. Mildred wanted to know if Ruth had roots in the county. "No, all my family is from Pittsburgh. This is as far south as I've ever been."

When Mildred left, Paul said, "You've been to Florida."

"Flights to the beach don't count."

And it was true that the Virginia Piedmont was farther south than anything in Florida, except maybe for the Florida panhandle.

Paul drove Ruth through the farmland. Paul believed that there were soybeans growing on his section of the old Wadsworth farm. He led Ruth down a dirt road to the Wadsworth family cemetery in a copse on the edge of the field. Paul was thankful for the overcast day. He was usually sweating by the time he got to the graves of Walker Wadsworth and his children. He did not like the idea of adding any more of the family sweat to this soil.

Paul had never been able to establish where any of the older graves were and the site of the slave cemetery had eluded him, but they were somewhere on the acreage that surrounded the remnants of the main house, so Paul owned them too.

Ruth asked Paul if the soybean crop was all that was being cultivated. Paul didn't know. "The guy who rents this sends me a check every year. These are supposed to be soybean plants, but he could be growing poppies for all I know." A few years ago, Paul had seen what he guessed were a few Mexicans laboring in the field, but there was no one in sight this time around.

He also owned his great-grandfather Hales' entire farm, but the land there was uncultivated. He just paid the taxes on it and let the weeds grow. There had been a time when he thought he might build a retirement home there. It became clear that he was mistaken about this. Paul was not going to leave Pittsburgh. He was not going to make his home in Lunenburg County. As Ann Page had told Mildred, "His grandmother was born here." Paul had decided not to die here.

Their last stop was at Rosebud Cemetery, where some of the more recent generations of his family had been laid to rest. His Hales great-grandparents would have been hard to find if a cousin had not shown him. Now that cousin was dead and he had no idea where her grave was.

Ruth bent over to pull some weeds away from one of the grave markers and Paul saw an insect crawling up her leg. He watched it for a while. Probably a tick, he thought. Ruth did not handle insects well and he knew that she was already on edge from the flies in the motel bathroom.

"Ruth, is there something on your leg?" He said it at the same time that he reached to pluck it off. But he was not quick enough. Ruth Gable had a conniption fit. She was out of control, dancing on his ancestors' graves. The tick was oblivious. Paul deftly grabbed one of her flailing hands, making it look like they were jitterbugging together. Then he hugged her and brushed the tick to the ground.

"You've always been quite a dancer, Ruth." Ruth looked at him wide-eyed and mouth agape.

"I think we're done here, ma'am. It's time to move out. I guarantee you as much excitement in Hillsborough and Mebane as you've had here in Kenbridge."

Ruth was quiet as they walked back to the car. Then she said, "Thanks. You know, I really am having the time of my life." This embarrassed Paul and he pushed the silliness button. "Tomorrow we have an appointment at the Eno River Saponi tribal office. You just nearly got us put in a minstrel show. Please don't audition for a pow-wow."

Paul put a compilation of Art Tatum piano solos in the CD player and pointed the car in the direction of North Carolina.

HIS MOTHER'S COUNTRY

It wasn't until he had escaped the draft and returned to Germany in 1970 that he began looking for his mother, Ursula Kowalzik. It took him nearly four years to find her address and he needed the detective work of one of the teachers at the high school where he taught. She lived in Munich, quite a distance from the Rhineland where, by then, he was mired.

If this were a movie, one would see an aerial shot of Paul making his way along Hüttenstraße carrying his wash home from the laundromat. He would come out from under the railway overpass and turn left into Arminstraße, switching the bag of laundry from his left hand to his right. He was walking directly toward the brothel now, Hinter dem Bahndamm, where he had watched the women in negligee the summer of 1968 and gotten his first shot. He seldom went behind the wall, even though he lived only two blocks away. Just on rare occasions, he would find himself there, see the women circling, hear the proposition "Kommst du mit?" He would watch and remember his summer of the ice pick and the Himmelfahrtskommando. He never bought.

He turned into Industriestraße at the wall that shielded the brothel's courtyard from public view. There was one more turn at Vulkanstraße and a short walk to the corner at Dreieckstraße, where he lived. It was a seedy, resolutely drab neighborhood. A few sex shops catered to the spillover from the brothel. Paul dodged numerous and enormous deposits of dog shit because not even lip service was given to German cleanliness in this part of town. This was where the whores walked their poodles. There was a tavern on every block in a quarter filled with mostly lower-income families clinging to their German identity, crowded by Turks and southern Europeans clinging to their work permits in the face of rising German unemployment.

He had become a gambler of sorts. If the weather was pleasant, he would get on the trolley and ride out to the Grafenberg woods, where it was his practice to put a hundred marks on the longest shot he could find, and then watch his horse circle the track. Most of the time his selection would trail from start to finish. He never won any money. But he had seen a long shot named Gegenwind, Against the Wind, win on the same track in 1968. Paul was waiting for another Gegenwind. The next Gegenwind was long overdue.

Paul was also playing the nationwide lottery: six out of forty-nine. He had calculated the probability of winning and found it to be just slightly better than one in fourteen million. The circles on his entry sheet were filled in with an emphasis on prime numbers and perfect squares.

Paul walked into the building that housed the foreign employees of a fashionable Königsallee hotel. He then continued through the hallway and outside again into a courtyard, the Hinterhof, and threaded his way around garbage cans and ducked under clothes drying on the line. On the other side of the courtyard, dwarfed by the surrounding buildings that faced onto the street, was a one-story structure where he rented a room and shared a bathroom with the other tenants. Paul could see the eighty-five-year-old Oma waiting at her window, the only window the building had. The other rooms had skylights that could be opened thirty degrees by a crank kept in the hall, skylights where water condensed and rained back into the room on cold days; on the days when they cursed the underperforming radiators and boiled water to steam themselves warm. No doubt that the Oma was waiting for Paul.

The Oma finally scrambled out into the hall after fumbling with her door key. Time and again she locked herself into her room and then had to fight the lock to get out. "Paul," she whined. "Paul." Well, she knew the rules and she was going to have to live by them.

"Paul, are you going shopping today?"

"Oma, what is today?"

"Today is Thursday."

"And what time is it?"

"Four-thirty. "

"I gave you a shopping schedule three weeks ago. Monday, Wednesday and Friday at two o'clock."

"I just wanted some cigarettes. Tu' mir den Gefallen." She was standing hipshot and it drew attention to her slightly humped back.

"Asthma and cigarettes don't go well together, Oma. Besides, today is Thursday. I thought we had this settled."

Resigned, she started back to her room, the long, chestnut-dyed hair tied together with a rubber band and swinging at her back. She turned to ask if he would watch television with her that evening. Paul said that he would. He would also get her cigarettes, but he didn't say that.

She was called the Oma because she was old, not because she was anyone's grandmother. In fact, she had no children and, at this point, Paul was the only person standing between her and an old folks home. There was a family that had taken some interest in her. The children had run errands. But they moved away. Tremors, asthma and near blindness prevented her going out on the streets alone. So, even though all the stores were within easy walking distance, Paul remained the only means. He had been there four years and, at this point, he was the only one she trusted.

The restriction of the Oma's shopping privileges to certain days and hours was more than just a common-sense remedy to the fact that she had been running him ragged. It was also part of a more general dependency that had evolved between Paul and the other Hinterhof tenants over the years that he had lived there.

Ibrahim, a middle-aged Turkish laborer, depended on Paul to check the meat labels to ensure that Gisela, the woman he lived with, was not feeding him pork. He also relied on Paul to read his bank statements and other business mail to check that his money was being handled according to his wishes. Paul had bought a separate mailbox for the Hinterhof when he moved in. He held the only key.

What little German Ibrahim spoke was devoid of grammatical sense and conceptual vocabulary. When Gisela tired of this, and she tired very quickly in this regard, she turned to alcohol and sometimes to Paul.

As a kind of anchorman, there was Max Schadlich, forty-five years old and living on a state dole. Schadlich was deteriorating, a defective bladder and sensitive stomach, a bad heart and no teeth. His hair was white and he suffered from insomnia. At five-foot-two, he had barely more substance than the Oma and looked just as old.

Max had found in Paul what he misconstrued to be a good listener. Like a museum guide who had waited decades for a visitor, he eagerly took Paul on tour, the foreign legion, his stint as a professional boxer, flak duty as a teenager during the Second World War. None of the stops on the tour corresponded to the facts of his personal history. But he wanted badly to believe that Paul believed him. That would be enough.

"I don't understand you, Max. You said you were with the foreign legion for eleven years. That would mean, if I'm not mistaken, that you were in Indochina at the age of fourteen. Didn't you say you had..."

Paul was constantly threatening in this way to close the museum in one fell swoop. Then, in the very next moment, he would rescue Max and, in the process, create another museum display, adding to the tour. He felt perverse, like an adolescent scouring Superman comic books for contradictions.

"I see, Max. I see. I'm probably confusing that with the time you were with the small mercenary band of paratroopers. You never did explain how you got out of the jam in South America. You remember, the time you guys parachuted in broad daylight into a fortification."

And Max, speaking a coarse Low German dialect, would hastily construct a fitting conclusion. Although he couldn't remember telling Paul about a band of paratroopers, anything to save the museum. Anything.

"Yes indeed, those were rough times. Nothing but tough Jungs in the paratroops. You have to be tough to be a Fallschirmjäger."

Paul balanced his part-time employment with many hours a week cruising the streets of Düsseldorf. There was a small contingent of Africans, African students, and African scoundrels. Paul had taken up with the scoundrels. He would usually run into them at the train station when he bought the daily paper, the Rheinische Post. Some of them were selling their bodies, their brown faces cold and gaunt in the Rhineland winter.

They came and went, the Africans. There was the Ethiopian in his twenties who spoke English and Italian, but no German. He wanted training as a mechanic, but in the meantime was lubing rosy German rear ends so that he could eat. But most were West Africans. Paul had met dozens of them, all of them going straight to hell.

A man from Senegal had broken Paul's heart one day. He broke Paul's heart while they sat in the train station's cafeteria and Paul ate spaghetti. He was about Paul's age and spoke to Paul in French, while Paul worked very hard to follow. Paul's French was weak. The man described the beginning of French colonization in Senegal. When the account was finished, the man returned to his newspaper. But as Paul stood to leave, the son of Senegal asked him in German if Paul would give him five marks. "Hast du fünf Mark für mich, Paul?"

And this broke Paul's heart because over the two months Paul had known him, no German had ever been spoken. German was apparently the language he begged in. Paul fished a five-mark coin out of his pocket and placed it on the table. The returned expression of gratitude was also in German.

That same day, walking through the main staging area of the train station, he saw Pell Dobbins. At least he thought he saw Pell Dobbins, looking cheery with a knot of people who were obviously Americans. Paul turned and walked away, losing himself in the crowd. Maybe it wasn't Pell, but he couldn't take the chance that it was. On days when he didn't have to teach, he didn't look much better than the deadbeats he hung out with. He couldn't risk a greeting from Dobbins. He could hear it now. "Hey, Paul, what a coincidence. What are you doing here?" Paul didn't know what he was doing here. He now knew where his mother lived. It was a five-hour train ride away in Munich, the city he had passed through in 1968, where the woman had fed him fruit from the bottom of her wine glass. Since then, Paul had managed to get himself stuck in a Rhineland dystopia. It was way past time to go to Bavaria and reunite with his mother.

There was at least one African in Düsseldorf who was not in a bind, at least not financially. Saedy Gaye was a Gambian with bad teeth and the complexion of dark slate.

He always had money, but no visible means of support. Paul had met him through Hans-Joachim Pruger. Hans-Joachim was from New Jersey and Paul had known him since the ice-pick summer of '68. Hans-Joachim had dropped out of high school and moved to Germany to squat with relatives. He spent his days sponging drinks in the Altstadt and dealing drugs on a small scale. In fact, Paul had no doubt that Saedy and Hans-Joachim were involved in multiple criminal enterprises. But they never discussed how they made their money and Paul never mentioned the urine-soaked body on the train. Paul would not have been able to explain why he spent any time with either one of them. It was frequently the case that if he saw them on the street and believed that they had not seen him, he would steal away.

The Oma didn't like Hans-Joachim because he had a German name, but spoke German with an accent. She didn't like his slicked-back blond hair either. That's what Oma had told Paul after one of the visits that Saedy and Hans-Joachim made to the Hinterhof, visits that she viewed as suspicious. "That Hans-Joachim is no good. He thinks he's German. He's no German. You're more German than he is."

She didn't like Saedy either. When she talked about Saedy she referred to him as "der Neger." Paul felt he had to explain that he was a Negro too.

"Du bist kein Neger!" she scolded. No, her grandson could not be a Negro. She didn't know what he was, a Mischling maybe. Yes, maybe he was mixed. But he wasn't a Negro. She knew what Negroes looked like. She had seen a few of them after the First World War. Negroes are black.

Paul was gentle with her. "Oma, listen to me." He always addressed her as 'grandma.' "I am a Negro."

"No, you are not!"

"Well, then what am I?"

"Du bist kein Neger. Das weiß ich ganz genau!"

Paul insisted. "Doch!"

That made her fly off the handle. "From now on I'm going to call you Negro!" And she stormed down the hall. Of course, she never did call him 'Neger.' But Paul had made the Oma mad. He had gotten on her bad side for a moment.

Two weeks after the man from Senegal broke his heart, Paul was thrown out of a bar, the Rhinoceros, in the Düsseldorf Altstadt. He was there with Hans-Joachim, swallowing beer, pretending to celebrate his birthday. It was the first time that Paul had seen Hans-Joachim in months. They stood at the bar, Hans-Joachim bullshitting, as usual, embedding dramatic pauses in the mundane discourse. The volume of the music supplied them with an excuse to lapse into silence.

A man tapped him on the shoulder and Paul thought at first that it was a joke. The man must be drunk or crazy. He looked too young to have any authority, too young to stick his thick, yellow beard and wire-rimmed glasses into Paul's face. One glance at the barmaid's face convinced him otherwise. He was being told to leave. Apparently, the man had overheard his conversation with Hans-Joachim, which inspired him to address Paul with bizarre chunks of English. "I am the chief. You are going."

Hans-Joachim didn't hesitate. He sprang into the chief's face asking him rapid-fire, "Do I have to go too? Do I have to go too?" His profile was rodent-like.

Paul gripped his beer glass more tightly, while Hans-Joachim raged, his nostrils flared, his face gone red, all the filth of northern New Jersey beginning to flow over his lips.

"I'm gonna kick your motherfuckin' ass." He could go for the Chief's throat at any second, so Paul readied himself, feeling an obligation to move before he did, before the teenagers sitting at a nearby table joined in. If it was going to be a brawl, he would do the honors, try to break his beer glass in that sweaty, obnoxious, bespectacled face, watch the blood run down through the blond beard.

But the brown-skin woman prevented bloodshed, slipping between him and the Chief, putting her arms around him, almost a lover's embrace. She spoke quickly in a whisper, pleading in soft, warm, southern German tones.

"Araber," she explained. It was Arabs. They caused a disturbance the night before and put him in a bad mood. "Nothing to do with you. It's not personal. Anyone who has a dark skin." Paul let go of the beer glass. "Come back tomorrow. You'll see. It's just tonight. We can talk outside..."

It was with the same abruptness that he had planned to use to jerk the beer glass into the Chief's face that he did an about-face and moved toward the door. He heard Hans-Joachim threatening to come back and burn the place down, down to the ground in fact.

"You defend him?"

The brown-skin woman said nothing.

"I asked if you're defending him?"

"If you come back some other time, everything will be different. I know him." She smiled and Paul wished he had planted the beer glass in her face.

"What's your name?"

"Gretchen. Gretchen Traub."

"I don't understand, Gretchen. The man's a pig."

"I wouldn't live with him if he were. I wouldn't stay under the same roof."

And he almost began his sentence with "You mean," but he knew what she meant. "You live with a pig. You're a black sow. No wonder he doesn't throw you out. He's fucking you."

She started back into the bar, tall and graceful. "You have no right to judge me. Who are you to judge me?"

Paul turned his back on her and walked away. Hans-Joachim left the bar and ran to catch up. "What did she say, Paul?"

"She said she sleeps with him."

***

Paul's mother was still using her married name. Paul and his colleague at the high school had found the address in the summer of 1974. It was several months before he mustered the courage to board a train and take the ride from Düsseldorf to Munich.

He stalled in Munich, spending a day trying to find the hotel where he had stayed six years earlier, where he had been intoxicated for the first time. It was the summer of the Himmelfahrtskommando on the train between Düsseldorf and Cologne. But he couldn't find the hotel and began to think that the only real thing about that summer was the killing. That perhaps he had been called to Germany for a changing of the guard. Kill one, take his place.

Paul waited two days before hailing a cab and directing the driver to the Englischer Garten, leaving himself a fifteen-minute walk and time to compose himself. Paul wore the suit he had bought soon after he finessed the draft and established that he would not be in army khaki.

Even on a crisp autumn evening, a brisk walk would leave him with sweat on his brow, so he took care not to walk too quickly. Only hours earlier, he had traced the route on a map. Now he emerged from the Englischer Garten and glanced back at the considerable expanse of high grass that he had traversed. There were street signs to follow. Paul had made no attempt to formulate a speech. He would let her talk.

When Paul rang the doorbell, he was at ease, having done all that he could do. The name next to the button read Ursula McCarahan. Never having heard his father mention divorce, he assumed that his parents were still married. A man appeared, a short, dumpy man with gray hair and gray eyes that protruded as if for fright. He greeted Paul and the muscles in his face tensed the way he had seen other German faces tense when they anticipated an outpouring of broken German. "I would like to see Frau McCarahan. I'm her son."

"ihr Sohn," the man said. And it was not a question, but an acknowledgment that something had registered, a verification of impact. "Please come with me." Paul followed the man with the Bavarian accent and the slight limp down a hallway to a flight of stairs. He could have written to his mother first, but he hadn't. Paul did not want the cushion of preparation.

"Ursula, there is someone here to see you." Then he gestured for Paul to enter first and followed him into a small living room. Still, he did not see his mother, but heard her in the kitchen, running water, dishes being washed. Then she came to the door and saw him. She had to steady herself in the door frame. Ursula McCarahan stared at him;

her square, flat features gone slack in disbelief. "Bist du Paul oder Fritz?" He answered that he was Paul.

She came a bit further into the room and then backed into a chair, her shoulders arched, her right fist tightly clenched. Paul took one step toward her, just one step forward, and she broke down, the clenched fist at her mouth, rocking rapidly back and forth in the chair. The man limped to her side, hovering helplessly, undoubtedly saying to himself, "ihr Sohn," the impact registering at a yet deeper level.

This continued for some time, with Paul standing in the middle of the room waiting for her to talk to him. When she finally settled, her friend left. He kissed her on the forehead and shook Paul's hand. Then he limped away. That this man, this white man, could share a level of intimacy with her caused Paul a brief flaring of anger. He had not shared anything with her for an eternity, had not even known what she looked like. All he had was a bad snapshot, almost two decades of still life.

"Robert threatened to kill me. I wrote him a letter that I wanted custody of you and Fritz. He wrote back that he would kill me. I was afraid of him. He was my husband, but I was afraid. When he came to the village to court me, he would always bring a rifle with him. The whole village was afraid of your father. How was I to get you? I was not even an American citizen. I didn't have the paperwork I needed.

"A couple of years later, he came to Germany looking for me. Maybe I should have seen him when he started asking, but I was frightened. Then when I had almost changed my mind, he told my adoptive father that he would kill me if he ever got the chance."

She spoke quickly. "You know your father was very cruel to me when I was in America. He would get angry if I spoke German. I have very little education. Robert always made fun of me. No one in Germany had ever made fun of me, not even in the bad times, the way your father did." She didn't tell Paul about the fear she endured when word reached her village that the Third Reich was doing something mysterious with the brown children who had been fathered by occupying French colonial troops in the Rhineland. The shadow never actually reached her door in the Swabian region of the country. Many years later, it came out that the mysterious action was forced sterilization.

If Paul were to hazard a guess, it would be that his father was sorry. "He doesn't talk about you very much. Most of what I know about you my Aunt Loretta told me. When I was a child, she gave me a snapshot of you."

"Loretta had a good heart, but she wanted to be your mother from the moment I entered the house. Right from the start, I didn't have my own family life. You know I felt uncomfortable speaking German to you and Fritz, but I couldn't speak to you like a real mother unless I spoke German. When I spoke English, I was just a child myself.

"Your father could speak some German. It wasn't good like yours, but it was good enough. He was a smart man, very resourceful. Sometimes, when we were alone, he would speak German. But he said it wasn't right. It got in the way of being an American, he said. I'm surprised that he let you learn it."

Paul shrugged this off. "Decisions like that were always up to me. He wasn't around much anyway."

"You probably think that I'm not a very strong person. And you're right. But I would have been a good mother if I had gotten you back. I just couldn't face your father. He never hit me or anything like that. Looking back at it now, if I had returned, I don't think that he would have done what he said. He wouldn't have killed me. But he would've tortured me with his words for the rest of my life. He would've picked me apart."

Certainly, Robert McCarahan would never kill. Threats were his province.

Ursula held his hands and asked him about Fritzi, eager to know if he spoke German too. Fritzi did not and the disappointment in her eyes was clear. "I will write him a letter. You can translate. I have forgotten most of the English I knew."

She examined the gold ring and its translucent bluestone, his class ring. It was the one excess that he had allowed himself as a student. Ursula had never heard of Yale or any other American university, but he told her about Fritzi going to Antioch anyway, just for completeness sake.

Becoming more relaxed, she giggled, while divulging that she had used the money that she snitched from his father to start herself on the way to an apprenticeship and licensing. She was a hairdresser. "I could never do anything with my hair, that's why." She pointed to her hair smiling, "Is it okay?" Her hair was done in a curly afro. "Du siehst sehr elegant aus, Mutti." They both ignored his saying 'mom' to her for the first time since he was a small boy.

Ursula gave him ice cream and watched him eat as if he were still a child. He had never been able to eat ice cream without getting it all over his lips. "I just remembered that last week was your birthday. You were such an earnest child, my little Scorpio. Now you are grown and educated.

And you have ice cream on your lips." She laughed almost as hard as she had been crying, and Paul laughed with her.

"My Fritz was so chubby. Is he still?" Paul nodded, fearful that she would question him too closely about Fritzi. "Like me when I was little. I'm starting to get that way again. My chubby Fritz... As soon as I get your bed ready, I'm going to start writing the letter."

"I have to go back to the hotel. I don't have a change of clothes"

"Don't leave me, Paul." She reached for the hand with the ring. "Bleib doch."

"I'm not leaving town. I came to Munich to see you."

But there was uncertainty in her expression, possibly resignation as well. As if he could really walk away from her. She didn't know him yet.

And after midnight she called him at his hotel, crying again. "Paul, bist du enttäuscht von mir?" He assured her that he was not disappointed, that she had made him happy.

They spent the next three days together. Twice, her friend Georg Merz joined them, and although Paul was uncomfortable with his presence, he knew the man was harmless, deferential to Paul and respectful of his mother. Paul made every effort to be attentive as Merz talked about his employment as a minor union official, questioning Paul about the state of unions in America. Harmless and respectful of his mother. That was all Paul felt he should care about.

At his mother's insistence, he put in an appearance where she worked. She cut his hair while her bedazzled colleagues watched. She explained how important it is to get down well below the damaged part of the shaft. Paul thought she was cutting it too short, but let her have her way. She claimed to be a specialist for frizzy hair. "The best in Bavaria."

***

His brother Fritzi had never seemed interested in learning German. Paul could only remember him asking about their mother a few times when they were growing up. There were a few German words that Paul continued to use after she left and that Fritzi somehow picked up from him. They didn't realize that the words were German and these words took on specialized meanings. Perhaps the strangest of these, 'beugen', meant a funny bending of the upper lip. Maybe it came from when Ursula helped him brush his teeth. They used the word when making silly facial expressions.

Paul had not lied when he told her that Fritzi had gone to Antioch, but he had not reported fully. Fritzi was smart, but Westinghouse had not prepared him for Antioch. He did not have Paul's academic bent. And he already had been dabbling in drugs when he left for college. Before the end of the first semester, he had been arrested. Fritzi had gotten into a fight with some stock boys when he tried to help a friend, who was caught shoplifting a package of wieners. Loretta spent two days on the phone getting a lawyer and arranging to pay for the lawyer's services. Fritzi received a thirty-day suspended sentence. By the time he came home for the winter break, he had converted to Islam. He wanted to learn Arabic and move to Cairo.

A few months later, Fritzi and two of his black classmates were arrested in Antioch and charged with abducting two people from nearby Springfield, along with assorted other crimes. Paul was still in New Haven and didn't learn all the details, but knew that it was a skirmish over drugs. Fritzi was accused of pistol-whipping a man. This time he got off with a six-month suspended sentence. Before the end of the second semester, he dropped out of college. Loretta dropped dead while at work shortly thereafter. He did not tell his mother any of this.

When he returned to Munich two months later, Ursula cut his hair again. She cut it close to the scalp this time too. He wanted her to tell him about her childhood. She claimed that there was little to say. Her circumstances were extraordinary. The day-to-day events were not. Her knowledge of her ancestry was close to negligible. She was told that her grandfather Kowalzik had married a woman in Ghana named Amma and their daughter gave birth to Ursula. Her father's name was never revealed to her, but he was also Ghanaian. Günther Kowalzik left Ghana with Ursula when she was two years old. That is all she knew. She did grow up with an awareness that she was different, but this fact had not preyed on her constantly.

"I met this girl a while ago. I didn't really get to know her or anything. She was in a bar and we talked for a few minutes. She's black, a mischling. My guess is that her father was an American. And her accent is like yours, southern." She went on with her trimming, waiting for him to continue.

"She has a boyfriend. A German."

Ursula stopped cutting, but just for a beat. "That's natural, Paul. German girl. German boy."

Paul could feel his face grow warm. "Did you ever have a German boyfriend?"

"Georg is German. You're starting to sound like your father."

He meant before she met his father. He was botching the whole line of inquiry. "I'm sorry."

"Alright. Your father was my first real boyfriend. I had a crush on one boy, but he was killed in the war. None of your business, but I've told you. Aren't you embarrassed to ask such questions?"

"More afraid than embarrassed."

"Now I feel free to ask you a question. Do you want to be this girl's boyfriend? Up until now, I haven't heard you say much about women."

"I said I don't know her. I just mentioned her because of the similarities."

"What similarities?"

"Her southern accent. And she's a black German."

"She was born after the war. I was born before it. I lived through it."

"Well, you never tell me much about those years anyway, so…"

"You're terribly grumpy today. I've told you before. There's nothing to say. There was nothing. I managed to grow up. But there was nothing really. Nothing for anybody and especially nothing for me. Then your father came, and for a while I had something." She was almost through cutting and Paul could tell that she was certainly done talking about this.

His mother leaned over and put her chin on his shoulder. "I have a surprise for you. I've put some money aside and I have enough to buy Fritz a plane ticket. The three of us can be together, as soon as you talk to him and make the arrangements. I'm as excited as when you were born. If you really want to know about my past, we can go to the village. All three of us. They're good people. They'll enjoy meeting you."

This should not have been a surprise. Even an idiot would have anticipated it. He should have told her right away, instead of the foolishness about Fritzi and Antioch. Now he was forced to tell her without the proper preparation. "Mother, Fritzi can't come here." There was no sense giving her time to protest. "Fritzi is a heroin addict. He wouldn't come here unless we guaranteed him a supply of dope. He wouldn't come. He would try to cash in the ticket. Besides, at the moment I don't even know where he is."

"What are you telling me, Paul? What are you saying?"

He repeated, "Fritzi is an addict." And he thought she would cry as she had done when he found her. But she didn't. She just looked away, away from everything. "He's your little brother. How could you let this happen? He's just a baby..."

He could have shifted the blame back to his mother. After all, it was Paul who had hovered over Fritzi for years. Had consciously hovered since the day when Fritzi had started home from kindergarten without him because the traffic guard saw him standing alone in the deserted schoolyard and told him to be on his way. Paul ran in panic for a half mile before he saw Fritzi in the distance wearing the new winter coat and battered, but serviceable winter hat with the ear flaps strapped down. But he would not shift blame. Taking the blame made it easier for both of them. He did feel guilt. He had gone away to college and left Fritzi behind. A few years later Fritzi left for college and ended up putting out a cigarette on a man's forehead. He had left it to Loretta to lie on her bed crying as she tried to find a lawyer.

"It's very hard to bring up your own brother." He slowed his speech, like a driver on an icy road. "He's only three years younger than me. It's very hard. Especially if you're worried about going down the drain yourself. Kannst du doch verstehen."

She came back to him and began brushing the hair off his collar with short, vigorous strokes. "I should never have left. It was the mistake of my life."

***

Paul was in a holding pattern. Every year he said that he would go back to the States. At this point, he had been in Germany as long as he had been at Yale. Paul had found his mother but had little else to show for the time he had put in. He had gone so far as to give notice at the high school, only to then reverse himself and scramble awkwardly to have his contract renewed.

It was not clear how much longer he could hold onto the position. A few parents had advanced the charge that he was teaching American mathematics. This was, of course, absurd on its face. They could not make headway against him by taking this tack. But nonetheless, it was irritating. He had ten classes with pupils ranging in age from fifteen to nineteen. Each class was a sermon in mathematics. There was no chance to intimidate by threat of failure. The grade in algebra carried too little weight at a commercial high school. And there was not much chance that he could wear them down, since he met each class only fifty minutes a week. So, it was sheer force of personality. That was all that was left. Paul learned all two hundred and fifty names and proselytized twenty-five pupils at a time, fifty minutes at a time, only to find that most had backslid by the time he saw them the next week. With American mathematics, repentance was a weekly affair.

Every year he expected to be arrested and somehow, despite having returned to the scene of the crime, he was not. Ice Pick Killing...

***

The Oma was waiting for him when he reached the Hinterhof. As he crossed the courtyard, he noticed that her light was still on. She heard Paul at the door and met him in the hallway.

"I took your shirts off the line. It felt like it was going to rain." Paul had indeed forgotten that he left his shirts hanging on the line when he brought them back from the laundromat.

"Oma, you're not supposed to go out into the yard. It's slippery. Just let the shirts get wet next time..." He paused because he could feel the increased tension and volume in his voice. The week before he had made her cry. His tone had come home from school with him. And, anyway, she was just using the shirts as an excuse to wait up for him. He tried to soothe her by asking about the weekly lottery. There was little chance she hadn't watched the drawing on television. Paul always put in an entry for her.

"8-38-27-41-35-29. Lots of high numbers. Will you check my slip?" The Oma was proud of her memory. Her eyes were too bad to read or write anymore. She had tried writing the results down when Paul wasn't there on Saturday night, but the scrawl was generally illegible.

"I'll check your slip tomorrow. I'm tired now. I'll check them first thing."

"There was a Heinz Rühmann film tonight, Paul." And Paul did love Heinz Rühmann, his bland face, utter helplessness, maintaining a measure of civility to the hilarious end. Rühmann never failed to make him laugh, even though these were films made in a Germany he would almost certainly not have survived, but his mother somehow managed to.

"I'm sorry I missed it."

"I wish I could get out like you. I wouldn't mind missing a film if I could get out."

He had never offered to take her for walks and she was too proud to ask him directly. This woman was almost as close to him as his own grandmother had been and yet he was ashamed to be seen walking her around the block. Ashamed simply because he was a young black man and she was an old white woman. He refused to chance being viewed as her walking stick.

"If I could get out and go like you, Paul, I would be happy." He would regret it. He already knew he would live to regret it. If he had just been willing to take her for a walk...

What was he doing anyway? What was he doing with his time, with that golf club, that putter in the middle of the night on the Hofgarten grass? Putting by the light of a park lamp at an imaginary hole. And rarely allowing himself to imagine that it went into the cup, consistently pretending that he left it short or that it rimmed out. Paul didn't even like golf. He should have taken her for a walk every day, his Oma.

Hadn't he indulged Max? Hadn't he accompanied him on a visit to his distant relatives on the far side of town. The two of them arrived unexpectedly, but this was the mode in which the host household seemed to run, unexpected and unlikely. There were four adults, two male, and two female, along with scads of children. Paul was not able to unravel the relationships; which children belonged to whom. What was clear, was that there were too many of them for the four rooms. The toilet was so filthy that Paul had left in full retreat, kicking the door open with his foot because he was unwilling to touch the doorknob.

After Max downed a few beers, he strutted around the dining room flirting with two teenage girls, bellowing, thrusting his jaw forward, his lone rugged feature. It was Max's social event of the year. But in a few more days Paul and the Oma would be bridging the gap to the first of the month, bridging it for him with bread, soup, and lies about not having room for the food in their tiny refrigerators.

One of the men had not eaten his dinner earlier and was eating late, stopping at intervals to swat away a young boy. The boy stood beside the table sucking in air, making little noises at each swallow. The man had meat in his stew. The boy wanted meat.

Paul putted an imaginary golf ball in the middle of the night. He indulged Max with a white-trash escapade. But no walks for the Oma.

And each evening Paul wrote a few more lines of his story. He kept the picture of the boy in his mind, sucking in air, wanting meat, and wrote a story about chance. About gamblers who followed a model of probability that had a dubious relationship to the way the universe operated. Three ridiculous, sad and funny colored boys upping the ante. He wrote and knew that he should take her for walks, arm in arm.

***

Ursula McCarahan learned of Fritzi's death before Paul did. When Fritzi died in Chicago in what was described as an altercation, the only identifying information that he had on his person was the letter from his mother that Paul had translated. It included Ursula's return address. Fritzi must have gotten the letter from Thelma. The authorities contacted the woman who was identified in the letter as his mother, a cruel trick of fate served as the conclusion to their mother-son relationship.

Oma walked to Paul's room to tell him that his mother was on the phone. He took a train to Munich the next day. A flurry of correspondence with his sister Thelma followed and revealed that his father had died a few months earlier when he fell from a second-floor balcony while drinking with friends. Thelma claimed to have misplaced Paul's address. She had buried their father and she would bury their brother. The house would be sold, the proceeds to be divided between the two surviving siblings. Thelma already had a house and Paul was in Germany.

Life was a lot simpler after that. Ursula McCarahan was a wreck for months, but the plan for a reunion, which would have been complex, was no longer in play. Paul and his mother could focus on each other.

To his mother, Paul said, "He got the letter. He knew your feelings. He died with them in his pocket."

***

Five years in Germany without incident and then the police had appeared from nowhere. And on the Königsallee with hundreds of well-dressed Bürger out for an evening stroll. With the noise that tires make before a collision, they pulled up near the base of the canal, where Paul was leaning against the rail. He was contemplating the swans asleep on the water's surface, their heads turned back and tucked in.

There was a flash of identification by a young plainclothesman. His partner kept his distance and Paul could see that another car had stopped with additional policemen who looked on. And, absurdly, his first notion was that he was about to be cited for playing golf in the Hofgarten, not for the mess he had created years earlier on a train.

"What were you doing in front of the stock exchange, Herr...Herr Paul?" He was reading from Paul's passport and was either confused or reluctant to attempt pronouncing his last name.

"McCarahan. Paul is my first name."

"What were you doing in front of the stock exchange, Herr McCarahan?"

"I don't remember being in front of the exchange. I'm just out walking. Out to enjoy the evening."

"Out to enjoy the evening? I'm going to have to frisk you this evening. Are you carrying a pistol?"

"Nein." There was the one syllable and the facial expression like a boxer's jab. But he was thinking that the time had come to return to Pittsburgh, to the East End.

"What's this?" The policeman tapped on his jacket pocket.

"A wallet."

"Let me see it, please."

Paul removed his wallet slowly.

"Please come over to the car."

They held his passport. One waited with Paul, while the other got on the radio. Paul leaned against the automobile trying to appear nonchalant as a crowd of onlookers enjoyed an unexpected treat on a quiet Sunday evening. The man who had frisked him returned his passport. "You may go, Herr McCarahan."

"That's all you want?"

"That's all. Enjoy your evening."

Paul watched the two cars drive off. The crowd watched him watch.

***

It was getting late and Ibrahim was due home from work. Gisela refused to budge from Paul's bed. She lay there and, in her anger, resisted all reason. Force was not a consideration. The prospect of carrying her naked, screaming and, almost certainly, kicking out into the hall was the deterrent. Max Schadlich was already jealous and so was the Oma. The Oma could not bear to share Paul with anyone. Schadlich had his gray head against the wall listening every time Gisela was with him. Paul believed he could hear heavy breathing through the plasterboard.

"Gisela put on your clothes." And it was damn nigh impossible to reason with her when she had been drinking.

"You're scared because you think Ibrahim will catch us, but I don't give a shit. Scheissegal! You're a coward. Feigling!" This was his control. He was practically caretaking for these human odds and ends in a back courtyard. No one had asked him to do it. And now it had degenerated to the point that he felt he belonged there, screwing Gisela and running errands for the Oma.

"Gisela, come on and get dressed."

"Feigling!"

Paul dared let his eyes move across the map of the world that was thumbtacked to the wall directly opposite him. He dared try to measure the distance he had covered all the way to here: a series of trysts with a drunk. Before too long he would look back to discover that he had widened his base of humiliation. The only question would be the extent. In looking back, he was always impressed by the accumulated damage.

Sometimes he believed it was all a test, that he was being put through his paces for the scrutiny of some unseen judge, that if he just held out, the opportunity to rally would present itself. The rally would justify all, make it look as if he had drifted into decay just so he could display his restorative powers. Restoration as casual as the sweep of the hand, that would be the answer. He leaned heavily on the belief in some future upsurge. This quest for justification was consuming his present, relentlessly squeezing his here and now into nonexistence. There were only further additions to the past. It all demanded an increasingly decided sweep of the hand.

And how was this going to look, this middle-aged Neanderthaler lying in his bed, full of his ejaculate and calling him a coward? It was going to have to be a hell of a rally.

"Du Feigling!"

She was good for repetition. When Ibrahim was home, he often heard her playing a tape recorder, listening to her own voice again and again. Apparently, it was an excerpt from a discussion they had about her going back to Turkey with him. Gisela wanted to know what would happen if she went to Turkey with him and it didn't work out. She played the question repeatedly with no response from Ibrahim. "Und wenn wir uns nicht vertragen?" Her voice winding off the tape. But Ibrahim didn't understand, hadn't understood the first time and wasn't going to understand no matter how many times she played the tape. He didn't care that he didn't understand. Paul thought that should be answer enough.

"You get yourself dressed and get out or don't bother to come over here again." Gisela popped out from under the covers. "Okay." She staggered from the bed, sweeping sheet and blanket onto the floor ahead of her. "You don't like me, do you? No, you don't. You don't like me." She pulled on panties and dress. "You don't like me when I drink." He put a hand on either side of her waist and steered her through the door, down the hall, and into the neighboring room, where he seated her on the edge of the bed. She had left her teenage children and husband for Ibrahim. She was taking afternoon vacations from Ibrahim with Paul. There was no salvaging this. Paul hatched a new model daily to help him grapple, a theory each day, each gloomier than the last. Reality was viewed as a supersaturated solution. One little jolt and something had to precipitate out. One false move and you would see crystals of the unmentionable forming.

Jolts were unavoidable. Besides, there was a perverse streak. "Oh, it's clear now, but one touch and you'll see it all. Scum will float on the top."

This drivel - and he reminded himself time after time - is not going to get you past the first sewer. Much less past the first plainclothesman, one who wanted to know if he carried a pistol. Paul turned and started out of the room. Gisela followed as if obeying some sort of imprinting mechanism, a forty-seven-year-old duckling, plump, with dark brown hair. He guided her back to the bed, where she broke into tears. "My god, you're always crying." That was all he could think to say.

***

Hermann Stender could not justify keeping Gretchen Traub. But in a world out of sync, you hold on to what you can, even if principles have to be bent. In the frightening scheme of things, she was his due.

It was early evening. Hermann looked through his apartment window out onto the square. A few children played near the fountain as an old man watched from a bench nearby. It was fall and Hermann could see the other side of the square. In the summer, the trees mercifully blocked his view of where his parents usually sat on warm summer evenings. He had not always disliked the balcony. There had been a time in his childhood when he looked forward to the evening on the balcony with his parents. He could sit there after completing his schoolwork, listening to them talk, sometimes sharing coffee with a neighbor. But that had all ended the summer when his father befriended two French-speaking Africans.

Before his father was forced to leave the Gymnasium because of failing grades in mathematics and science, he had intended to study French language and literature. But without an Abitur to qualify him for study, his ambition could not be realized and he had reconciled himself to taking over the family's furniture business.

That summer had served as an outlet for his father's frustrated aspirations. The Africans came three or four evenings a week to drink his father's wine. Behind his back, they snickered and flirted with Hermann's mother. But his father had been happy. Oblivious. Hermann watched him struggle to regain contact with the language, strain to earn a nod of approval for the correct use of an idiom, a smile of acknowledgment for an especially well-turned phrase. The summer passed leaving the balcony in total ruin for the young Hermann, his father a bitter joke.

Unlike his father, Hermann had earned the Abitur, but he had not gone on to the university either. He spent two years in one of the furniture stores and then decided to buy into a bar. The business would be his eventually, one way or the other, and he had not enjoyed working for his father.

So Hermann looked across the square at his parents' balcony and frowned. The same way he frowned at Africans. The children had left the square now, but the old man still stared at the fountain as if in anticipation of a main feature scheduled to follow, bending forward a bit for yet another raising of the curtain. Hermann knew the old man's habits. As soon as it was dark, he would leave too. He remained at the window watching the old man on the square. The balcony was visible.

It was simply that he did not like foreigners. No one asks you for a reason when you say you do not like the color red or classical music. It was a matter of taste. Conceivably it was true that every last one of them could have turned out differently under other circumstances. He had even met a few who at least tried to maintain appearances. But no matter what they might have become, you still have to deal with what they are.

And those people who argue against generalization might as well argue against thought. What would thought be without generalization? Some people are dirty. Other's aren't. Some people are dumb. Some are smart.

It would be ridiculous to say all groups are equal. The differences are there. Average height, weight, average anything. One group would almost always have a higher average. Why not better on the average? In Germany, the Germans should judge what is good. But no one wanted to. They were all afraid.

Where did they come from, swarming at the train stations, building ghettos, overburdening the school system with their offspring? There was no reason why Germany should allow itself to be turned into a three-ring circus. But everyone pretended not to see the disruption, the ugliness. The fabric was dry-rotting. If you let them into your group, compromise will follow. It was wrong to give up your values for a compromise with theirs. Like his father on the balcony, once you are down to their level, they laugh at you. And flirt with your wife. Maybe she even flirts back. Women are always trying to make things uniform, smooth over differences. They have no sense of territory, dealing in and living from confusion. And probably in the terrifying scheme of things Gretchen Traub was his due. She was half German. Salvaging had to begin somewhere. Gretchen was learning. She had helped throw that colored man out of the bar and put him in the street.

***

"If you wanna kick his ass, then we could. But it would be a real stupid move." Hans-Joachim was running out of patience

"Just the address."

"What are you gonna do?"

"I want to talk to the girl. Just get me the address."

"Paul, like there's thousands of good-looking women in Düsseldorf."

Paul wasn't even attracted to Gretchen Traub. He recognized the fact that she was good-looking, but that wasn't it.

"I need to tell her something."

"What the fuck do you need to tell her? Do yourself a goddamn favor and tell somebody else"

"I need to tell her that there's been a mistake. She was born in the wrong country."

"Paul, you're off. Way off."

Paul was angrier than he had been when he was talking to her on the Altstadt street. Nappy-headed piece of war fallout. That was the latest put-down he had invented. She was a consequence of the massive movement of New World troops through Old World cities. The label was pure conjecture. He did not know. He guessed. He surmised. It was something of an enigma that he didn't view himself that way.

***

Paul had found a piano at the Jugendgilde, which was not far from the Hinterhof. He gave English lessons there a couple of times a week to new arrivals from East Germany, mostly teenagers and young adults, and donated what he was paid for the lessons back to the settlement house. In return, they let him use the piano whenever he liked. It was while he was in Germany that it became clear to him that he was missing something. For years he dreamed that he could play the piano, really understand the instrument, associate chord progressions with changes of tension in his left hand, only to wake up and know that he could not. But he had continued to hold out hope that this would change, that he would slowly converge to his dream state. What he had converged to was the realization that he didn't have all the pieces. And he was not going to find them. The lofty state that he had aspired to, as late as when he played in the Berzelius Tomb a few years earlier, was closed to him and there was no fooling himself on that score.

But he loved the piano and it liked him a little. Paul played in the corner on the first floor of the Jugendgilde and kept his limited repertoire alive. He had composed one piece during his first year back in Düsseldorf. It was in the key of G-flat. Paul gave it the title *Platt and Deutsch* as an allusion to the flats in the key and the place where he had given birth to the tune.

Occasionally, a few people would stop and listen to him play and he would garner some applause, but it was on the Rhine that he became fully aware of his pianistic limitations. Sometimes he would find himself staring at the keys, wondering how it was possible to coax anything out of them.

***

Hans-Joachim did his part, address, age, place of birth. His guess was confirmed. She was a product of the American occupation after the war. But six months later Paul still had not found his way to Gretchen Traub. He had not even seen her. He felt time was running out. He had been frisked on the Königsallee. Frisked for standing in front of the stock exchange, they claimed. Maybe he had stood there trying to decide what he should do about Gretchen Traub. It must have been like that. If he really had been standing in front of the stock exchange, that's the only thing he could have been thinking about. He couldn't remember.

Paul could feel a malignancy setting up shop. Several nights a week, a stroll through the central city in the vicinity of the address, imagining an encounter. What would he do with her then? What would he do with her and her lover? There was something growing and it was not benign. And still, he did not leave. It was his mother's country. He was just in the wrong district.

***

He did the things he had done from the beginning, groping to find security in habit, sweeping through the train station in the afternoon. There were the Germans hurrying to catch their trains, hurrying past swarthy foreigners huddled in small groups, the pimps, and other elements that earned a living in the city's central station.

This afternoon, Paul patrolled the train station yet again. He had not slept well. In the middle of the night, his sleep was disrupted by Ibrahim's hack cough and he had cursed him for being a Turk with bad lungs. The rain had streamed down on the squalid Hinterhof, sweeping in from the West, pounding on the skylight. And he was wide awake. Think the rain would get tired after all these years and find a new gig? No, it was the same old set. At the station's main exit, he had to fight his way through a crowd of men. A train-station whore in bobby socks was busy enticing customers with flashes of her pale, bare right buttock.

Like an abandoned child, Gisela was waiting for him at the entrance to the Hinterhof. Paul gave her the Nazi salute, arm fully and rigidly extended. One of his students had greeted him that way as he walked into his first class of the morning. Paul had let it pass. The kid had no other way of showing affection without losing face. It was the perfect device.

"I thought you had forgotten me."

"Why? I'm no later than usual." Paul opened the door to his room and let her in. "Everybody treats me like shit. My husband did. Ibrahim does... And you're no better."

"I've never done anything to you. And I'm in no mood to be lumped in with Ibrahim and your husband."

Someone knocked at the door and Gisela squeezed herself into a corner. Paul opened the door cautiously, remembering the time her husband showed up looking for Ibrahim. He had cursed Ibrahim, called him the worst kind of Mohammedaner. In return, Ibrahim had bounced him off every wall in the room, chased him through the courtyard and through the front house out into the street. But it wasn't her husband. It was the Oma.

"Saw you come in, Paul."

"What is it?"

"I want you to talk with Ibrahim when he comes home from work. You know the flower box outside my window? He's been letting onions sprout in there, right next to my beautiful plants."

"I'll have a talk with him."

"Eine Unverschämtheit ist das."

"I agree. In fact, it's despicable. And I'll have a word with him when he gets home."

"One other thing."

"What's that?"

"I need some orange juice."

"Okay, Oma." Paul's patience was running out. He looked down on the Oma, stooped and small. "Is that all?"

"Jo. Vorläufig besten Dank." Paul closed the door, heard the Oma whisking back down the hall.

"Ibrahim's been a naughty boy. The Oma's only been out of the hospital two days and he's already got her stirred up. If things go on this way, she's going to have the shakes again inside of a week and I'll be stuck taking care of her parakeet another three weeks."

"I hope you have better luck with Ibrahim than I do. I can't get through to him." Gisela looked hopeless.

"Teach him, German."

"I've tried, but it's no use. He says he knows all the words he needs to know. And he's not going to teach me Turkish. The only thing he's taken time to show me is how to make yogurt. Yogurt is the only Turkish word I know.

"You know what happened? Max and Ibrahim traded televisions. Max wanted a smaller one and Ibrahim wanted a bigger one, so they traded. When I get home from shopping, there's a different television in the room. And when I ask him where it came from, he says he doesn't know. I'm going to go crazy. We can't even hold a conversation. The man doesn't understand half of what I say."

"He's been in the country for eight years. You've been with him for more than three. You've got to figure he's not going to learn. He's over fifty...."

"What am I supposed to do then? I threw out those old shoes of his with the holes in them. He's so damn cheap. When he found out they were gone, he beat me. You must've heard..."

"Yea, I did..."

"So, I told him off and got drunk. He goes to Max and tells him he wants to swap back because ever since he brought in the new set, I'd done nothing but drink. I can't live with this nonsense..." Then, without looking in his face, "I wish you were older..."

"Then what?"

"I feel you like me."

"Gisela, I'm not a safe bet. For you, I'm a really bad bet. Even if I were older, it would be a mistake. If it weren't for Ibrahim, you and I wouldn't get along at all. You're just running away from him."

"Maybe I should stop coming over." She sounded insulted. He didn't believe he had given her any reason to be. Yet he could hear the hurt.

"I didn't say you should stop coming over. "

"Well, then I'm allowed to come over and screw if I want?"

He had his opening, a clear cut. The voice was so resentful. She wasn't even drunk. Gisela was sober and asking for it. "You shouldn't keep coming to me if you don't think it's in your best interest to do so."

"Asshole. You sound like a lawyer. Arschloch!"

She had probably been sitting on this for a while, waiting for an excuse, waiting for her anger to build. But this had caught them both unprepared. Neither would have thought they could slip into animosity so easily.

"I don't really need anyone like you. You're a snob, Herr School Teacher. Mr. American with your High German. Do you know what you can do for me? Do you know?"

Within a month Gisela had also left Ibrahim, had left the Hinterhof entirely. And this had surprised Paul. He would not have believed that she could simply go. It was a demonstration of strength that he would have deemed impossible if anyone had asked, if anything had caused him to consider the possibility. Poor excuse for a girlfriend, but up to then it was as close as he had come. He should have treated her more gently.

The same month he had sent his manuscript, *The Due Set*, to New York, to a publishing house randomly selected from those publishers whose names he recognized. He fully expected a rejection slip. And, ironically, he conjectured that this additional comeuppance might simply be his *due*. Certainly, Gisela's departure was.

His mathematical sermons at the high school were delivered with even greater zeal. In a quite abstract way, it became clear that killing Gretchen and her lover would not be a move beyond his depth. He could do it and walk away as before, as if from some act of sanitation. It would be a service rendered and worthy of a Himmelfahrtskommando.

***

Paul had decided to go home and study mathematics seriously. He pulled a book from underneath his bed, Apostol's calculus. For now he started at the beginning with elementary but foundational material to build his strength.

Tomorrow night it would be set theory, infinite cardinals. Tonight, it was Apostol's take on the relationship between the integral and the derivative. That was how his schedule alternated. Paul carefully read four pages on continuity. Then he turned off the lights and fell asleep, already entertaining second thoughts about everything.

***

Due to the charity of the Arbeiterwohlfahrt, the Oma received two second-hand dresses and a light coat for autumn. It hardly mattered that she never left the Hinterhof. The arrival of the garments in a flat cardboard box represented a departure, an escape from the irregular layers of cotton and wool draped about her, all clinging to now nonexistent contours, to some other time.

She stood before him wearing her new dress, wheezing with the excitement of the newly acquired, her lungs taxed by the exertion of change. She tried on both dresses, presenting herself each time in a near frenzy of anticipation for Paul's approval. The cords in her neck stood out as she strained to fasten the belt, to find an overlooked button. He only managed to say that the dresses fit. If he said more he would have been moved to tears and he didn't want that, couldn't afford that.

For fifteen marks, she said, for fifteen marks she could have the hemline altered. The waist was fine. And then she had whispered to Paul, although there was no one there but the two of them, that she no longer had a bosom. "Nichts." But the dresses were alright, weren't they? Again, Paul confirmed that the dresses fit.

"I'm so tired, Paul. I think I'll wait until tomorrow to try on the coat. You can tell me how it looks." The Oma smoothed away an imagined wrinkle.

He spent his spare evenings with the Oma. In the beginning, Paul had only watched television. He soon discovered, however, that the Oma much preferred to talk. She lapsed into discourse without the slightest warning. Paul's determination to ignore her was to no avail. His resistance was ineffectual, the pictures flickering across the screen serving no other purpose than that of inducing a trance. And in the trance, she could shuttle him back and forth through whole eras.

Right after the first World War, there were some American soldiers stationed near where we lived in the Mosel Valley. From Texas mainly. But there weren't any of the colored soldiers there. They were all stationed farther away in Trier. I saw a few of them once. They had a skin color like yours. But where we lived there were only the white ones and, like I said, they were mainly from Texas. And some from Oklahoma, I think. We could watch them out in the pasture playing with their mules. Sometimes the mules made them angry and they would scream and curse. We tried to repeat what they were saying so that we could learn to curse in English. All except my brother. He had been wounded at Flanders and was hard of hearing ever since. Not because of the wound. The wound healed. But when he was shot, he was left for dead. He lay in a cold puddle for a whole day before someone found him frozen half to death. By then he had lost most of his hearing.

There was one American who had such a beautiful voice. He could sing better than anyone I ever heard. Such a beautiful voice, you wouldn't believe it. But he was always downcast. Whether he was homesick or not, I don't know. But you could see the sadness. One day one of the farmer's sons got sick and this man went down to see if there was anything he could do to help. I saw him afterward and he looked even sadder. The farmer's son got better, but a week later the American died.

That was right after the end of the war and we weren't allowed to have much contact with the Americans, so I hadn't gotten to know him well. His death hurt me all the same. I don't think he was from Texas. He was probably from Oklahoma. At least he was a decent man. And he could sing. Like an angel. His voice would fill the meadow.

Back then we had large families. I was the youngest of eleven. Eleven, if you count the brother who died of whooping cough and the one who drowned in the cesspit. I never knew either of them. They died before I was born. The Americans, I mean Texans, were always looking for girls and there were six girls in our family. Now I don't want to say the Texans were bad. If the farmers hadn't given them all that alcohol to drink, they wouldn't have done it. None of the boys lived at home after the war except one, the deaf one. And our father was dead. So, when they came bursting into our house that night there was nothing we could do. My mother ran to the commandant's house for help. They tore our clothes off. My mother said I was as white as chalk. After that, we always had an MP in front of our house and they claimed to have locked them up. At least they were taken away. But I was still afraid. So until they all pulled out a few months later, I slept in the vineyards. That's why I sometimes have pain and stiffness in my hip. The doctors say it's sciatica.

Paul sat and the pictures on the screen flowed by.

I didn't marry until I was thirty-five. He was younger than me by three years. My mother told me not to marry Werner. She told me he was a good-for-nothing. It lasted exactly nine years. The divorce became final on the day of our anniversary. I should've known it would come to no good, considering the way it started out. That was during the inflation and we were paying twenty thousand marks for a loaf of bread one week and thirty thousand the next. I remember him complaining when he found out how much the ceremony was going to cost. It cost two million marks and he thought a whole week's pay was too much. He paid it though, because my mother couldn't. And I couldn't. The only jobs I'd had were the kind working in the homes of well-to-do families. You didn't get much more than room and board. Some were nice enough to give you a little wardrobe. I had some beautiful things from one family, tailor-made. Then they were stolen one weekend while I was away. I got so depressed that I quit. I just didn't want to see that house anymore. The fortunate thing for me was that I was wearing my best dress that weekend, blue with pleats. I quit the job and on the way home I decided to make a side trip to Koblenz. There were some friends of the family living there and I thought it might lift my spirits to see them again. But I didn't get to. Instead, I was arrested for telling an American army officer to kiss my ass. When he asked to see my papers, I didn't understand him. It was such bad German. And I didn't know the Americans were making checks. So I went on without showing my papers and told him to kiss my ass. If I had known he could understand me, I wouldn't have said it. But I didn't know, so I landed in jail for three months. Maybe if that hadn't happened, I wouldn't have met Werner. Maybe I would've never moved from the Mosel to the Rhineland. No use talking about that though. The fact is I married him and suffered with him for nine years. Until I found out that he had another woman. She lived right around the corner from us. When I finally found out about it, he had already gotten her in the family way. He knew I couldn't have children. I guess he thought of it as a way out. At the place where he worked, he got a warm meal every day. I didn't begrudge him this, although I was almost always hungry. He had to work so hard that I figured it was better for him to eat all of it than to bring part of it home to me. Then I found out that he was giving this food to her. Every day he stopped on his way home and gave her his dinner. I took an ax and demolished all the furniture in the apartment. Then I left him.

It was well past midnight. The Oma paused and swallowed, then continued. It was as if she had actually carried him back there. Only her history remained real.

The Kaiser visited our village when I was five years old. The whole village went down to the train station to see him. All of us. Even my sister Hildegard. My parents were ashamed of her then. They thought she was pregnant and they weren't going to let her come along. But they changed their minds. As it turned out, she wasn't pregnant. After ten months and still no baby, they took her to the doctor. What it was, was a thirteen-pound growth. The operation nearly killed her. And she had an enormous amount of excess skin on her stomach for the rest of her life. She had nine kids, too.

Anyway, we all went down to the depot. Everyone was standing around and I was so young I didn't know what was going on. I wanted to know where the Kaiser was, so I yelled out, "Wo ist der Kaiser?" I was standing right next to him. He reached down and patted me on the head. Everyone laughed. My mother whispered that this was the Kaiser. I looked up at him and said, "Ach, du!"

The Oma offered him the box of chocolates. It was their late-night ritual on the Rhine.

I knew a woman who had a baby when she was fifty-one years old. She didn't have any luck, though. One day she was bringing the baby back to the apartment after a walk and she ripped her leg open on something in the hall. Instead of going for help right away, she went into the apartment and opened a bottle of whiskey. It could be she wanted to kill the pain.

When her husband came home from work, the blood had run all the way out under the door. She had fallen asleep and bled to death with the whiskey bottle in her lap. This was a woman I should have hated, but I don't carry a grudge. It was nineteen thirty-eight. She and another woman went to the Nazis and told them I was living with a man. The Nazis believed them and cut off my welfare checks.

I was living with a man but I didn't get any support from him. He was on welfare himself because he could only get temporary employment. That's because when he was a teenager, he lost one leg up to the knee. He was a good-looking fellow with wavy hair and the finest features you would ever want to see. Other women envied me. It was jealousy that made them do it. I had to live on bread and potatoes for weeks before I finally got back on support.

A few months after that, he got a letter from his parents asking him to return to Ludwigshafen and that was the last I ever saw of him. He sent me a postcard. He had married a seventeen-year-old. It's like they say. You never have a good man for just yourself.

And there was a Heinz Rühmann film on the television screen. Heinz Rühmann, forever on the verge; twitching, stammering, a half-clown picking his way through a heap of twentieth-century German debris, winning a smile. Play-acting for Paul. Her history had no right to impress him, to make him ache as it did. But he listened and grew through it, holding it close, the Oma's personal gift.

The thing that bothered me most was the way the Nazis twisted the communists' arms. You'd think they were going to tear them right out of the sockets. They twisted their arms and then twisted them again. They would drag them through the streets that way. Some people stood at the windows and watched, but I couldn't stand to see it. It made me sick. I don't know why they felt they had to wrench their arms like that. But they did. And then they pitched some of them into the river. The only good thing about the whole business was that I got a job. As soon as Goebbels started running around screaming about Total War – "Wollt ihr den totalen Krieg?!"- everybody got a job. One of the first things I did with my money was to buy myself a little pistol from one of my friends.

He gave it to me for almost nothing. He was glad to get any money at all for it. I didn't really think that I would have to use it. It was just that fear nagging at me that a few of them would come to drag me away someday. The thought of them wrenching my arms was more than I could bear. I told myself I'd have them shoot me before I'd be mistreated like that. And I meant it. They would've had to shoot me. I wasn't a communist, so I really shouldn't have been afraid. But sometimes I dreamt my arms were being twisted by two of those huge men. It always turned out to be my rheumatism acting up or that I was sleeping in a funny position, but I'll have you know it scared me. It really did.

Paul was having trouble with his wake-sleep cycle. He slept irregularly. And it was only with difficulty that he was able to establish when it was he had fallen asleep, or if he was awaking to sunrise or the rays of sundown falling through his skylight. In more bitter moments of reflection, he was given over to the proposition that sleep was simply taking him, like death. He slept and was well aware that if his Oma could buy a pistol that she didn't know how to use, he could buy an ice pick. He could kill them. You walk in. You do it. Who would know? Hans-Joachim, maybe.

The worst that could happen was that he would have to get out of the country. And it was time to go anyway. He didn't have to be in Düsseldorf to visit his mother in Munich. It was a five-hour train ride away, almost as long as a flight from the East Coast to Germany

The Oma packed her new clothes from the Arbeiterwohlfahrt into the flat cardboard box again.

Paul dreamed that Gisela came back to the Hinterhof. And they made love.

***

In the winter, Paul's manuscript was returned from New York. The publishing house had kept *The Due Set* for three months. But then it came back. A letter accompanied it containing a flattering appraisal, encouraging his efforts. They inquired as to whether he was writing anything full length. Something full length was required, but he had nothing full length in him. He tucked the manuscript away in his dresser. The Oma asked him several times what had become of his story. Each time he answered that it just hadn't turned out like he thought it would. His story of youth casting the die was consigned to the shelf, an ignored account.

By the time the Karneval season arrived, he had steadied himself. He was still to be found patrolling the inner city, frequently in Gretchen Traub's neighborhood. It was a habit now, like sweeping through the train station. As far as Hans-Joachim knew, she was still in town, still at that address. He claimed to have seen her in a Königsallee store during the Christmas holidays.

Paul had never liked parades, but Max had just bought a record player secondhand and his records were driving Paul mad. There were three LP's devoted to the Schlager of yesteryear and one recording of Irish folk songs sung in German. Paul chose the parade, chose the madness that came of watching Germans run drunkenly through the streets.

He reached the Königsallee and pressed himself into the crowd to begin inching along the canal. Mammoth speakers that had been tied to trees blared forth the music of good cheer. The ducks had disappeared from the canal and traffic had been banned from the streets. People stood squeezed against buildings blasting beer breath and the Karneval's battle cry 'Helau' into the nearest person's face. It was the sort of atmosphere that would have permitted Paul to play golf in broad daylight on the Hofgarten lawn, putt at an imaginary cup. But he wouldn't give the Germans this satisfaction.

His attention was drawn to an African in a knee-length, tweed coat. The man moved into view briefly and then disappeared into the crowd. His face was made up for the festivities with chalky white hearts pierced with arrows. He had the look of someone who had been double-crossed and didn't want to admit it. A man dressed in drag and wearing a purple wig careened by, about six-foot-four with shapely legs. After a half-hour and progress of six blocks, Paul tired of the struggle and stopped. A band in monk costumes played and a drunken old woman, her head tossed back in song, projected spittle towards the sky. The first float appeared, one of forty announced for the parade. The women on the float showered the crowd with candy and red plastic balls, one of which Paul caught in flight. The sentence 'Es ist noch Suppe da' was printed on it in white. If there was a reference, he missed it. 'There is still soup there.' Paul had no idea what it meant. And as the floats passed by, he puzzled over it as if it were a clue in a crossword. There was no figuring it out. He remembered the hungry boy in the filthy apartment, where he had been taken by Max Schadlich. Stew with meat in it. Still soup.

McCarahan became a focal point of the candy bombardments, his autumn complexion a well-defined target amongst the pallor, something those up on the floats could easily home in on. Children crawled around his feet stuffing some of the candy into their coat pockets, unwrapping and eating the rest.

Following the flute and drum contingent, came an entry representing the American consulate. A half-dozen men on horseback, dressed as nineteenth-century cavalry, led a scaled-down replica of a covered wagon. He was passed a sticky bottle of cherry brandy by a middle-aged man with a ragged, red goatee. To warm against the cold, the man said, and Paul drank without protestation.

There had been difficulties with the German authorities again. His request for an extension of his residency permit was denied. He was given as the reason an entry in his file listing his residency as officially discontinued for not reporting a change of address. "We would not make a mistake, Herr McCarahan. We have competent personnel. You no longer live where you were registered as living and you have not lived there for months. A man from our office was at the supposed address on Dreieckstraße and established the grounds for termination."

Two days later Paul returned with receipts for rent paid at the Hinterhof for a period covering the past two years. The termination order was rescinded. Just bureaucratic bungling. That was what rationality would require him to conclude, but there was no reasoning with paranoia. When he faced the bureaucrat and saw him tapping his fat fingers on the desk, he had almost lost his temper. He had almost blurted out that if they would just stop harassing him, he would be out of their hair by the end of the following summer. And he had no plans to kill anyone between now and then. Not Paul.

On the other side of the street, a section of spectators broke into song. Linking their arms, forming a chain, they swayed from side to side as the king and queen of the Düsseldorf Karneval rode by on different floats. The man passed him the cherry brandy and he took another swig.

The day grew clearer and colder. He was chilled through from standing in one place and his mood had gone completely sour. He decided that he had seen enough of the parade. Paul tried to find a way back, but everywhere he went he was blocked by the density of the crowd, a barricade, or the parade itself. He made it back to the Königsallee just in time to see the U.S. Cavalry pull by again. Right behind the cavalry, the African with the white hearts on his face had, to the delight of those watching, joined the parade. Somewhere along the way he had acquired a green paper wig and was dancing while tooting on a toy horn. Paul was seized by embarrassment at the sight of a black man performing in this way and it made him talk to himself in English. "Asshole's trying to be accepted I suppose. Goddamn asshole."

The parade again prevented his continuing along the route he had chosen, unless he wanted to join the African and dance his way out. So he fought his way back past the shining facades of banking houses, down and through to where the Altstadt began, not far from where he had worked during his perfect summer at Commerzbank in letters of credit. The crowd became thinner as he turned in the direction of Haroldstraße. Paul's legs, which had gone to jelly from standing and cold, began to come alive again. The main commercial thoroughfare, Graf-Adolf-Straße, was choked with thousands of people, so he went four blocks farther before turning into a narrow street so quiet that he was stunned. A lone couple walked on the opposite side toward him. It was a young couple, both had a head full of straw-like hair, easily manipulated by the wind. The woman carried a baby papoose style. Her baby, to carry it, so unconventionally... And if their baby were to fall, so unconventionally...

Paul circled back again crossing Aderstraße, thinking he could make it to the train station to buy a newspaper, but the crowds were too deep and the parade was everywhere. The place where Jehovah's Witnesses usually stood, with their magazine 'Der Wachturm' held dutifully before their breasts, was swarmed over, the tiny spot in front of the tobacco store captured by the Karneval.

When he got back to his neighborhood, the diner was half full. He rarely ate out, but after his bout with the parade he didn't feel up to cooking. Gerhard was also there, one of the worn-out men who worked as errand boys at the brothel. Gerhard was sulking. The woman had forgotten his order of Frikadellen and when she finally brought them, she had not sliced them up. Gerhard had failed to put out his cigarette before he began eating, and its smoke, smelling strangely like perspiration, filled the side of the room where Paul sat. Looking for all the world as if he would burst into tears at the outrage, Gerhard pushed bits of food into the side of his mouth. His lopsided face was fruit-punch red and his hair stuck out in all directions. Trying to pacify, the proprietress winked at him from behind the counter. "Come on, Gerhard! You can do it! Smile. Ja, das ist ein guter Junge."

Paul got up and went over to the window. It was already dark outside, the beginning of Lent. A group of children dressed as cowboys and Indians ran past. In the distance, a series of firecrackers went off. Someone yelled, "Helau."

"Helau," came the answer, the echo. But it was already over. Like the shrill notes of a seventeen-year cicada one week late, Helau was suddenly inappropriate. Misplaced. Back there in the winter.

***

He was like a man on the verge of recapturing some distant and exquisite sexual encounter. There was a tremor whenever he thought of using the ice pick again. But this time, unlike the first, the corpses would reach the headlines. There would be prominent mention. They were not derelicts. Additional risk was involved. But minimal, he thought. It was a matter of timing at the door ... and no surrender to minor points of self-indulgence. Paul had a preferred order: the blond-beard and then Gretchen. But no concessions would be made to this. He would hit whichever one came first. Paul heard the Oma shuttle by on her way to the john. She had already reported her diarrhea to him early in the day. "Ich hab' den Durchfall."

"Sometimes I don't mind killing," he muttered and felt the tremor.

"Sometimes I don't mind killing at all."

***

Hans-Joachim tapped the side of his half-empty beer glass with his index finger, making sharp little ringing noises with his fingernail. "I don't know. But the guy makes me feel unsafe. He says he's going to leave this summer. If he's going to act like this, he should get on an airplane back to the States right now."

"Well," and the Gambian's sigh was full of practiced Weltschmerz. "He's always been worrisome. I've heard some rumors about him that make my skin crawl..."

"You hear rumors. I don't need no rumors to tell me he's not right. I seen it with my own eyes. Couple of weeks ago, I'm out riding with a friend at three in the morning. What I shoulda done was keep on rolling. But me, like the New Jersey ignoramus I am, I jump out, 'cause I was headed home anyway. It was just a few blocks. Did you know he won't talk English anymore? Maybe a few words, but then he's right back to German."

"I haven't talked to him for months, which is perfect. The longer the better."

"Buy me another beer?"

"I suppose." Saedy put up one slate-colored finger to attract the waitress's attention. Hans-Joachim licked his thick, pink lips wet.

"So, I get out and start walking with him. He's carrying one of those little golf clubs, a putter. Tell me he's not in space. The first thing he wants to talk about is the mischling girl who hangs out at the Rhinoceros. I think he's in love or something. Bitch helps throw him out of a bar and he gets a crush. I'm tired of talking about her. After a year or so, it gets on your nerves. I told him, 'Paul, you're getting on my nerves.'

"We're walking along one of those side streets off Graf-Adolf-Straße, down where the strip joints are. And I swear to God he takes the putter and puts it through the display case. It was like nothin', like he was in his backyard swattin' a fly or somethin'. He leaves all the pictures alone except two of a black girl. Takes those out and throws them in a trash can. He's standing there saying he 'can't stand it when they do this', stuffing the pictures into the trash. And he's not drunk. He never drinks much. I told the mother fucker he was on his own and split."

Saedy said, "Paul thinks he has a guardian angel."

After the Gambian left. Hans-Joachim took the glass of beer from under the bench. Took it from behind his leg, where he had been hiding it ever since he saw Saedy come in. It was the only glass he had bought himself all evening. No need putting a crimp people's generosity, he reasoned. Then he downed his beer with satisfaction.

***

It was a small matter. So small in fact that he felt that by concentrating hard enough it would be remedied. And if it couldn't be, it might very well mean his undoing. Paul's water faucet was broken. The water was running. It was a holiday and the landlord did not give a damn. He didn't even know what holiday it was. He only knew it was one of the several bizarre holy days when the bars were allowed to open, but couldn't play music.

A worn-out washer. He had seen it coming for weeks. And despite this, he had gotten up in the morning betting that it would be alright, good for at least a few more openings and closings. So now the water was running and he couldn't turn it off. He borrowed a wrench from Ibrahim, who stood in the door to watch. But Paul had not gotten underway. He didn't have a washer. He didn't even know where the water main was.

Ibrahim's German seemed to have gotten worse since Gisela left. Or maybe he was intentionally formulating mocking banalities. His mastery of the language didn't allow him to rise above the grimmer fundamentals.

"Maybe turn and okay. Maybe turn and kaputt. Total kaputt. Then later the specialist man come."

No, Paul had not turned at all. He sent Ibrahim away and left the Hinterhof. The day was cool and overcast, too cool for that time of year. It was a Monday holiday. Pigeons thrown out of their accustomed rhythms, clearly disconcerted by the lack of workday litter, strutted about as strut they must. The people were all hiding inside. Yet another gray day good for nothing but mourning or lying about, grooming a peace of mind. Their plumbing functioned, so there was no reason to mourn. No doubt the specialist man was hiding in there someplace as well, knowing that sooner or later he would have to sally forth.

Sooner or later it would be too late. A specialist man could not bail him out. Goddamn Ibrahim and his specialist man. He thought of going back to get a jacket, but first he would follow the crumbling brick wall surrounding a boarded-up factory. No sidewalk, just damp earth and a shroud of trees and bush, all wrapped around an organization at whose core the ovens had gone out.

Paul circled the factory several times. He intended to go around exactly three times, but lost track of his revolutions, thinking of the water that was keeping him from going home to sleep. On the edge of his awareness, a burglar alarm sounded a warning for someone, perhaps for one of those hiding inside. Surely, he wasn't responsible for the siren. Surely the alarm wasn't for that guy, the specialist man. He stopped and leaned against the wall, the palms of his hands sweaty.

He circled back around, still moving along the wall. There was the vague hope of closing it up, winding it back together. But the last advantage had been lost and the flow went on unimpeded. Water, colorless and odorless, was seeking its own level, while he stood by with a wrench.

Paul returned to the Hinterhof. Halfway across the courtyard, he could hear the water or at least imagined he could. He took a jacket from his room and went down into the basement. There would have to be a cut-off valve somewhere. The Oma had lived in the basement after the Second World War; before the landlord consented to give her a room on the surface because of her asthma. Dust covered everything and he could imagine her straining against spasms and contractions to breathe. There was a small room at the end of the corridor with steps that led up to a wooden toilet seat. Criss-crossing the space was a network of pipes that had some relationship to his own. He searched for a cut-off and found none. It did not matter to him if it ever flowed again. He was willing to seal it once and for all.

Towards evening he returned to the streets. The water was denying him escape into sleep, the most precious option he had. Instead, he sat in an empty park adjoined by a playground. He was reminded of the swings that his father had put up in the backyard, the one project that his father ever completed. The earth was soft and the support had not been anchored well, so that whenever he began pumping his legs and going for height, the whole framework would begin moving with him, upwards and almost out of the ground. No matter how slowly or quickly he began, no matter how cautiously he developed the arc, the accompanying rise and fall at the foundations was inevitable. Paul had found himself trying to get the whole frame out of the ground, if only for an instant, all four supports out of the earth and in the air as he swung. Discovering that this was impossible, he left the whole apparatus to rust where it stood.

An intimacy with the growing darkness began to develop. There were corners into which one would never venture had the darkness been there at the outset, corners that seemed quite secure when the darkness was taken in progressive doses. He searched the ground for pebbles, stuffing them into his pockets. It was as dark as it was going to get. His landlord lived on the other side of the park and Paul found himself there, throwing pebbles across the street at the window. He kept this up until a light went on in the apartment, the signal for him to retreat into the night, back in the direction of the Hinterhof.

***

As the spring of 1976 took firm hold, he followed the school's soccer team, watched them fight their way to the city championship. More than half the team received instruction from him in algebra. They could have been his long shot come home, these boys of the working class. But he had not thought to bet. Paul had gone to all their games, pacing the sidelines, the only teacher present. He was on the sideline as the team won the Düsseldorf championship, in an upset, 4-0.

His colleagues at the school viewed him as a walk-on, not a professional teacher and civil servant, as talented as he might be in his area of expertise. Sometimes he joined a group of younger teachers for a picnic or went along for lunch, but he remained a peripheral member of that smaller group too. He cared about the soccer team and followed them. He had been an athlete once. Now his youth seemed far behind him. He stood on the sidelines and watched his boys' offense penetrate and dissect the opposition while thinking of his own plans for dissection and penetration. It would, of course, have to be a smoother, less rambunctious sort of assault. He couldn't just march down the field... Hans-Joachim had told him flatly that he would supply him with no more information about Gretchen Traub, had told Paul that it was a waste of time. He had even hinted that he thought Paul was obsessed. Paul had not broached the subject with him again.

Gretchen Traub was not a subject that he could discuss sensibly, not with the Oma. The only time he had brought it up, the Oma had scolded him for his trepidation. She had teased him, saying that maybe Gisela had taken the guts out of him, made him gun shy. He should introduce himself to the girl. He hadn't told her about the confrontation that had led to his meeting Traub. In his state of mind that could have led to a discussion of ice picks. It would be foolhardy to put himself under more pressure. He couldn't discuss it. Not with the Oma. Not with his mother. With no one. Besides, the Oma had suffered a relapse and was back in the hospital. She left him her key so he could watch television and take care of the parakeet. Her room was the same size as his, somewhat longer, somewhat narrower. It was so crammed full of furniture that the only open floor space was where they pulled up chairs to watch television, where he now sat alone with only the memories of her memories.

Perhaps frightened by the severity of her latest attack, the Oma revealed to him where her money was hidden. It was in the pocket of a robe in her closet, more than six thousand marks rolled into a ball, money she began saving in the fifties. "If I die," she said, "don't tell them about it. You take it. Give some to Max and keep the rest. Don't let them get it back."

The string finally ran out. The soccer team lost, was eliminated. There would be no Nordrhein-Westfalen provincial championship for Kaufmännische Schule IV. He stood on the sideline and watched it happen, was crushed by it. A few more victories and the team would have been in Berlin for the final round. He had planned to go with them, his first trip to the city that was blockaded the year he was born. He harbored the sentiment that they would not have lost if he had placed a bet on them, if he had given more. Increasingly certain of this, he went into depression for more than a week. They were his Gegenwind. All the bets at Grafenberg, all the lottery sheets, and still he had let his dark horse pass by. Worse, he had allowed his dark horse to lose. Paul discontinued his gambling. He put in only one lottery sheet a week, this for the Oma.

And the Oma remained hospitalized. With Gisela gone for more than a year and the Oma sick, there was no female presence at the Hinterhof. The summer with its final oral exams approached and Paul prepared his pupils for a display before the other faculty members. He honed them to a fine edge, polished their American mathematics. Peachy, ice-pick keen.

***

Max Schadlich had walked out of the Hinterhof into the blaze of the summer sun, hailed a taxi and checked himself into a hospital. Three days later he was dead. Max Schadlich, the perpetual loser, taken in summer, away from the small room and the secondhand furniture. A white-haired forty-five-year-old, who had had nothing from life, the constitution of a sickly eighty-year-old, a subsistence check from the Sozialamt and a twenty-mark whore at the beginning of the month. A quickie. That had been it for Schadlich, a miserable, desperate and doomed attempt before someone hollered, "Next!"

When Max walked away from the Hinterhof, he might have thought that he still had a chance. But more likely, he turned there in the courtyard and took one last look at the shabby one-story building and saw the hideousness of it all. All men were not equal and he was at the bottom of the heap. There was no final fantasy, just a walk to the corner and a ride alone in the summer heat, a final passing in an overcrowded ward in a bed placed temporarily at the end of the hall. Max Schadlich was dead.

"Everybody's dying, Oma."

"Was sagst du?"

"Everybody."

"Paul, it's just Max who's dead. I'm not dead yet. And nobody's killing us."

"But no one's helping you live."

"You should get hold of yourself. You're a very young man. Get out and meet people. If you weren't so shy, you'd have a girlfriend by now. That with Gisela was not good for you. She was too old. Should've been ashamed of herself. Really. I never liked her."

"She was okay."

"But she was bad for you."

Paul smiled and he thought, "Just as long as they don't take away my Himmelfahrtskommando badge."

Two men moved into Max Schadlich's room. Both were Turks working illegally and on the dodge. The Hinterhof was a perfect hideout. There was no chance of the real estate agent talking. Only someone like Max or Turks looking for cover would be willing to rent the room.

The Oma never returned to the Hinterhof. When Paul told her that he was leaving for America, she arranged to go directly from the hospital to a home for the elderly. She didn't believe she could make it at the Hinterhof without him and admitted she was unwilling to stay there surrounded by Turks. The nights when Paul was out prowling Düsseldorf, she had waited for him to return, uneasy, knowing that Ibrahim was at the other end of the hall. In this matter, there was nothing Paul could say to assuage her.

"Take the money, Paul. Take it." The Oma had begged him. And so, before her closet was cleaned out by personnel from the Sozialamt, Paul took the six thousand marks. Her plan was to have him send the money back to her little by little every month, money from a relative in America.

"I'll get someone at the home to write for me. If I stop writing, Paul, you stop sending."

At midnight he walked across the city to the river and moved north along the Rhine in the direction of the government buildings and consulates. But he stopped before reaching these structures, turning east into a park he knew well. As always, he was comfortable alone in this nest of grass and trees. It was almost six years since he had come to Düsseldorf and during that time an American president had fallen for spying, a German chancellor for being spied upon. America had celebrated its bicentennial without him. Saigon had fallen.

"I'm still here." He assured himself, mostly in German but then and again an English phrase erupted. "I'm still alive. And I have found my mother."

There were rabbits throughout the park. They would stand like statues as he approached. But they would stand for only so long, only let him get so close, before bolting into the shrubbery. He called for them to come back, called to the rabbits. "Kaninchen, kommt zurück! Kaninchen!"

He left the Hinterhof the next morning, not looking back. Someone was waiting for the room. Then he flew west, moving against the rotation of the earth, his manuscript, *The Due Set,* buried in his suitcase beneath his underwear. The Oma's money, still wrapped in a tight ball, was stuffed into a sock next to Apostol's calculus and Fraenkel's set theory. After nearly six years he was done with Düsseldorf. He had visited his mother in Munich and promised that he would come to Germany to see her at least twice a year.

Ten months later the Oma stopped writing. Paul stopped sending.

DEEPER INTO THE
ANCESTRAL LANDS

The hotel in Hillsborough, North Carolina was palatial compared with what they had settled for in Kenbridge, Virginia. Ruth spent an hour in the bathtub scrubbing herself and looking for ticks. Paul stuck his head in after a while, wanting to know if she was sufficiently prune-like. What he wanted to do was get into the hunt and Ruth was holding things up with her bath. There were cousins to see and an off-chance that he could find one who was a direct maternal descendant of his McCarahan great-grandmother. She was the only paternal great-grandparent whose haplogroup signature had not been captured. Paul wanted a clean sweep. He had a kit in the car if he could find the right cousin.

By the time they reached his cousin Jenny's house on Highway 70, it was three o'clock in the afternoon. All of his family lived in close proximity to Highway 70. The stretch from Hillsborough to Mebane was packed with them. He had lost track of the number of married couples, who were both his relatives.

Paul met Jenny's mother, his grandfather McCarahan's half-sister, on his first sortie into North Carolina. He was forty years old and the Geometry Killing was only a couple years behind him. Paul would travel around the country knocking on doors of people he had never met, but believed to be his blood. As was the case with most old women, his grand-aunt had seen some virtue in Paul. Before she was even convinced that he was right about being her relative, his Aunt Clara had allowed Paul across her threshold and into the living room.

His cousin Jenny respected the memory of her mother so much that year after year she had continued to extend Paul the same hospitality that her mother had offered him. Most recently, he had been hunting DNA.

There they sat on Jenny's porch at the edge of Highway 70 under a gray sky, dripping sweat in 90-degree heat and waving at every second car that went by because Jenny recognized a relative. Ruth waved manically each time. Paul's wave slowly degenerated into a stiff-armed Nazi salute. He was exploring Jenny's brain for his great-grandmother's surviving maternal line. Jenny wouldn't do. She was a maternal descendant from Plese McCarahan's second wife, not his first.

They had discussed and eliminated a dozen candidates when Jenny looked at Paul and said, "Robbie."

Jenny knocked on Robbie's door for several minutes before the three of them gave up and started back to the car. Jenny was pouting a bit and Paul caught her and Ruth in profile. There was something like a resemblance, both dejected because of Paul's disappointment.

Paul had said nothing, just asked Jenny to stop knocking. If Robbie was asleep, Paul didn't want to wake him up to ask for a cheek scrape. Robbie did shift work at a factory in Burlington. Jenny hadn't known which shift. As much as he wanted the sample, that was not the way to meet your cousin for the first time.

They were in the car and Paul had the key in the ignition when Robbie came lumbering out of his house looking befuddled.

There they stood, while diminutive Jenny introduced Robbie to Ruth and Paul. Ruth smiled and waved like a little girl. Maybe because that's the way she had been signaling to Paul's relatives all afternoon from Jenny's porch. Paul stepped forward awkwardly and shook Robbie's hand.

"I hope we didn't wake you up."

"No, sir," Robbie said gently and smiled. "I couldn't hear you over the TV."

Paul launched into his pitch. Still feeling clumsy, he explained how they were related. Their shared great-grandparents made them second cousins. Plese McCarahan and his first wife, Louisa, were their common ancestors. Louisa was the only one of Paul's great-grandparents that didn't make it to the twentieth century. She died in 1892.

"We know next to nothing about her. There's no picture. But there's one thing we still have... You still have." Then Paul popped the question.

Robbie took a half step back and ran a hand through his graying locks. He didn't seem angry, just perplexed, the way he looked when he had come out into the late afternoon sunlight to find them sitting in the car.

Paul said nothing. Ruth and Jenny were turning into twins. They stood side by side with their arms folded over their breasts.

"Can I think about it a little and get back to you?"

Paul hesitated. It was a reasonable request.

"I mean, are you going to take me to a doctor for this?"

"No, we can do it right here."

"Here?"

"I have a kit."

"I don't want to give my blood without a nurse or something."

"No, there's no blood involved. You just swab your cheek. You do it yourself."

Jenny and Ruth nodded at Robbie.

Robbie said, "Oh, I can do that. I hope they don't think I'm a poppy. I've been eating poppy seeds."

The next morning on their way to the ten o'clock appointment at the tribal office of the Eno River Saponi, Paul dropped off the envelope containing Robbie's sample at the Mebane Post Office.

His meeting with Robbie had him feeling off his game. It had ended well enough. He got his sample. Robbie got some brochures from the Genographic Project and the "Journey of Man" CD that came with the kit from the National Geographic. But he had nearly fumbled the opportunity away. He would rather have a one-on-one conversation with the tribe's Federal Acknowledgement Officer, but he was going to have Ruth with him, wearing his letter sweater. There was no telling what she might say.

"Ruth," he began. "Ruth, there are some points that I need to make with this woman. I don't want to put a muzzle on you, but my guess is that this is going to be a one-shot deal. I've got to get it right the first time. I don't want it to be like those interviews we had with the Post-Gazette."

Ruth said, "I'm more mature now than when I gave that interview."

"You gave the interview last week."

"Yes, and it aged me."

Paul accepted this as agreement and went on, "What I want her to admit, in some shape or form, is that the whole tribe business is nonsense, recognition of the great state of North Carolina notwithstanding."

"They should have gone ahead and offered you membership in the tribe."

"They call it 'enrollment.' I should have realized that they're serious about this shit. I thought I was trying to join something that is basically a club, the Descendants-of-the-Saponi club. These people are talking about a nation with this Saponi stuff. They have their heads way up their asses. Either that or they smell casinos." Paul paused. "Just do me one favor and leave the sweater in the car."

There were three exchanges that he was going to have to get right this summer. At least he believed that there would be three. The first was this meeting with the Eno River Saponi. There had been a time when he thought he might start a scholarship fund in his grandfather's memory, the last on that line to be born in the Piedmont, land of the Eastern Siouan speakers. That wasn't going to happen now.

In two weeks, he would see Ernest Robinson in Philadelphia and try to reconcile being the author of "Topological Avenues in Analytic Number Theory," without even knowing of its existence until preprints arrived in the mail.

There would be a third meeting; this with Pell Dobbins, up-and-coming jurist rumored to be on the President's shortlist for the next Supreme Court vacancy. Dobbins had sent email to all the Berzelius alumni on the fundraising committee, which he chaired, with some ideas to consider before the summer meeting. After he read it, Paul had been tempted simply to donate a chunk of money and forgo the committee work, but then he thought better of it. Paul would sit down with Pell again in the Berzelius Tomb.

Perhaps there would be a directive from his Y-chromosome. Then Paul recalled that neither of his killings had been premeditated. Pell was probably safe. This line of reasoning landed him in alarming proximity to Ruth and her death-evasion-by-preconception notion. He shook his head back and forth in a motion that resembled a shudder.

Wanda Jeffries was short and thickset with dishwater blond hair, as much a white woman as Paul was a black man. Ruth had peeled off the letter sweater without protest and left it folded neatly in the car. Now she sat next to Paul braless in a tee-shirt and summer skirt. And the air conditioner in the tribal offices gave her goosebumps and made her nipples stand up.

Wanda sat in a chair facing them. Since she graduated from UNC-Chapel Hill, Wanda had spent almost all of the intervening thirty years researching the Piedmont Siouan tribes and helping to resurrect what was now called the Eno River Saponi. She had been the force that helped push them to state recognition. Paul admired her drive, but not what she had done.

At first, they discussed linguistics. None of the Eastern Siouan languages had been viable for nearly two centuries. Paul wanted to know how they really believed that they could build a tribe from scratch with neither cultural nor linguistic backbone available.

"So," Paul asked. "So what languages are the tribal members studying? Lakota?"

Wanda put her hands together as if praying. "We don't have any formal language programs. Catawba was probably the last of the Eastern Siouan languages spoken, if it was even Siouan. There's no telling how long the Lakota and the eastern tribes have been separated. Five hundred years, probably more."

Then Wanda started talking about the studies done by Frank Speck, the Tutelo Spirit Adoption Ceremony, the Catawba Texts. She followed with what Paul viewed as successive admissions of malfeasance.

Paul worked his way to the DNA question and Wanda shook her head. "I don't think that many of the tribal members want to do that. Why should people have their whole self-image upset by a sheet of paper with lab results?"

"Well, you don't have to make the results public. You don't even have to tell them the individual results if they don't want to know, but you could see what the tribes average blood quantum is." And he pushed further. "When my application for enrollment was turned down, you said it was because you couldn't quite connect my great-grandmother's Chavers family to your tribal history, which for some reason you keep hidden. You could do the same with the DNA. Keep it a secret. Stay biologically and historically under wraps."

Wanda shrugged and Paul softened. This was what this woman had. She was not going to budge. It was time to sum it up and leave. "Wanda, if you just called it an association and not a tribe you might have a chance to build something real."

By the time Ruth and Paul spoke, Ruth had put the sweater back on and they had driven six miles north in the direction of Caswell County. "Well, Paul, she wasn't what I had expected. I mean she had really hairy arms."

"It doesn't matter much to me what they look like. Their Chief is a black guy like me. I met him a few years ago. For all we know, modern Germans don't look anything like their ancestors did fifteen hundred years ago. But they're Germans because of continuity. I would put my mother in this category. She's German." He rarely mentioned his mother in her presence. It was an awkward matter. Ruth was only four years younger. "The Eno River Saponi are not Indians. They have no continuity. A few people survived the hippie years and, when they got off drugs, they decided to start a tribe. North Carolina went along with it, and now they're using all of their resources trying to seduce the federal government and get recognition at that level. Most of them know less about the Saponi Confederation than I do and probably have less Indian blood, as they say, if any. But they can almost taste success now. Once they made it a tribe, you're either out or in. You can't just share a common interest. I'm out. I just wanted to make it clear to Wanda what she is *in*."

They drove north for another twenty minutes to Yanceyville, the Caswell County seat. Paul had never been there. It was where his McCarahan line was rooted in the 18th century. Ruth took a picture of the courthouse and then they made their way back to the comfortable motel in Hillsborough.

***

I believe that there is a quantum nature to Truth and Falsehood. I confess that I do not have a good feel for science. My intuition is faulty whenever I go there. I feel a much stronger kinship with linguists and philosophers. People always assume that I know something about science because I'm a mathematician. They're wrong. I would say that my unorthodox take on truth and falsehood is not science, but an exercise in language aided by a quirky philosophical perspective. But it is science that influenced me in this.

If a photon can be in a superposition of opposite states, why is it not possible for any statement to be suspended between truth and falsehood, neither the one nor the other? If you observe a photon in superposition, it is collapsed into one of the two possibilities. Perhaps certain fundamental statements are neither true nor false until an intelligence, whatever that is, formulates it, effectively interacting with it and collapsing it into a truth or a falsehood, when it was neither. Maybe that is how human beings shape the reality of the universe. Maybe there is an inexhaustible list of things yet unshaped.

That's why I think that posing questions is the most important thing that I do and the most terrifying. Perhaps when you are passing into death, the ability to question becomes acute. Could that be what I saw in those dying men's faces? Of course, who knows what ramifications these very questions are having, even if they are rhetorical.

***

Paul straightened and eased himself from the pull-up bar. Then he stood there in the entrance to the piano room, posture perfect. That was the way his daily workout always ended, with three sets of ten pull-ups each, one set overhand, one underhand, and the final set with his grip on the handles perpendicular to the bar. There was always the slight buildup of lactic acid in his biceps near the end of the third set. It reminded him of the pain in his buttocks during track workouts a long time ago in New Haven.

In the ten days since his swing through Virginia and North Carolina, there had been another email from Pell exhorting the committee to arrive in New Haven with energy and ideas, reminding each of them how valuable their year in the Berzelius Tomb had been. Paul wondered how much he would even remember of the experience if it were not for having his collision with Pell.

There was also a letter from the Eno River Saponi Tribal council, which he was sure Wanda Jeffries had written. It thanked him for the interesting ideas he had presented. "The tribe always looks for opportunities to foster ties with the larger community of Indian descendants."

In a moment of weakness, he had mailed back a reply scribbled on the letter that they sent him: "People of multi-racial heritage should not be in the business of forming tribes. We should be building interest groups."

Paul grabbed the bar and did one more pull-up for good measure and then glanced at a photo that Ruth had propped up on the piano. It was an 8x10 of her cavorting with the steers that Paul owned with a cousin on their great-grandfather's farm in Pittsylvania County in Virginia. It had been the last stop before returning home. In the corner, written in Ruth's extravagant hand, were the words "The time of my life!"

It was surprising to Paul how comfortable he had been having her along. It was something that was even better than being alone and he really enjoyed the simplicity of being alone. That's the way it would be when he left for Philadelphia and New Haven. This trip would not be good for her. Both trips were really about the past, but he didn't have enough distance to the recent past, which is what the upcoming trip would have him take on.

If truth be known, he was more concerned about seeing Ernest than his anticipated showdown with Pell. There was already a buzz in the department about the paper. When he went in to check his mail earlier in the week, Arnie Landau flagged him down in the hall wanting to know about his new "venture" in analytic number theory. Arnie had gotten a call from a colleague at Syracuse and thought that Paul should organize a departmental seminar series in the fall to examine this "fresh view." Then he wanted Paul to know how much he respected him for having the resilience after all these years to move into a brand-new field and make a contribution.

"I know how much pressure you're under. People have long memories only when they shouldn't. The Post-Gazette is never going to let you go."

Paul responded that it had never really bothered him very much.

"But they even dragged your girlfriend into it."

"I don't think it bothers her either. We're both old and callous."

Arnie said, "Nothing beats maturity, I guess."

Paul said, "Unless it's death."

Paul liked Arnie. He was one of the few people in the department he had managed to hold a sustained conversation with. But he had never socialized with any of his colleagues and that included Arnie. It didn't matter. If there was any place a maverick could feel at home, it was in a mathematics department.

In his quarter of a century of academic life, Paul had supervised twelve master's theses. His Ph.D. production was even more meager, one. She was from mainland China and by some fluke latched onto a few notions in topological groups that Paul had been entertaining since his college days. In eighteen months, with very little guidance, she built it into a full-blown dissertation with some interesting dimension-theoretic results for factor groups. Paul still got a photo-card from her every year showing herself, husband, and two kids. She was married to a physics professor at the University of Kentucky and held a position at a small college nearby.

Mei- Ling had surprised him by marrying a white guy. It felt a bit like betrayal, which he recognized as utter nonsense. He had never put any such restrictions on himself. When her future husband sat in on the first part of her thesis defense, Paul had wanted to interrogate him. "What, sir, makes you a fit suitor for my daughter?" In a far-fetched genealogical sense, she was his mathematical daughter and Paul's line went back one doctoral advisor after another until it reached Euler, and then the Bernoulli brothers, who were forming the foundations of modern mathematics just as America began the more ambitious project of socially constructing race.

***

The evening before Paul left for Philadelphia, he and Ruth had dinner at his house. Paul fried shrimp with a light coating of bread crumbs, using his Aunt Loretta's recipe. Ruth brought a bottle of wine and drank half of it herself. Paul hadn't had a drink since he left Germany and that had been thirty years. His father's fatal fall from the balcony had something to do with it. It wasn't as if Paul feared that he was on the path to alcoholism. He had been a social drinker and he simply wasn't very social these days. He stopped drinking because alcohol had killed his father and he didn't much like the taste.

Paul drove Ruth home and as they approached the steps that led up through her terraced front yard, he yielded to impulse, lifting her and carrying her up the fifteen steps to her front porch. She felt amazingly light and bony. He could have run up the steps with her if he had wanted to. She started to laugh when he put her down and her laughter bent her at the waist. Paul kissed her on the top of the head and she said what she always said to him when he traveled, "I want you to be good." Paul was sure that this had nothing to do with fidelity, but he didn't know what she did mean. He didn't ask for clarification.

In the morning when he called Ernest Robinson, he thought he was just calling to let him know that he was on his way, but then something like insanity took over. Paul started blabbering about not being able to stay more than a day on this visit. "I have to do a hit in New Haven. Remove a fragmented piece of humanity."

Of course, Ernest had no idea what Paul was talking about. Paul was talking about Pell Dobbins. It was inappropriate and Paul said he was just kidding. "No, I can stay two days. I don't have to be in New Haven until the end of the week."

Ernest said, "Good."

***

Paul followed the Pennsylvania Turnpike and listened to Keith Jarrett piano solos on his CD, "The Melody at Night, With You." He wondered if he could ever play just one piece at that level. Jarrett made the recording as he was coming out of Chronic Fatigue Syndrome. He listened to Jarrett for 150 miles until he needed to pull off the road onto the shoulder, so that he could walk into the woods and relieve himself. This was one of the glories of traveling alone. There were thousands of unmarked rest stops. Feeling free, he ate some dried fruit, nuts, and yogurt, then put himself back on the turnpike with an Ahmad Jamal CD, "The Awakening."

Soon after Paul entered Philadelphia proper, he got lost. He asked a pedestrian for directions, but couldn't follow them. It took him a full hour to find Rittenhouse Square and, after he did, it was another twenty minutes to a ferret out a parking place that he didn't have to pay for.

Ernest Robinson greeted him wearing his doorman uniform, even though he wasn't on duty. His first words were: "Paul, I never really believed you would come."

Ernest was a half-head shorter than Paul with a dark chocolate complexion and keen features. His skin was so smooth that Paul assumed that he didn't shave. He followed Ernest down the hallway to a door tucked in next to an elevator shaft and was shown into a modest apartment. "My place. The commute to work is short."

The walls were covered with photographs, some of which Paul recognized as having been taken in either Pittsburgh or New Haven. There was snapshot of a chubby Ernest in an earlier version of the doorman uniform. Ernest was not chubby now. He had the proportions of his college days. Pointing to the bedroom, Ernest told Paul that's where he would sleep.

"Ernest, I don't want to put you out. Where are you going to sleep?"

Ernest looked at him triumphantly as if he had walked Paul into a checkmate. "Upstairs someplace. The tenants ask me to take care of their pets and plants while they're away. This week I have my choice of five apartments. I haven't decided yet. But it'll probably be the Berman place. Mrs. Berman is not here much now that she's a widow. In fact, she's in Israel this month."

What Paul really wanted to know was how this had come to be, from bright college years to doorman on Rittenhouse Square. But he held his tongue.

"Ernest, I brought an inflatable mattress with me. It's state of the art, really comfortable."

"These people love me, Paul. They don't care what I do. They're glad to help me any way they can. You have this bedroom. I'll have Mrs. Berman's. Are you hungry?"

By the early evening, they were into the mathematics, going over Ernest's paper lemma by lemma, theorem by theorem. They took only one break and Paul called Ruth to tell her that he arrived safely, but only got the answering machine. He left a message. He had almost forgotten to call and he knew that would make her fret and ultimately angry. She wanted him to get a cell phone, but he resisted because he just viewed the cell phone as another "Negro affliction" and he wouldn't be a party to it.

By midnight, Paul satisfied himself that he understood Ernest's perspective on the significance of the results and how the pieces fit together. It was quiet for a while and then Ernest started to talk.

"I had a nervous breakdown senior year and I had to leave. It had reached a point where I couldn't take tests anymore. I got down on my knees and prayed. But I wasn't delivered. I broke and went home. Left Yale. When I started getting back on my feet, I tried to find you. Your sister said you were in Germany and she didn't have the address."

"She was lying. She could always find my address when she needed a hundred dollars."

"Well, at any rate, the neighborhood was going downhill and I felt I had to get out. We had some family friends here in Philadelphia and they got me this job. It was supposed to be temporary, until I could move on. But as you see..."

"You were probably right to leave Pittsburgh. I'm back on the street where I grew up and I don't know a single person on the block. They don't own their houses. They don't talk to me. I don't talk to them. If I had a family, I wouldn't be there. But I'm something of a pervert. I guess I like being cozy in squalor."

Ernest winced. "Don't call yourself a pervert. How come you don't have a family?"

"Because I only like looking backward in family trees. Forward scares me."

"Didn't you ever get close?"

"No, I did not. If Yale hadn't waited until our senior year to admit women, I might have had a chance. Some girl might have made a project of that boy. But it didn't happen and I threw away my young adulthood in Germany. I thought that maybe I would drift into a relationship somehow, but I didn't. I know how relationships end. I don't know how to get them to start." He considered telling Ernest about the old-lady thing, but thought better of it. Why burden him with that?

Ernest said, "I see." And then they were quiet again before he resumed.

"I was terrified of going back into the classroom. As I said, I couldn't face being tested. In high school, I used to love it. Pop quizzes, SATs, anything. Before I knew it, I had gotten comfortable with being a doorman. But I started studying mathematics on my own and then I struck up a relationship with Daniel Berman. He got me hooked up with some people at Temple and I did some independent study courses that Yale recognized. They had pity on me. I became a Yale graduate a decade after I left the campus. I'm a doorman with a Yale degree."

"Ernest, you could have come to Pitt. I'm sure I could have gotten you a graduate fellowship. At worst, you could have worked with me. Shit, this paper that you wrote and stuck my name on could've been the centerpiece of a dissertation. And we have Arnie Landau..."

"I'm frail, Paul. I'm fragile. I can't take tests. I wouldn't have been able to take Ph.D. qualifying exams. I got into a routine here. I got comfortable. Church on Sunday, my little apartment, my own mathematics. If I had wanted to get into that world, Berman would've helped me. I didn't want to. I still don't. I'm frail. I thank God for you. For your willingness to carry my work forward."

"Honestly, it's not a role I would have volunteered for."

"I know that I'm using you. I like to think that it's God using you."

"Well, if I'm God's instrument, he sure has been moving me in some mysterious ways. Mysterious."

"You've always been mysterious to me, man. If you're not quite ready for bed. I want to show you something in the Berman apartment."

"What?"

"You'll like it. Just be surprised."

They took the elevator to the eighth floor. Ernest pulled a key off his key ring and opened a door to a darkened apartment. "Ready, Paul?"

"No, but go ahead."

Ernest flipped a switch and they were in a room completely dominated by a concert grand piano.

"Daniel Berman was a pathetic pianist, but he loved the instrument. He got this piano and his wife nearly had a fit because they had to remodel the apartment. And he still couldn't play worth beans. Would you play something, Paul? Play something from the old days."

"From the old days? I can barely remember the old days." Paul sat down at the piano and played a few scales and then one Hanon exercise. "From the old days, you say. In the old days, you were a lamb of God, weren't you?"

"I'm not sure."

"And you say I'm an instrument of God. So, I'm something like a lamb myself." Paul laughed and he sounded hoarse. "I think we've lost our way. Poor lambs. But maybe only Jesus can be a lamb of God."

"It's how you look at it, Paul."

"Well, I'm looking at it as an intro. The 'little black sheep' line works for sure. *The Whiffenpoof Song* should be our anthem." He began playing and singing *The Whiffenpoof Song*, Pell Dobbins' song. "We are poor little lambs who have lost our way." He had to feel his way through because it had been so long since he had played it. He could feel the muscles in his ear tense. "Gentleman songsters off on a spree. Doomed from here to eternity." He heard Ernest murmur, "Beautiful."

As he finished, Paul sang in a gentle baritone, "Lord have mercy on such as we. Baa, Baa, Baa." And then he vamped for a while and segued to *Taking a Chance on Love*. It had been a long day, but he felt relaxed and played a second time through, slowed it down and sold it as best he could. Playing it softly at the end, he just tapped out the melody with his right hand. And when he was done, he looked down at the keys and sighed, "Sometimes it does take a leap of faith, and I'm not joking." When he turned, he saw that Ernest's face was covered with tears and Paul wondered if this meant that he really knew how to play the piano after all.

"There's more I should tell you. As a young man, I took a lot of things to God. But the one thing I did not take to God... was my love for you."

Paul still had one hand on the piano. He sat on the bench and faced Ernest, but his body was twisted away.

"I always wanted to tell you, but I was ashamed. We weren't even very good friends. We just had that Pittsburgh thing going. And I could tell that you were pretty much oblivious. I knew you were straight. So I never told you and I pretended that God did not know.

"Back in the eighties I fell in love with a man here in town and I think he loved me. I didn't take this to God either. My lover is dead now and whatever is listed as my cause of death someday, it will probably be due to my unwillingness to handle love the way God would have had me handle it. I've now learned to take everything, without exception, to God. I'm HIV positive and most likely I'm going to die from AIDS. With the Lord's forgiveness, I'll live with Him in eternity."

Paul didn't sleep well in Ernest's bed. The mystical role of the Y-chromosome that he had fantasized into existence haunted him. If the Y-chromosome really was a divining rod showing him to his next kill, driving his fetish for old women, then he should be looking over his shoulder. Ernest Robinson had a divining rod too and, at least for a while, it was pointing straight for Paul. Maybe it still was. What better way for Ernest to marry him than to take on Paul's name. God wouldn't mind that. The paper wasn't by Dr. Paul Edward McCarahan. It was by Mr. Paul Edward McCarahan. Dr. and Mr. Paul Edward McCarahan, man and man. Mr. Paul Edward McCarahan, nee Robinson.

He finally drifted off and then woke up again after an hour, his torso damp. And he feared that the fever of unknown origin was back again. In a dream, he saw Ruth as she was telling John, the reporter, what had appeared in the paper - that no one would be interviewing Yaros twenty years after he killed the black kid if Yaros were still alive. Paul saw himself standing behind Ruth and saying "Bravo!" Cindy snapped a photo and their picture covered the front page of the Post-Gazette with a caption that read: "The Gospel according to Ruth and Paul. Plain Geometry."

When Paul woke up again, it was morning and he could hear Ernest moving around in the kitchen. After a few minutes, he stood up and walked to the bedroom door. Paul cried out, "Ernest Robinson of Pittsburgh."

Ernest stuck his head around the corner, eyes big. He smiled and responded, "It is I." And the uneasiness that Paul had felt during the night evaporated. The courage to be silly and state the obvious was all that was needed. This was his old friend from Pittsburgh and his Yale classmate. Paul had run track. Ernest marched with the God Squad. Here they were in Philadelphia decades later, somehow still managing to stumble forward.

They ate cereal and Ernest described his situation in greater detail. As long as he could work, he would be fine. He was afraid of what would happen, if he moved into full-blown AIDS. Even now he had bad days and his endurance was in decline. A doorman that sat all the time would be no doorman at all. Ernest was hatching survival strategies. He wanted to hunker down and do mathematics as long as possible.

They cleared the dishes from the table and went over the paper once more, but quickly this time. Paul said something about follow-up and then let fly the idea that had occurred to him when he was in North Carolina, when he finally understood Ernest's general approach.

"Ernest you might as well take this and go for broke. Go after the Twin Prime Conjecture. I'm not saying that you're even close. But when I look back, I sometimes regret that I never went after any of the big problems. I do believe that what I've done mathematically is important. I went after the questions that were important to me. I had my personal agendas. But I never went after a single big problem head-on. But this machinery of yours is so original. It might lend itself to taking down this problem. You could wrap yourself in glory."

"That's not the kind of glory I should be reaching for at this point."

Paul wasn't as patient as he might have been. "Yes, I know that adulation for having settled one of the great open questions in number theory won't get you one step closer to heaven." Then he stopped himself. "Listen. Something occurred to me a couple of weeks ago. You're starting off with this quirky family of topological spaces that are metrizable in a canonical way. You port all the machinery of complex analysis to the topological space intact. Then you pull a sequence of integers almost magically out of the hat. You then read off all sorts of information about the sequence from the structure of the original space.

"What you need to do is find a way to reverse the order. What I'm saying is maybe you could start with the sequence of twin primes and find the topological space that corresponds to it in your family."

Ernest was unmoved. "Why do you think that would be easy? It doesn't sound easy to me."

"I doubt that it's easier than anything else people have tried. But what they've tried hasn't worked. This is different and it's yours. Maybe it would work. Or maybe it wouldn't. Maybe there's no corresponding space in your family. But what the hell. If you could prove that, it would be interesting in its own right; a fruitful failure. All the examples of sequences in your paper are monotonic and strange. Maybe they are cousins of the twin primes."

"Paul, I could squeeze on this thing until all the magic is gone for me."

"Or you might squeeze out some more magic. There are all sorts of questions that you could consider. You haven't even begun to look at cardinality arguments. How many of these spaces are there? You should mine this, Ernest."

"That's what I have you for. You're the professional mathematician. Some days I'm so tired that the proof of the Pythagorean Theorem looks hard. You carry the ball, Paul. Run with it."

***

In the evening they went for a walk and passed Paul's car parked a few blocks away. Ernest walked around it twice. "I've never driven a car, not even once."

"I hadn't either, until I finished graduate school. The Auburn job forced me to go out and buy a used VW Rabbit. I knew I couldn't survive down there without a car. I barely passed the road test and I had to spend some of my savings, which I didn't like to do." In fact, he had not needed much of his savings. The Oma's money, Loretta's insurance money and the proceeds from the sale of his grandmother's house remained untouched. He had simply drawn on some of the savings he put aside while living in a hovel and teaching at the Kaufmännische Schule IV.

Paul looked at his car. "They're a nuisance, but once you have one you develop a dependency. It would be really hard for me to wait for a bus now with the temperature in the teens."

Walking back to Rittenhouse Square Paul thought about how many times he had gotten on buses and streetcars with his feet so cold that he could barely feel them. He looked up and saw a stately, elderly black couple walking towards them. They were old enough to be his parents.

"Ernest, where are your people from?"

"I don't know exactly. Virginia and Tennessee. But I forget what towns. I think my grandparents were country people."

"Wouldn't you like to trace it back?"

"Well, I won't say I'm not curious. But I'm done with following my curiosity. I'm probably better off letting it rest. And who would I pass it on to anyway? I don't have children. I don't have nieces or nephews."

"I don't have children either. I do it for myself. It's like a religion for me. I feel I owe it to my ancestors to find out as much as I can. I'll write it down and maybe someone will care about it three hundred years from now. Maybe they'll find the photographs quaint."

"We'll know everything about them in the sweet by and by."

"Ernest, you have to be kidding."

"Well, yes. Sometimes I kid."

They went up to the Berman apartment and ate pizza while they watched a DVD, "The Last of the Mohicans."

***

By the time he was making his way through New York City, Paul had already begun to regret the things that he had not said in Philadelphia. He had given Ernest very little beyond his mathematical insights on a paper that Ernest wrote. He gave Ernest nothing about corpses, nothing about elderly women in short skirts. Dr. McCarahan had nothing to share. He had never told anyone about the train in Germany. He had never spoken in a forthright way about Yaros. Ernest was the one person on Earth with whom that might have happened and it did not. And he had not offered Ernest the comfort, which he was in a position to give: "Ernest, if things start going downhill, you can stay with me. I have a big house. I have money." It was not because he feared living in the same house with a man who loved him. It was because he didn't want to share his refuge with anyone. And it was because he didn't want to watch Ernest die.

***

Paul reached New Haven and the Berzelius Tomb in the late afternoon. The committee meeting wasn't until the next day. He used his key and was for some reason surprised when the heavy metal doors swung open. He didn't need to search his memory for the combination lock on the interior set of doors. They had been left open. But it took him a while to find the light switch and then finally the hall was illuminated with that swooshing sound that he remembered from so many years before. He could see through the sitting room all the way to the dining room at the end of the building.

Ruth had asked him to be good. "No," he said to himself. "No, I will not take the opportunity to kill Pell Dobbins." It wasn't going to happen anyway. Paul reminded himself again that premeditation was not his thing. It would be hard to promote Ernest's work from a prison cell. But it did feel like something was in the offing. His twenty-year cycle screamed for it. He walked through the sitting room, through the hallway and into the dining room, where he dropped his suitcase and the box with the inflatable mattress next to the fireplace. He couldn't go around killing the Pell Dobbinses of the world. He wouldn't know how to live without them.

Paul found an outlet and inflated the mattress. Then he dragged it over to the piano. The last time he had slept in Berzelius, it had been downstairs on the couch next to the pool table and the National Guard was right outside the Tomb's green plot. He woke up and went outside to find them practicing fixing bayonets. The campus was roiled by protesters. It looked like the Warsaw Pact about to enter Czechoslovakia. But the campus survived that sticky weekend.

It was a warm evening. By the time he walked across the campus and returned with food, he was sweaty. One of the negatives about camping out in the Tomb was the lack of a shower. That meant washing up in the bathroom off the passageway between the sitting room and dining hall. When he came out, he was face to face with a young woman and there was another one right behind her. All three of them jumped. Paul was wearing boxer shorts and socks. He was carrying his pants and shirt over his arm. This is the way I go down, he thought. After all the things that I've done – morals charges, lewd in the Tomb. The clock was ticking and Paul found his voice.

"I'm the ghost of Berzelius's past." He held up his free hand. "Just wait. Give me a second." And Paul retreated into the bathroom and put on the clothes that he had intended to stow in the dirty clothes bag. This was a screw-up. He muttered, "Should've told them I'm the goddamn Berzelius spook."

When he reemerged the two of them were laughing.

"The show's over, ladies." Paul tried to establish himself. "I'm Paul McCarahan. There weren't any women, non-members generally, allowed in the building when I was here. I apologize for the awkwardness." The only good thing about this was that Ruth was going to love the story.

He could see now that one of them was really a girl, who appeared to be in her mid-teens. The other one was older, robustly built. Both of them had eyes that were set close together. The older one offered Paul her hand. "I'm Sandy Dobbins. This is my sister Carla."

Pell's daughters had come to call and caught him with his pants off. They stayed long enough to tell him what it was like to grow up in the home of a distinguished jurist. None of Pell's children had gone to Yale. The youngest, Carla, was older than he had guessed. She was going to be a freshman at Boise State in the fall. There were three boys. All of them knew Berzelius inside out from frequent trips to the campus. Pell was at the hotel with friends. He had given his daughters the key to the Tomb.

After the Dobbins girls left, he lay on the inflated mattress in moonlight filtered by the skylight above. Paul realized that his basic occupation description could be simply 'entertainer.' He wrote stuff to entertain other mathematicians and the classroom was his stage. He read his reviews, which were called teaching evaluations, at the end of each semester. "Sometimes he's funny." Or others might say, "I'm terrified the whole time I'm in his classroom." A real testament to his versatility as an actor. This was the first time that he had resorted to strip-tease, except maybe the one time that he taught ninety minutes of differential equations with his zipper down.

Before Pell's daughters left, Paul would strip himself bare in another way. Berzelius had internet access in the second-floor study, next to the ceremonial meeting room where Paul had given his Plecker speech. The reason the Dobbins girls had dropped in was to check their email and ended up checking out Paul.

He could have said, "Don't mention this to your father because he'll be pissed." He could have said that right after he said, "I know your father. He was in my delegation." But he did not. They were excited by the coincidence. He was still feeling nearly naked and, as a result, talked more than he might ordinarily.

Eventually, he discovered that the older daughter, Sandy, was majoring in anthropology at Washington State. Paul's quick rejoinder was that he would have majored in misanthropology if Yale had offered it. It was the one quip that neither girl laughed at. They just shook their heads very seriously. Of course, the email was the reason they were there. So Paul followed them up the stairs to the computers and offered to show Sandy, the future anthropologist, around the Genographic Project website. He could not have known that the analysis of Robbie's sample was complete. He had conducted a dozen tests and none had gone through in less than four weeks. His own had required additional testing and taken over two months. But when he put in the password, the legal fine print describing the 'Terms and Conditions' flashed to the screen. The Dobbins girls were leaning over his shoulder. He knew that if he clicked once more, the next thing that would appear on the screen would be his great-grandmother Louisa's ancestral DNA signature, her mitochondrial haplogroup.

Paul lay on his back and watched the skylight darken then lighten again. He conjectured fast-moving cloud cover and wondered at it all. Maybe he was an exhibitionist. He had clicked 'I ACKNOWLEDGE' and revealed that his great-grandmother Louisa belonged to a branch of the mitochondrial DNA Haplogroup A, a branch that was a Native American signature. Actually, this result surprised Paul because the McCarahans had no oral history about Indians at all. He thought they had married into it through the Chavers. It was becoming clear that the native ancestry was pervasive in both his Virginia and his North Carolina branches. For a moment, he forgot that the Dobbins girls were in the room with him. The two of them followed the ancient migratory path, which was pictured next to the list of mutations that defined the signature. It led out of Central Asia, across the Bering Strait and one line branched to the Atlantic seaboard.

The younger girl, Carla, looked at him bewildered. "You have Indian blood?"

Paul said, "That's not the way I would put it."

"I mean, doesn't that make you feel kinda funny?"

"What about that would make me feel funny?"

"Well, you're black."

"The black part of me has no problem with the Indian part. It just feels kinda funny about the white part."

"You have white blood?"

Sandy stood by helplessly, squirming and apparently embarrassed by her younger sister.

***

Of the eight committee members who showed up, Pell was the last to arrive. He saw Paul sitting on the piano bench and walked toward him with what might pass for a warm smile, except that his nostrils were slightly flared. Paul had forgotten that Pell was shorter than he was. Pell's hair had gone completely white. Unlike Paul, he hadn't lost any of it.

Paul rose to the obligatory handshake. Pell took his hand and looked him up and down. "The girls say you have great abs."

"Well, we surprised each other in many ways."

"Did you play the piano for the girls. They're both quite musical."

Paul had, in fact, played the piano. Berzelius had acquired a new baby grand and he enjoyed playing it. But he hadn't played for Dobbins' daughters.

"Pell, actually it didn't come up."

"What did come up?" Pell's tone sounded as if they were on the verge of renewing the Paul-Pell wars.

"Your daughter Sandy is a budding anthropologist. We talked about her field."

"All I know is that they came back to the hotel talking about your abs and your DNA. They actually asked if I would let them have some money for DNA testing. To find out if they're mixed. Paul, you're like a disease. What were you doing walking around in the Tomb naked?"

"I wasn't naked."

"In a state of undress then."

"Maybe I divined that you were sending your daughters over." Paul immediately regretted saying this. He had enjoyed talking with the girls. Even if they were a bit dim, they were innocent.

"I apologize, Pell. They're nice girls. They didn't make me feel like an idiot. And they could've done that very easily. I was still living in the days of the all-male preserve. Embarrassing."

Pell appeared to be mollified. "You were always a little off. I guess not much has changed."

"All in all, that's probably a good thing." He hesitated, wondering whether or not he should get into it. "Are you in a frame of mind to accept a Supreme Court nomination if it's offered? You know the president is Skull and Bones. Maybe you wouldn't accept the tap from a Bones man."

"Paul, you're a delightful jerk. At any rate, I would never pass on the opportunity to help ensure that the Constitution remains the supreme law of the land."

Paul waited for the go-ahead from his Y-chromosome to smite Pell and wondered why it didn't come.

Pell chaired the meeting and it lasted all afternoon. The goal was to come up with some preliminary recommendations for assuring the long-term financial viability of Berzelius. Paul said nothing the whole time. He loved mathematics. He hated verbiage rife with ugly bits of references to financial arithmetic. As the energy level in the room wound down, Paul raised his hand and accepted Pell's acknowledgment.

Paul said, "We need to lead by example. First, we all plunk down a chunk of money and say this is what the committee has been able to do to get the ball rolling. Then we tell our fellow BZ alumni how much more we need to make the picture look rosy.

"Second, we turn the Tomb into a bed and breakfast. This place is hardly used at all in the summer. I slept here last night. I'm going to sleep here tonight. The two hundred dollars I save by not staying in a hotel will be added to my gift to Berzelius. Of course, any guest would have to get permission from the resident delegation in advance. Maybe the first few thousand dollars that we earn this way should be earmarked for having a shower installed. I certainly could have used one last night...

"Finally, since this is a tomb anyway, we should create a crypt. The capacity would obviously be limited and that should drive the bidding for the privilege to have Berzelius as the final resting place. I might even jump into the bidding myself. I'm single and there's no family plot."

Pell looked away into the fireplace.

The woman from the 1985 delegation cleared her throat and volunteered to write up the promising ideas that had been put forward and distribute the summary electronically. "Paul, will you be hurt if I leave crypt management off the list?"

Pell stood up quickly, not giving Paul a chance to respond. "Let's think about how to move forward over the next couple of weeks." Turning to Paul, he said, "I need to get a proposal ironed out for the board by the middle of September. We can't dilly-dally. I'll see everybody at Mory's in an hour. I think we could all use a drink." The meeting was adjourned.

As the others drifted through the sitting room and out the door, Pell made one more attempt. "Why the hell did you volunteer to be on the committee. You don't give a shit about this effort."

"I do. I'm just bored by the standard approaches. Fundraising should be either cut and dry or you sell nothing for something. I offered a little of both. There's nothing worse than a solicitation that's both boring and complicated, and from what I heard today that's what you're going to get."

"We'll iron it out."

"Here's another proposal. I wasn't planning to go to Mory's, but if you promise to try recapturing your youth by singing the Whiffenpoof Song. That might get me over there." Paul sang the opening phrase, "To the tables down at Mory's."

"Paul, you ought to come and sing. My voice isn't what it used to be. No, I don't think so."

"Well, then I guess I won't be going."

Pell looked at him and for a moment Paul thought he saw the question in Pell's face. But it was fleeting and Pell still stood there before him, very much alive. "Suit yourself, Paul."

Paul didn't want to shake his hand because Pell had been picking his nose all afternoon long, just like in the old days. But not shaking his hand would have made him feel small again, like in the old days. And these were supposed to be the new days.

Paul watched Pell follow the others through the Tomb door and out into the summer evening, Pell with his finger again mining his nostrils.

The next day Paul did not hurry. By the time he finally got his things bundled together and left the Tomb, it was midday. He had a bad taste in his mouth. He had not handled things right and he felt he had fouled the Berzelius nest. And that was probably why he left I-95 when he reached Philadelphia. He got lost again trying to find his way to Rittenhouse Square. It was Sunday and the one thing he knew for sure was that Ernest didn't work on Sunday.

When Ernest opened the door and saw Paul, he got flustered. "Did you find something wrong in the paper."

"There's nothing wrong with the paper, Ernest."

And Ernest relaxed. "You didn't say you were going to stop on your way back. I'm always afraid someone's going to find an error in it."

"It's a beautiful paper, Ernest. Meticulous. It's done. It's published in Transactions."

"I've had a dozen dreams about someone finding a flaw. I thought you had come back to tell me." Ernest looked comfortable again and realized that he hadn't let Paul across the threshold. "Come in, Paul."

"Actually, I need to get on to Pittsburgh. I just wanted to show you something out in the car. If you could take a look now? I'm parked illegally."

Ernest followed Paul to the car and climbed in when Paul invited him to.

"I lied, Ernest. Only a part of it is in the car. We have to take a little drive to find the rest of it."

"I hope you're not taking me someplace where I'm going to be around people. I'm not dressed for it and I need a shower."

"You're perfect. There are no people involved."

Paul drove until he spotted what he needed. He pulled onto the parking lot and got out of the car. Ernest wondered aloud, "This is it?"

"Get behind the steering wheel and I'll show you."

Ernest didn't move.

"Ernest, go ahead."

They got out of the car and switched sides. "Turn the key forward. Go ahead. It won't move, it's in park."

Ernest turned the key forward and started the car. Paul put his hand on the gear shift. "Put your foot on the pedal on the left."

Ernest fumbled around with his left foot. "Use your right foot. Got it?"

"Yeah. My mouth feels really dry."

"We'll be done soon. I want you to keep your foot on the brake and pull the lever down until it's on the 'D.' It won't move if you keep your foot pressed down." Ernest complied without saying a word.

"Now take your foot off the brake."

Ernest drove for a half-hour, at one point nearly sideswiping the only car on the lot. Finally, he asked to stop. "Man, I'm drenched. I really need a shower now."

"You want to drive it around the block?"

"No, I don't think so."

There was something that he felt Ernest needed to know. "You know, it's not unusual at all for a mathematician to have the anxiety that you have about the first paper. I thought for sure that someone would discover a problem with the first two or three that I wrote. But what you've done; it's original. No mistakes. No duplication."

Then Paul drove them back to Rittenhouse Square, where they sat in the car and talked a while about some ideas they planned to collaborate on as a follow-up to the paper. Ernest asked him to come in, but Paul begged off. He wanted to get back to Pittsburgh.

***

This time was no exception. As usual, Ruth had left some items for him in the piano room. That's the way it was after every trip. She did this even though Paul told her every time that he didn't like her coming into the neighborhood when he was away. She would counter that she always took a taxi and asked the driver to wait.

There were two large manila envelopes. One had "More stuff on my family's genealogy – a surprise!" The other one carried the instruction "Some legal stuff, etc. - for your files." Paul was tired and wanted to go to bed, but he opened the envelope to see the promised surprise. There shouldn't be any. Both of her parents were born in Slovakia. She even knew the names of the towns. There were two smaller envelopes and inside the 'read-me-first' envelope were three certificates attesting to the haplogroup memberships for Ruth, her daughter Bobbi, and her granddaughter Giselle. There was another Ruth note taunting him, "I can play the DNA game too. I had this done three months ago." If Ruth thought these results were a surprise, she was slipping. The lists of mitochondrial mutations were identical, as they should be for mother, daughter, and daughter's daughter. They were Haplogroup H, the dominant female haplogroup in Europe. She could have just done her own and saved herself four hundred bucks. Paul was beginning to be irritated. But she hadn't consulted with him first because that would have spoiled the surprise. He pulled three certificates along with three CDs from the other envelope, still muttering. She had also tested the threesome with a leading autosomal company, a bad investment, given the known roots in the mountains of Eastern Europe. She wasn't thinking.

Ruth's Certificate read:

European	100
Sub Saharan African	0
Native American	0
East Asian	0

Bobbi's was the same.

There was another Ruth note that instructed him to look inside the piano bench, where he found Giselle's certificate.

European	88
Sub-Saharan African	6
Native American	6
East Asian	0

Paul nodded in appreciation. Ruth had tripped him up. Her granddaughter was a Plecker gem. So Giselle's father must have been too. This was practically the only way that Ruth would have had to get a fix on him since Bobbi had been closed-mouth about the man. This was a good enough surprise to justify waking her up. But she had the answering machine set to pick up immediately and all he got was, "This is Ruth. I love messages. Leave me one." So he went to bed actually smiling, marveling at tricky Ruth and slept better than he had in a long time.

***

Paul had paid no attention to his letter sweater, which was dry cleaned and hanging in a plastic bag on the door to the piano room. In the morning, he discovered that there was an envelope pinned to the sweater. Paul opened it and began to read.

My Love,

I hope that you'll understand the decision I have made to wrap a ribbon around my life and make a bow. You might see it as more like binding it with a piece of twine and a knot, but I hope not. I was diagnosed with cancer eight months ago. During our trip, I started into what a pilot calls the "final approach." I had prepared for this and am fortunate to be in a position, as well as have the strength, to make a rational decision on my departure. Giselle will be with me and, I hope, Bobbi. I couldn't let you be present. It might make headlines (smile).

There are a couple of other envelopes on the piano bench. One just addresses a few legal issues. I've left everything to Bobbi and (mostly) Giselle. That's except for the house, which I am leaving to you and Giselle jointly. The other envelope has what I think is a nice DNA surprise for you.

You know me. I kept a journal over the last few months. Giselle has it and is under strict instructions to share it with you. I doubt that Bobbi's interested. Thanks for carrying me up the stairs on our last night together. Thanks for caring for me. And please never give up on caring.
All my love,
Ruth

Paul went to the telephone and tried to call Ruth once more. "This is Ruth. I love messages. Leave me one."

***

He stood at Ruth's door ringing the bell repeatedly. Finally, he let himself in with his key and worked his way through the entire house from the basement to the third floor. He found nothing that would lead him to believe that Ruth's letter described reality.

He had driven in Ernest-Robinson style from his house to hers and was not much better on the way back. When he got home, there was a message on the answering machine. "Dr. McCarahan, this is Giselle Gable. Please call me as soon as possible." Her tone was low key and the cadence was even.

Paul dialed the number as if it were urgent, imagining that Ruth's life hung in the balance. It was Bobbi who picked up. "Paul, I'm sorry. Mother didn't want you to know. She was adamant."

Her voice was a surprise. At first, he thought it was Ruth. He had only seen Bobbi a half-dozen times in the five years he had been with her mother and these sentences amounted to her longest sustained utterance.

"What happened, Bobbi? What happened?"

"Paul, this is how she always planned to go. I've known about it for years. She had prepared me and, really, Giselle too. She was determined not to have a lingering death. She said that she wanted to go out on her own terms, not anybody else's.

"And she wasn't going to let the medical treatments and nursing homes bleed her estate dry. My father made his money in pharmaceuticals. Mother knew what she was doing with money and she knew what she was doing with drugs."

Then she asked Paul when he could come by to discuss matters with Giselle and Paul answered that he would come over immediately.

***

She met him at the door with a handshake, Ruth's granddaughter. Paul thought there was a chance that he might recognize her face from the classroom years earlier, seeing her in person instead of viewing a portrait in Ruth's living room. But he didn't. She was a little bit taller than her grandmother, but still a half foot shorter than Paul. Giselle had blond hair and gray eyes. In these superficial things, she was more like Ruth than Bobbi. And it was Paul's immediate sense that she shared more than a mere superficial resemblance with her grandmother.

Bobbi had left before Paul got there. Giselle said that her mother had some errands to run. They sat down together in the family room and Paul reached for an opening, "Is there going to be a service?" He immediately felt silly asking this, as if he cared about ceremony. "I don't even know when this happened. When did she ...?" So now he had messed up further, getting stuck on the verb choice.

"I believe it was two days after you went to Philadelphia. She listened to your voice on the answering machine and then she said, 'He's a good man. I ask him to call me when he travels. Now I'm going to travel soon. It makes me feel a little bad.' And then I drove her over to your house and she left you a few envelopes."

For some reason, this made Paul think of Christmas. Had he been naughty or nice?

"She really wanted to make sure that you were far away from here when she carried it out. At any rate, there won't be a formal service. We'll have her ashes in a couple of days and she wants us to spread them in the backyard. You can say a few words if you like. I'm going to say a prayer in Slovak that she taught me when I was little."

Paul came back to life. "Do you believe in God?"

"No, I don't. But that has nothing to do with it. It's something she gave me. I don't even remember what most of the words mean. I just imagine it being handed down from generation to generation. It seems like an appropriate time to speak it aloud."

"I suppose that's about as sacred as it can get as far as I'm concerned, remembering the past as best we can."

"Are you sentimental?"

"Maybe. Maybe that's what I am. Did you look at your DNA results?"

"I did. It made me want to know my father even more than before. My mother says my father was from the South. I should say the man she thinks is my father."

"Does she know where he is?"

"He was in the army and there's a name, the same as his, on the Vietnam Memorial, Vaughn Jacob Jeffries. I found out that Vaughn Jeffries was from North Carolina. So it's probably the same man and probably my father. A lot of 'probablys.'"

The name Jeffries registered clearly with Paul, but he decided that it wasn't the time to discuss the history of the Eno River Saponi. Maybe someday.

"Is this where you grew up?"

Giselle nodded. The house was small and cozy. Bobbi had not married and Paul assumed that Ruth bought her the house to keep her close, but still at arm's length. The house was on the other side of Highland Park from where Ruth lived.

"I'm going back to California tomorrow to tidy up my affairs there. I should be back in a couple of weeks. I've always wanted to live in grandmother's house and now I can. It's terrible to say. But I feel sort of happy that I have this chance. I was just treading water in California. I want to come home."

Paul started, "About the house. I don't want..."

But Giselle stopped him. "I don't want to talk about the legal stuff. Right now, it's ours together. I'm comfortable with that. I hope you don't feel uncomfortable. Maybe it's her way of keeping the family together. What she thinks of as her family. This way you and I have a formal connection."

He was still feeling unsure of himself and relented. "I'll do whatever you say."

Giselle smiled weakly. She looked tired. And yet, there was something flirtatious in her manner, in the mold of her grandmother. "Will you?"

***

She asked him to drive her to the airport. Her mother had to work and she didn't want to leave Ruth's car parked at the airport for two weeks. She did not say too much on the way. She was concerned about her cats. She had been forced to put them in a kennel.

Giselle pulled the journal out of her carry-on bag just before she got out of the car. She squeezed his arm and said,

"It's good. I've read it twice already." Then she got out of the car and left for California, leaving Paul in his unstable state.

Paul thinks that he's settled, but he's not settled at all. I watched him take apart the woman at the Saponi Tribal Office on our visit to North Carolina. He was methodical and relentless. When he erupts, he's a force to be reckoned with and he's beyond most people's reckoning. Luckily, I sit in the eye of the storm.

Now that my life has wound down, I finally am starting to feel guilty about stalking him, then trying to put reins on him. He has a lot to offer, but I was not the right one to help him get it out. As much as I treasured our relationship, I recognize that it was curdled. I wonder what might have happened for the good, if I hadn't ambushed him at that bus stop five years ago. Probably nothing, but you never know. After all those years of eyeing him on the bus, I was brave enough to make an approach. I thought I just wanted to see if he was real. Now I know that he is and I hope that it's not too late to do the salvage job that I was not able, or even willing, to take on.

He doesn't know how close we came to having a fight when he told me that he was resigned to being a terminal node on his family tree. But how could I really fight him when I was a big contributor to his dead-end status? He has quite an edge to him because he is not putting his energy in the right places. I used to play that Eagles song for him, Desperado. He would even sing along sometimes. Maybe he was just pretending to be oblivious to the words. "You ain't gettin' no younger. Your pain and your hunger; they're driving you home." In his present state, he would be real lucky to get to anything that could be called home. Unless the abyss is his home. Paul should be a patriarch. He claims to have a divining rod. If so, he doesn't know how to read it. But I do hope Dr. E1a is reading this. Dr. E1a: You should be a Patriarch!

It was this journal entry that Paul read over and over again. Ruth sounded frustrated, maybe even angry.

He escaped into mathematics, giving in to Arnie Landau's cajoling to conduct an analytic number theory seminar during the fall semester. The focus would be on Paul's recent publication, of course. For the next two weeks, he became a graduate student again. He reread several chapters of Berman's book on analytic number theory and a few of the papers that Ernest referenced in his unpublished manuscript. Paul eased back into the exercise routine that had been disrupted by his trip to New Haven and Ruth's death. In the evenings, he played the piano incessantly and worked up a composition with a title reflecting his memories of Ruth, *The Time of her Life*. It was longer than most of his pieces and entertained many mood changes.

He called Ernest once to tell him that he would fly him in for one of the seminar presentations as a guest lecturer if he wanted. Ernest did not. "You handle it, Paul. You'll get it right."

Giselle called him when the plane landed in California. She called him every day after that for two weeks. Paul would have been hard-pressed to say what they talked about.

***

The day after Giselle returned from California, they sprinkled Ruth's ashes in the flower gardens in the backyard. It was the hottest day of the year and Paul could visualize Ruth wearing his letter sweater in July in North Carolina. Giselle said her prayer in Slovak and Paul completed the memorial by playing *The Time of Her Life* on Ruth's massive upright piano, which Paul had gotten tuned while Giselle was in California. Bobbi placed the urn on the mantle and wept. This got Giselle started. Paul remained dry-eyed. He had done his crying alone, walking on the railroad tracks, moving north to the Allegheny River. That was after he put in a call to his cousin in Virginia and told him that he wanted to keep one of the steers as a pet. It was absolutely not to be taken to market. It was the one with the pattern like a question mark on its side; the one Ruth was hugging in the photograph.

***

In looking back on it, I realize that I never recovered from Düsseldorf. With that Gretchen Traub saga, I solidified my position as a champion wallower, a counter-punching Prince of the Stagnation Empire. I never even bought an ice pick. Why did I think that I would use one? Now I'm homing in on the sixty-years-on-the-planet mark and all I see are shortfalls. I'm a second-rate killer. Twice does not a serial killer make, especially since the first one was that counter-punching business.

In Germany, I started and abandoned literary ambition. I learned the art of cultivating dead-end friendships and mismatched sexual relationships. I launched a career in mathematics on a trajectory guaranteed to produce nothing more than cute surprises. Arguably, my best paper was written by an ailing doorman. I adore the great pianists of Pittsburgh's East End and live in the neighborhood where their ghosts reside. I don't have the guts to play their music beyond the confines of my piano room.

I did one good thing. I found my mother. It is clear that I need to reassess before I die.

***

She claimed that he had nothing to lose. The last time someone touched him on the shoulder and offered him an invitation, he ended up in Berzelius. Nearly forty years had passed and now she touches him on his shoulder five days after they placed the urn on the mantle.

There were other ways, she said. But this was the way she wished to go. Paul argued the pros and cons, which was telling because he might have questioned the foundation instead. It was just that he could not dig deep enough or fast enough to find the foundation. He told her that she was talking about the beginning, while he was looking at the end.

Paul remembered that he had promised Ruth that he would "take an interest in" Giselle the evening that they drove toward Lunenburg County. This was not what she had in mind. At least he didn't think it was. To father Ruth's great-grandchild.

They owned the house jointly. "We're almost married now," she said.

"I'm older than your mother."

"But much younger than my grandmother was... You don't have any children. Grandmother said you should be a patriarch."

"Too late."

"It's not too late. We can take your child to see her or his grandmother in Germany. We can travel with our child to Slovakia or to the land of your Haplogroup E1a, wherever that is. We have the money to do anything we want. How is it too late?"

"I'm an old man."

"Then you're just in the nick of time. Our child will be too."

***

He was not up to it. He had never had a successful sexual encounter with a woman younger than he was. There was no reason to believe that would change with a woman who was something like his granddaughter. Paul turned off his answering machine and didn't pick up the phone for two days.

When he decided to come out of hiding and picked up the receiver, it wasn't Giselle. It was the woman from the Berzelius fundraising meeting, BZ class of 1985. And she told him that Pell Dobbins was dead. Pell had a mild fever for a week and didn't get treatment. There was a crisis and he ended up in a coma. His family struggled with the decision to take him off life support. Would Paul step in and help her finish the plan for the Board of Trustees? He said, "Yes."

It was not what Paul wanted. Pell dead. His daughters' close-set eyes pushing out tears somewhere in the Pacific

Northwest. He could see Pell once more walking away from the Berzelius Tomb into the light of a late summer afternoon. Pell had shaken Paul's hand and shown that fleeting enigmatic expression. His finger went to his nostril as he crossed the sitting room. It was not what Paul wanted and he knew that clearly now. Paul wanted to wrestle with Pell forever. He remembered that when he had driven back to his house, when he had his fever and before he started on the antibiotics, the sun through the windshield felt like a local phenomenon, a warm light bulb a few inches away. And he wondered if everything had gone local for Pell before everything went away altogether.

He drove to Giselle's house, the house that was his too, and in his manner of speaking said "yes" for the second time in less than an hour. What he actually said was, "I don't know how this would work."

He was fetish-ridden, so it took a while. A couple nights a week he stayed at what he still thought of as Ruth's house and slept in the bedroom next door to Giselle's. Paul would fall asleep thinking about her as if she were a theorem that he was trying to prove. Sometimes she would come to him in the morning and massage his shoulders. He would say, "That's good for an old man." But that was all they had for a time, adjoining bedrooms twice a week.

When the semester began, his mind was taken away. There was the introductory graduate course in point-set topology to teach. This was a challenge for him, even though it was his specialty and he had taught it a dozen time. The first-year graduate students were like gunslingers, always trying to see what the professor had in his holster. These days he was not feeling that he had much of anything. He was also teaching Calculus II, the same course that Giselle had taken with him.

Paul gave the first talk in the new analytic number theory seminar, providing an overview of Ernest's main results. Arnie shook his hand afterward and declared the venture to be off to a good start.

***

Two months went by and then Giselle came to him while it was still dark. He could see her in the faint light from the street and she was ageless. They made love effortlessly and then slept together in the same bed for the first time. When the sun rose, she massaged his shoulders and he said with conviction, "That's good for an old man." It was as if a curse had lifted.

***

In December Arnie Landau finished the draft of a paper detailing some results that he had gotten with a graduate student. The work was rooted in what was referred to in the department as Paul's "phenomenal" paper. They had found a new and interesting way to describe the family of sequences that were central to Ernest's work. Arnie gave a talk in the seminar and called them McCarahan sequences.

After the seminar, Paul suggested to him that they would be more appropriately called Robinson sequences. He mentioned the listing of Ernest Robinson's unpublished manuscript among his paper's references. Arnie said that he would compromise and call them McCarahan-Robinson sequences. Then Paul invited Arnie to attend the wedding, because Giselle said that she wanted a small ceremony in their house and neither of them knew anyone to invite. Paul dared not ask his sister Thelma. His relationship with Arnie was as close to friendship as anything he had, except for Ernest and Ernest wasn't in the mood to travel. Giselle invited her mother and the next-door neighbors on either side. She was a month pregnant.

In January, Paul moved his piano. He paid the movers a premium to be on call to move it on the first day that was dry and seasonally warm. With the thought that he might let a couple of graduate students use the house, he moved none of the furniture. Selling the house would not be possible. Nothing sold in that neighborhood anymore.

The rest of his belongings were taken over in a few carloads, the computer, all the documents and photos from the genealogy room, his pull-up bar. He took the note that Sandy Dobbins had written him in response to his condolence letter to Pell Dobbins' family.

In a postscript, Sandy Dobbins revealed that she had taken an autosomal test as part of a project for one of her anthropology courses. The result was 100% Indo-European and she was a little disappointed. She wrote further, as if she were merely describing the result of a test for blood type, that Pell Dobbins was in haplogroup E1a. She tested one of her brothers because "Dad is gone."

This could have been the last straw, he and Pell having the same brand of divining rod. But he already knew about other white men who carried the E1a signature. In desperation, a group of them had started an electronic forum. The subtext was to disprove the notion that E1a was unambiguously an African signature; to show that it was rooted in the Middle East, where it survived and then somehow made it to Western Europe millennia ago. Paul joined the group and, at first, did not reveal that he was black. When pressed by the Moderator to provide a description of his ethnicity, Paul responded with 'AFPOC.' The Moderator said that he had never heard of that ethnicity. Paul explained that it was the well-known 18th-century acronym for A Free Person of Colour.

The forum Moderator and Paul both had roots in Caswell County, NC. When the Moderator suggested that Paul's male line went back eventually to Europe, Paul's reply was that E1a was the aboriginal North African signature and Paul was African American. Maybe the Moderator should do a little more genealogical "spade" work to uncover his black ancestor. Within one month the E1a Forum shut down.

Paul had been the forum's only participant with acknowledged African ancestry. Many of the group's members traced their male lines to the 1700s and then lost the trail. He wouldn't care if the McCarahan line ultimately traced back to Europe. If there was a long-lost remnant of E1a in the British Isles, brought into northwestern Europe from Africa with the Roman Legions, then so be it. It just seemed unlikely. There was to date no evidence of E1a in Britain. You would have to believe that the whole demographic left en masse for the North American colonies or that what remained behind died out.

For completeness sake, Paul wrote to Sandy Dobbins and asked her if she knew the first names of her Dobbins grandfather, great-grandfather, and 2nd great-grandfather. He asked her if she knew where they lived. He didn't have the time for this, but letting this sleeping dog lie was not a choice that he felt he could allow himself.

In one of the boxes in his bedroom closet, he found several copies of the story that he wrote when he was in Germany. It was a story about three colored boys with a gambling scheme, *The Due Set*. He didn't have the courage to read it after so many years but toyed with letting Ernest or Giselle amuse themselves with his Vietnam-era tale.

***

Into the winter, Paul kept up a steady exchange with Ernest Robinson and they produced enough new results to justify a paper, which they called Generalized McCarahan-Robinson Sequences, following Arnie Landau's lead. They had been able to prove the rather curious theorem that if there was a McCarahan-Robinson sequence that included all the twin primes, then there must be infinitely many twin primes. It probably didn't bring the state of play on the conjecture any closer to resolution, but it was an elegant result and certainly provided a new angle on the sequence of twin primes, which begins with $(3,5)$, $(5,7)$, $(11,13)$, $(17,19)$, $(29,31)$, $(41,43)$, $(59,61)$,... Most mathematicians believed that there were infinitely many. No one knew how to prove it.

Paul offered Ernest his vacant house but Ernest refused. He didn't want to return to Pittsburgh. He said that it would kill him and he wasn't ready to die. He said that for the first time in a long time he treasured each day. And Paul did not question this because he was starting to feel that way too. He already felt that he and Giselle had been together for years. He worried about how many good years there were to come. Maybe he could summon up another quarter-century and escort his child into adulthood. Maybe he could live that many more years and still have his wits about him when he died. Every evening he played the piano while Giselle sang songs for the child in her womb. She did not have a great voice, but she could carry a tune.

***

With a certain grim and workmanlike approach, he took the information that Sandy Dobbins provided and was able to trace Pell's line back to his great-grandfather, back to Alamance County, North Carolina. Orange County sits on its eastern boundary and Caswell County was to the north. He did not manage to push it any further back. Her Jack Dobbins ancestor only added to the mystery of the existence of a small group of white men in the southeastern United States with the rare North African signature, Paul's signature. Beyond the Y-chromosome, there seemed to be no other African vestige. Sandy Dobbins autosomal profile was European, to the exclusion of all others. When the E1a Forum existed, before Paul's nasty exchange with the Moderator brought on its demise, all the reports of autosomal results by the white participants had been the same as Sandy's, 0% Sub-Saharan African. And there was no reason to doubt their veracity. This question was unlikely to be resolved. The answer was buried in time at some port on the Atlantic coast. Except for the slow-mutating Y-chromosome, Africa could no longer be detected in their genetic make-up.

Of course, the other question was: Why had Pell Dobbins died; was his fever Paul's fever? That seemed implausible. Beyond a few instances of night sweats, Paul's illness had been long gone by the time he met with Pell in the Berzelius Tomb and no one else had gotten it. Ernest had not. Ruth had not. It was implausible. But then what was that fleeting, questioning expression that passed over Pell's face as they parted. Did it have nothing to do with Yaros? Nothing to do with the Himmelfahrtskommando?

He wanted to be done with the questions on other men's faces. Paul now had faces of his own to worry about. He was a sentimental man. Pure and simple. He clung to bits and pieces of the past. Now that it appeared that he would not be a terminal node on his family tree, he had already begun assembling the fragmentary evidence that chronicled his change of orientation toward the future. Paul had saved the pregnancy kit that he and Giselle used to confirm their suspicions. It was understandable that he still had the golf club that had been his late-night walking companion during his final year in Düsseldorf, a year of madness. The putter was a gift from his mother's now-deceased boyfriend, Georg Merz. Georg had told Paul to sink a few putts with it for him when Paul returned to America. Georg did not think that he would ever get to travel across the ocean. He never did.

On this night, Paul went for a walk through the snow, traveling a path through the woods that took him down to Washington Boulevard. When he left the house, Giselle was on the phone with a contractor hammering out some details about remodeling the room that was going to be the nursery. Paul heard her begin the exchange as he went out the door. She said, "This is Giselle McCarahan." She used the surname McCarahan as comfortably as if it had been hers her whole life. She never inadvertently introduced herself as Giselle Gable.

Paul worked his way across the boulevard and close enough to the Allegheny to sense its power. He had hoped to see ice floes because there had been a week of sustained temperatures in the teens and single digits. But either there weren't any or it was too dark for him to make them out.

Paul would go home in a while and be warm again. But before he started his homeward trek, he made a few smooth strokes through the soft snow with the putter. If he were to climb the hill on the other side of the boulevard and walk a mile south along the railroad tracks, he would be back in his neighborhood, where his house stood vacant. But he wasn't going back there anymore. He began his climb through the woods back to Giselle. They were closer to the park and the zoo in Ruth's house. Their child stood a better chance of hearing the lions roar.

KNOWNS AND UNKNOWNS

Near the end of Giselle's senior year at the University of Pittsburgh, her mother Bobbi began a relationship, which after a few months became what is tidily termed 'abusive.'

His name was Elroy and he left marks on Bobbi's arms. Once, when they met inadvertently and Giselle glared at him, Elroy grabbed her by the hair and whispered in her ear, "You're next."

But Elroy didn't understand her. Giselle was not about to be "next." She went to her grandmother and told her that she was going to kill Elroy. Ruth looked at her for a long time and then said, "I'm going to give you some start-up money. I want you to move to California and get a job."

Giselle said, "I'll move to California, but I swear I'm still going to kill him."

She took the money and moved to Sacramento, where she landed a job with Pacific Bell in public relations. Three months later she took a flight back to Pittsburgh and called Elroy from the airport. He was drinking, as she had anticipated.

"What do you want, bitch?"

"You said that I'm next. I'm coming over to see if you can make good on that."

"Well, come on then." And he laughed.

She drove her rental car to his house. When Elroy opened the door, she stepped into his embrace and buried an eight-inch blade just below his ribs. Giselle would not have been able to say whether his expression was quizzical or not. She was focused on twisting the knife and pulling it out and putting it back in again, something she had actually practiced on thick cuts of meat from her butcher shop. It all felt intuitive. For a while, he didn't move or say anything, then he whimpered and dropped to his knees. She would have slit his throat, had she thought of it.

While his former calculus student and wife-to-be was killing Elroy, Paul was at home playing the piano. The woman who years later would meet Paul, and then pave his way to matrimony, was in Las Vegas with her daughter Bobbi on a four-day getaway.

Giselle had one meal before boarding her flight back to Sacramento. The knife ended up at the bottom of the Monongahela River. McCarahan's reporter, John, wrote the story in the Post-Gazette. The police work was uninspired. They postulated that it was a man with considerable upper-body strength and quickly ran out of suspects. There was no follow-up report in the newspaper.

***

The woman was far enough removed from him in time that, had she survived in the family oral history, Paul would have called it the family mythology. As it was, the 1735 landing in Yorktown, Virginia was lost to him, even though her arrival in North America was, except for his mother, the most recent of all his ancestral arrivals on the continent. It was another two centuries before a McCarahan paternal ancestor would cross the Atlantic again. That was Paul's father during World War II, who passed through Normandy and made his way inland to receive a Purple Heart when one of his comrades stepped on a landmine, tearing himself to shreds and distributing shrapnel to others nearby. This launched him into alcoholism. He stayed on with the occupation troops and eventually met Ursula Kowalzik.

Yaa and her five-year-old daughter were among seventeen captives who survived the passage from the Gold Coast to Virginia on a ship called the Last Resort. One hundred and fifty-six slaves-to-be succumbed to fever along with half the crew. As a result, for the remainder of the trip there was no dearth of provisions.

Before Yaa died, seven years after her arrival and purchase by Richard Wadsworth, she had one more child. This child was fathered by a light brown-skin man with whom she could only communicate using the bare bones of the English language. His English was not much better and for the three years that they were together he took care of her as well as one slave could be expected to take care of another. He taught her a few words in his Eastern Siouan language. The language his mother had spoken to him as a child. For him, his mother was the whole Saponi Nation, the only member of that nation that he had ever met. Yaa's child was named Ren and a generation later she became a part of Thomas Wadsworth's household when he moved west and became one of the founders of Lunenburg County. Her African-born half-sister Sork was also part of the Lunenburg household.

Ren and Sork were on a list in one of Paul's cardboard boxes. They were two names among eighteen included in Thomas Wadsworth's will. In 1789, he had finally succumbed to the effects of the wounds he suffered in New Jersey at the Battle of Monmouth Courthouse. Paul was Ren's descendant but did not know it. The oral history had gotten him to the list, but not to a specific name on it.

Ren's daughter Lucy bore three children by a free colored man who worked on an adjoining farm. His existence was also effectively unknown to Paul. It was not until the birth of his great-grandfather James Hales in 1856 that a record was written that would eventually tie Paul's family to the Wadsworths. James Hales was a man Paul's father had known as 'Popo' when he was a young boy. Paul had a photograph that had been taken of him at age forty, a heavily mustachioed man, who could have passed for white if hadn't been for the fact that he was brown.

In Paul's treasured birth-register find, 'Robert Wadsworth' was the entry under the column heading 'Name of father if child be born free and in wedlock. Name of owner if child be born a slave.' Robert Wadsworth had served valiantly for the Confederacy. When Lee surrendered at Appomattox, only sixty miles from the Lunenburg County seat, Robert Wadsworth was one of the officers who accompanied him. In 1868, when James Hales' younger sister was born, Robert Wadsworth was again the informant and is listed as 'friend' in the relationship column.

Paul had not been able to establish what other relationship might exist between the Hales and the Wadsworths. Y-chromosome analysis and access to the Wadsworth DNA results through the Wadsworth DNA project did not produce a hit. In fact, it was the Revolutionary war Wadsworth, who had produced a daughter with the woman who was the descendant of Saponi and African slaves. But Paul would never know this.

**

In 1989, Paul had completed a compilation of the correspondence written from Lunenburg County and neighboring counties to the Bureau of Refugees, Freedmen, and Abandoned Lands. The reports spanned four years and were written by army officers, most of them veterans of the Civil War. The Bureau was administratively under the War Department.

Paul was not able to find any reference that allowed him to understand how his ancestors in the region had survived Reconstruction. However, everything that he read about in the monthly reports happened to at least one of his relatives in some form or fashion. These stories were not passed down.

May 29, 1866

Sir,

I have the honor to submit the following report in regard to the general condition of the Freedman's affairs in this county. The condition of affairs is quieter than at the time of my last report, a sort of "calm after the storm." A little conversation I had with a carpenter who is at work on the new jail will perhaps best illustrate the state of feeling that exists between the citizens and freedmen. He said, "Lieutenant what rights do we colored people have under the laws?" I replied, just the same as the whites. He then said, "A man told me that he would sell me 25 acres of land, but the people said no niggers should settle about here. He said that we couldn't get any of our rights but for you Lieutenant. I do not know what we would do if you were to go away." And this man is as sober, industrious and law-abiding as any man in the county. A man has just reported to me that his employer had ordered his wife to leave and that he would not pay her for the time that she had worked. The offence was this. The employer's wife called the woman a "dirty slut." She replied that she was not when the gentle Saxon "Let out her left" and drew the "claret" from the African's nose. Yet the white man will put such a construction on it, that it will be difficult to obtain her pay from a civil magistrate. This is the second case that has been reported within two days. It is my impression that they will increase as the season advances. Employers will seek pretexts for diminishing a part of their laborers as soon as the crops are in such condition as their services can be dispensed with. This suspicion is concurred in by some citizens whose names I will not mention. I would like to report an affair of a serious nature in regard to myself, but do not care to trust it to the medium of an official report.

Very Respectfully,
Your obedient servant
J. Arnold Yeattley

Lt. and Asst. Superintendent

In 1868 Minerva, who had found work as a domestic, was beaten badly by her employer's wife after she had observed Minerva being groped by her husband. Minerva recovered, but the beating was so bad that she miscarried. Minerva and her husband had been married in a ceremony conducted by Freedman's Bureau officer assigned to Lunenburg County. The child would have been their first. The pregnancy was their last. Minerva was the sole surviving descendant of Yaa's African-born daughter Sork, the five-year-old girl who had not succumbed to the fever aboard the Last Resort.

June 13, 1866

Sir,

I have the honor to submit the following report in regard to Freedman's affairs in Mecklenburg County, Virginia. In accordance with orders received from Captain Barnes, Supt. on June 6th to take charge of Mecklenburg County in addition to this County, I started on the morning of the 7th to do so. At Christiansville I met a freedman who had been stabbed in the arm and both shoulders. He looked very weak and feeble. He had a dispute with a man about his work, when the man said, "You have disputed my word once before," and commenced choking him. He then struck the man. The man then drew his knife and called to another white man to help him saying, "d__n you, I will kill you now, all the Yankees are gone, and we can cut and kill 'niggers' just as we please." I talked with the magistrate and he said

*they would give the freedman justice, but I have no
confidence in them. I found the negro freedmen despondent
all over the County thinking the Bureau had been removed. I
assured them that it was not and that the government would
not desert them. They seemed much rejoiced and the
universal response was "You must not turn us loose yet,
Massa." The opinion (for some reason, I know not what) is
prevailing, among black and white, that the Bureau is to be
removed, and it produces sorrow to the one party, and joy to
the other.*

Very respectfully,
J. Arnold Yeattley, Lieutenant

On the land that Paul bought, exactly one quarter mile from
the grave of the last owner Robert Wadsworth and just inside
the property line, was the grave of Paul's 2nd great-grandfather
Stephen Hales, who was stabbed to death by a roving gang of
white men, while returning to his home after a day of digging
ditches. He never showed up in any US census, having been a
slave in 1860 and dead before the 1870 census, just days after
the last Freedman's Bureau officer was withdrawn from
Lunenburg County. Paul knew where Wadsworth's grave was
on his land. He did not know the site of Stephen Hales' grave or
even that he was buried on the land that he had purchased for
old times' sake.

October 1, 1866

General,

In compliance with existing orders, I have the honor to submit the following Report of the condition of affairs in the Counties of Lunenburg and Nottoway, Virginia for and during the month of September 1866.

Condition of the Freedmen

In Lunenburg County, the Freedmen are becoming dissatisfied with their employers, and not without cause, the frequent outrages and injustice practiced upon them have made them restless and suspicious. They do not appear to have any confidence in their employers and labor rather sullenly, certainly not with the same spirit they commenced the year's work. On the other hand, the employers complain of the laborer's laziness, and indisposition to work, which may be accounted for by the mutual distrust existing between both parties. This feeling has developed itself lately, as during the past months the Freedmen labored hard and faithfully which the size of their crops testify to. I cannot account for the present feeling, but hope it will not be of a long duration.

In Nottoway County, the condition of affairs is quite the opposite. The Freedmen are working faithfully and I receive but few complaints from either party. Complaints against the Freedmen upon investigation generally result in that he did not understand properly the contract. In this county, a feeling of confidence exists to a certain extent between both parties and as a consequence but little difficulty ever occurs between them. Quite a number of the Freedmen are already negotiating with employers for the next year.

The State of feeling existing

I am compelled to here again report each County separately as they can by no means be compared alike. In Lunenburg County among the majority of the citizens, a deep and bitter prejudice exists against the Freedmen, all Northern men, and this Bureau. For the least provocation, and frequently without any, large numbers of Freedmen have been drove off the plantations by their employers the past month and none of them have received any compensation for their services. They are frequently beaten by gangs of rowdies for which this county is famous, and they receive no attention from the magistrates who are really in dread of the same gangs of rowdies. Even if these Magistrates and the respectable community were disposed to protect the Freedmen they dare not interfere. It is my opinion that the authorities of this county are unable to enforce their own laws. Such being the case what justice or protection can the Freedmen expect?

In Nottoway County, the Freedmen are treated with a degree of fairness and justice which is very gratifying. The citizens of this county are far more liberal towards the Freedmen than in <u>Lunenburg County</u>. 'Tis true there are occasional cases of beating and oppression of the Freedmen reported to me. But I am happy to state that the majority of the people are disposed to act fairly towards the Freedmen, it being to their interest to do so. I do not wish this to be understood that no prejudice or bitter feeling exists in this County; for it does to a certain extent, but not so strong as to materially injure the Freedmen's prospects.

Freedmen's Schools

The want of some schools is felt badly. The Freedmen are all anxious to educate their children but no opportunity exists for doing so. I would earnestly recommend that a school be established here as soon as practicable.

The position of Assistant Superintendent

The above position is a very humiliating one for an officer to occupy in this Sub-district without any authority or protection whatever, the magistrates and citizens entirely ignoring the existence of such a position. I am not aware of what advantage or benefit it is to the Freedmen as it now exists unless armed with authority and bayonets to support it.

I am, General,
Very Respectfully
Your obedient Servant

Jerome Connelly
Captain U. S. Vols.

Assistant Superintendent in charge of
Nottoway and Lunenburg Counties, Virginia

The end of the Civil War gave rise to one hundred years of Southern Resistance. For four generations the Wadsworth family sheltered their black kin, the Hales, as best they could. Fifty years after Sork's line was brutally ended, two Hales men were beaten in Lunenburg County for having the temerity to return in uniform to Lunenburg County from France at the end of WWI. It was then that most of the Hales joined the black migration north, first to Baltimore and then on to Pittsburgh, where they traded curing barns for the open-hearth furnace, tobacco leaves for molten metal.

In Pittsburgh, they lived the immigrant life in their own country and were not assimilated. In 1957, Eisenhower responded to Captain Connelly's 1866 plea for bayonets by sending the 101st Airborne Division into Little Rock, Arkansas to enforce the desegregation of Central High School. Nine-year-old Paul McCarahan watched the newscasts with a sense of shame. His great-grandfather Hales was the same age when he saw Union troops sweep through Lunenburg County.

Three decades after Little Rock, he would sit in the parlor of Robert Wadsworth's great-granddaughter Ann Page and try to begin piecing it together. They would have lunch together at Mildred's Meals in Kenbridge.

WHEN TOMORROW IS YESTERDAY

Paul snapped at Giselle on the morning of the girls' violin recital. He was nervous, having butterflies. Their violin teacher had asked him to play the accompaniment. He had foolishly agreed, knowing that he was not disciplined enough to play behind anyone.

Giselle asked him if he was going to do a run-through with Ursula and Ruth before they left for the recital. Paul said, "Giselle, you know nothing about music."

Giselle asked, "What's that have to do with it?" Paul didn't have a ready reply.

After the recital, six-year-old Uschi hugged him and said, "That was good, Daddy."

He smiled at Giselle, as exhausted as if he had just raced a quarter-mile. "Your mother didn't think that I had practiced enough. I guess I showed her."

Ruth, the eight-year-old, chirped, "Daddy's always showing somebody something." And Paul was forced to laugh. His daughters were taking him back to another time, when he was a boy and the kids on the street would sit on their porches laughing heartily at each other's frailties. As an adult, things had gotten out of kilter. The neighborhood, as he had known it, went away. He continued to laugh at others. No one laughed at him anymore. They didn't know him well enough.

Sometimes it got to be too much. The girls were miniatures of their mother in every way and when there was anything like a real issue, they usually lined up with her. He would sulk, but not for long. Long-term brooding was for the young. He didn't feel that it was a luxury he could afford.

Paul and Giselle had had only one serious disagreement. He let her read the story that he wrote when he was living in Germany many years before, *The Due Set*. She entered it in a Post-Gazette-sponsored competition without his permission and it won. But even that flare-up died after a matter of hours.

The Due Set was published online by the Post-Gazette in four installments over four weeks. As a result, the reporter John, last name Winston, got to write another article on the 'multifaceted' mathematician from the East End and the Geometry Killing was celebrated once more. John did not bother to call Paul for an interview for the new article. He wrote a piece for the editorial page with what Paul viewed as a lame attempt to do psychoanalysis. This triggered a letter to the editor from Paul, which said that John Winston was attempting to do what not even Freud would have been able to accomplish.

Ernest Robinson heard about the Geometry Killing this time around. Just a few days after Ruth's second birthday Paul had persuaded Ernest to accept an endowed Research Associate position at the University of Pittsburgh. The position was "endowed" by Paul, a plan he cooked up with the department chair to get Ernest to leave Philadelphia. There really was no financial involvement by the University, but the department gave Ernest office space. Paul renovated his house in the old neighborhood and installed Ernest there. That was how he became Uncle Ernest to the girls. Uncle Ernest was upset by the whole Geometry Killing business. He viewed it as an insult to Paul and to Mathematics. And *The Due Set* didn't sit well with him either. It was too "salty." Ernest asked, "What will the girls think when they're old enough to read it?"

After his story won the contest, Paul decided just to go with it. He even delivered a talk in the English Department's Modern Authors seminar the following semester, presenting it as a modern fairy tale, a rough sketch with a tragic twist. The next year's anniversary gift to Giselle was a bracelet with the engraving: "Giselle McCarahan, Literary Agent."

***

Pell Dobbins' and Paul McCarahan's most recent common ancestor was a man who died 2837 years before they were born. With the exception of a few mutations that had accrued since that time, it was this man's Y-chromosome signature that they both carried.

The man and his two sons were members of a nomadic band of herdsmen, who began what was to become a slow push west from Northeast Africa, from what is now southern Egypt and northern Sudan. The sons feuded incessantly. Their father would say, "You're delivering the family to ruin." They appeared not to care. They lived for the quarrel. The last time that they spoke to each other was when they buried their father during a bad stretch in the Sahara. On his death bed, he grieved because of the great loss of livestock that the family had suffered. By the time the brothers' descendants reached Mali and the present-day site of Timbuktu, the only things the two lines had in common was language. Many centuries later, when these patrilineal lines made the passage to America, they didn't share even that.

Pell's Haplogroup E1a ancestor was the son of a woman whose father was a Portuguese sailor. The son and his father were sold into slavery. The father died before reaching North America. The mother remained in Guinea-Bissau. She was not considered marketable. Three years later, Paul's ancestor made the crossing on the same ship.

Within three generations, the racial identity of Pell's male-line ancestors became white, having been laundered through the intervention of at least one white man and an Irish indentured servant woman. The name Dobbins was adopted and the Dobbins were free in Caswell County, North Carolina. Paul's male line was not free until 1865 and lived as slaves on the McCarahan lands in Caswell County until that time. Paul found his 2nd great-grandfather Walter McCarahan living in Orange County, North Carolina, according to the 1870 census, and working for the North Carolina Railroad. He was still black. Walter's son Plese married a Chavers woman who was listed in the 1870 census as a mulatto, but their daughter remembered her mother saying that the Chavers were Indians, and that's why they had always been free. She would not be able to tell her grandson Paul the name of the tribe. He would have to dig that out himself.

After a hiatus of almost three millennia, the feuding between the two brothers was taken up again by their patrilineal descendants in the Berzelius Tomb.

***

It was something that approached being a lie. The girls had just finished the school year and packed off with their mother and grandmother for Shelter Island, where Bobbi had bought a summer home with the money that she inherited from Ruth. Giselle and the girls usually spent three weeks, but Paul never stayed for more than five days. There were lots of excuses: Graduate students to care for, the lack of a piano. But the truth was that he couldn't stand more than five days non-stop with his mother-in-law, a woman who was both trifling and younger than he was.

He would usually come up the first week and then drive back at the end of the stay to chauffeur them home. This time he told them that he would just come up the last week and put in his five days then because he had to go to Germany on business right away. The claim of business opportunities in Germany was the approximation to a lie.

Uschi was sulking the morning he left for Germany. She had been moody for a week because she knew that Ruth would be a freshman in high school in the fall, while she remained on the K-8 campus of their private school. Three mornings in a row she came down for breakfast with the same opening line. "Ruth and I are going to be separated for two whole years." This was a ploy to get Ruth to hold her. She was shameless.

"We don't get to go to Germany anymore," Uschi said. "If Grandmother Ursula were still alive, would you take us with you."

Paul said, "Sure."

In fact, the girls had only been to Germany twice. The first time was when Uschi was six months old. The second time was when they discovered that Fritzi had fathered a son Albert, who was a grown man when he approached Paul and made his claim. He looked a lot like Fritzi and DNA testing later confirmed his claim. Paul, Giselle, and grandmother Ursula, with all three grandchildren in tow, had gone to her village in southwestern German to show off her family. There was a picture of the whole family standing in front of the tavern where Paul had, in fact, been conceived. An ancient Ursula has her arm around Albert and Albert is holding an enlarged copy of his father's high school yearbook photo in front of him.

The only time that Uschi truly remembered seeing her grandmother Ursula was when she visited the family in Pittsburgh. The visit became something of an ordeal for Paul. His mother had a panic attack and didn't want to fly back to Germany. She said, "The last time I flew to Germany, I lost my children." Paul solved the problem by flying to Munich with her.

***

Paul worried about how his sensitive girls might handle it if his health went into decline and he went off the edge. Bobbi was their only living grandparent and she was not around much. He resolved once more to live until they reached adulthood, then he followed this pledge with a Lufthansa flight across the Atlantic Ocean. If the resolution had been firm, he would have steered clear of flying, which he increasingly feared as he grew older, and he certainly would not have flown to Düsseldorf.

On a whim, Paul had tried an Internet search for Gretchen Traub and in seconds found her still living in Düsseldorf, the owner of a bar in the Altstadt. In an apparent effort to raise cash, she was offering to sell a one-quarter share in the business. Paul started an email exchange with her in English, expressing an interest in meeting with her to discuss specifics and to take a look at how the business was being run. So that was why he was sitting in the Düsseldorf train station eating lunch once again, four decades after he had admitted defeat and left the country. That's why he was in Düsseldorf, while his children frolicked on Shelter Island. He had a two-p.m. appointment to talk business with Gretchen Traub.

Paul had been in Düsseldorf two days, two days of walking the streets and trying to remember how they were glued together. He would never have thought that he could forget, but more than forty years had taken their toll. Near the end of each day, he felt his energy level drop. He compensated by hiring a taxi and then continuing to snake through the city. The building in the Hinterhof was gone. At least that's what he was told when he came to call. The lady who answered the doorbell wouldn't let him through to the courtyard to look for himself. "Only residents," she said. He knew that the Oma, Ibrahim, Gisela, and Max were long gone. He said, "I used to be a resident." Then he left.

His ear for Rhineland German wasn't what it used to be, but he was quickly adjusting. When he entered the train station, he remembered the day when he thought that he had spotted Pell Dobbins there. He never got around to asking Pell if he had visited Düsseldorf in the seventies. And then he actually waved his hand and muttered to himself in German that it didn't matter.

When he began what he had come to describe to Giselle as his "long years" in Germany, he had stayed for a while in a pension until he found lodging in the Hinterhof. It was owned by a couple, but the wife did more work than the husband, the husband's body having been sapped and his spirit broken in a Russian POW camp. She was a vigorous woman in her fifties with a substantial bosom and muscular calves. And Paul had not minded when she came to his room to talk. They didn't get much foreign trade, she said. She claimed curiosity about America. The second morning she asked him quite directly if he found her attractive. The years at Yale had passed and he might as well have lived them in a monastery. He did not know what to say to a woman who wanted him. He did not know what to say to a woman if he wanted her.

At first, the woman had tried to please him in a way that was unacceptable; the way that had forced him to use the ice pick three years earlier. But they had found other ways to accommodate each other. For seven days, the rail-thin twenty-three-year-old with skin the color of a buckeye and the woman with light brown hair and suffering blue eyes had given each other comfort. In the afternoons, he roamed the streets and occasionally met up with Hans-Joachim or

Saedy. Saedy was the worse than Hans-Joachim, with his stories. All lies.

Paul found a room to rent in the Hinterhof. On the morning he was to leave, Frau Brugge did not come to the room as she had on every previous day. Her husband came instead and stood in the doorway looking at Paul's suitcase, at Paul. Then he handed him the bill. All was in order except for the six hundred Marks that he had added to the three hundred Mark bill with the notation: "Special maid service."

"You people think you can come here and fuck German women." He was out of breath, almost wheezing. "Destroy families. Na, gut. But you're going to pay for it. You're going to pay or I'll make trouble for you with the police."

Paul paid the extra money, but not because he was afraid of what the man could stir up. He paid because he thought the man was right about everything, with the possible exception of being able to put a price on it. He couldn't remember the woman's name. Now he was in a taxi headed for the Altstadt and a meeting with Gretchen Traub. He remembered her name all this time, even though they had been face to face for no more than a few minutes.

Gretchen Traub's nightspot in the Altstadt was the Sonnenuntergang. The sign over the door offered a graphical depiction of the sunset by using the door frame as a horizon swallowing the sun, which adjoined the last part of the word in dark lettering "Untergang."

Paul paid the driver and stepped toward the setting sun. He knocked timidly on the door and sensed that there was no one inside. He had not contacted her for a week. He had not confirmed the appointment. He realized that he had stacked everything on her being conscientious and mindful, at the same time half hoping that the appointed hour would pass without the spectacle of their meeting. He stepped back looking at the sign over the door and wondered if he should walk the few hundred yards to the edge of the Rhine. Then the door opened and it was Gretchen Traub, forty-five years older than just seconds earlier.

She explained to him that the establishment would not open until 4:30. That was Paul's chance to beat a retreat, but he held his ground and told her who he was, the prospective investor Paul Edward McCarahan.

"I'm sorry. Please come in." And Paul followed her. They took seats at the bar and she asked if he would like something to drink. Paul declined and Gretchen apologized again for not realizing that Paul had come on business. "I was not expecting you to be black. You never said... Of course, why would you? I didn't either." She forced herself to laugh.

Paul said, "You needn't apologize."

"All of your correspondence was in English. How is it that you speak German?"

Then Paul explained that many years ago he had lived in Germany and taught high school mathematics. Then quickly, before she could ask him where in Germany he had lived, he waved his hand and said, "Let's talk business."

Apparently relieved that he was not put off and that she would not have to speak English, Gretchen moved into a presentation that she was clearly not giving for the first time. She owned the business outright, but did not want to borrow money for the changes she felt needed to be made. She preferred to sell interests in the Sunset to a sufficient number of investors to raise the equivalent of eight hundred thousand dollars for renovations. Gretchen had owned the business for twenty-five years and it had turned a good profit every year. She spoke essentially uninterrupted for fifteen minutes and then walked him through the physical plant. Paul followed her upstairs, where there were restrooms and additional seating. She wanted to renovate the restrooms, add an elevator, replace the sound system. Gretchen was not as tall as he remembered. As they went up the stairs, he noticed that she was a bit stooped and quickly corrected his own posture as he felt the weight of his years.

Gretchen said that she was not expecting the investors to be silent partners. She fully expected them to serve as advisors. Did Paul have any experience? He shook his head to say no. Then Gretchen said that she had in mind being able to meet with the co-owners at least twice a year, preferably more. She suspected that it might be excessive for someone based in America. Paul responded that it might be more than he would want to take on, given that he hadn't retired yet and he had children who didn't see enough of him as it was.

Gretchen seemed surprised. "You have young children?"

Paul said, "I got a very late start."

She said, "I didn't start at all."

Paul stared off and he felt that she was sizing him up. She sighed and asked if he would like to walk over to the river. On the way, she asked him where he had lived in Germany and he replied, "I'm sorry. I didn't say? I lived here."

They found a bench near a tree and sat there, the two of them with weathered, brown complexions in dappled sunlight. Paul gazed across the river to Oberkassel. He had only been in that part of town once. A number of the younger teachers had gotten together for a party there. A red-haired, physical-education teacher made a formal proposal to Paul in front of the whole group. She proposed that she and Paul address each other with the familiar "du" from that moment on. The whole gathering toasted the new arrangement and suggested that the two kiss to seal the deal, which they did not. He struggled to recover yet another forgotten name and it came to him. Rosi. Paul wondered why he had never followed up on that. Probably too busy with nonsense.

When Gretchen spoke again, she said, "I think I know who you are. You're the fellow I pulled out of a fracas in my bar. Well, it wasn't my bar then. But you know what I mean. Or am I wrong?"

It was one of those one-two punches and Paul was stunned. He had no idea that the bar he had just toured was the Rhinoceros, except for a name change. And that she could actually put him on that spot after all this time... His only fear had been that it might all spill out of him. He had never thought that she would have retained anything of that night. "How is it that you remember me?"

Gretchen said, "I could ask you the same thing. You know, that little incident was the nudge toward the exit as far as my relationship with Hermann was concerned. It lasted another year or so, but he became increasingly irrational in his behavior in the bar and he became obsessed with controlling me at the same time. He stopped seeing me as a human being. When I bought him out years later, I think he believed that I would reach out to him for guidance. That was not the case. He died last year. Otherwise, I would never have sought investors. He might have tried to worm his way in through a third party.

Instead, I got you. That's what happens when you fish." She smiled at him and, unlike her laughter earlier in the day, it was not forced.

"You remind me in some ways of my mother. Maybe it's the southern accent."

"Your mother's German?"

"She's passed away, but yes."

***

The next morning, on his way to the Düsseldorf Airport, Paul called Giselle to tell her that the deal had fallen through, but that he had enjoyed his stay nonetheless. "It just wasn't a good investment fit," he said. The girls got on the phone and he promised that he would come up to Shelter Island earlier than planned. They wanted him to bring Uncle Ernest along. "Just don't let him drive," Ruth said.

***

Near the end of the summer, they took the girls to Washington for sightseeing. Giselle wanted to see her father's name on the Memorial. Contrary to his usual practice, they stayed at a fancy hotel. They also booked two rooms instead of a family suite. The girls were getting older, Paul said. They needed more privacy. He confided to Giselle that after a person makes a wise investment decision, he feels flush. That was true even if the decision was not to invest in a German bar. At this, she revealed that she had been thinking all summer that Paul had meant to see a woman from his past.

Paul told her the whole story. She seemed not to be breathing as she listened and when he was done, she said that it was quite a tale. "Unbelievable, really. You should write it down."

"If I write it down, will it end up as an entry in another Post-Gazette contest?"

"I don't know. The literary agent moves in mysterious ways."

The last stop on their three-day visit was to see her father's name on the wall. Early in their marriage, they had gone to North Carolina to meet Vaughn Jacob Jeffries' surviving family, a sister and two first cousins. His sister Vickie was a member in good standing of the Eno River Saponi. She thought they might have some black ancestors too. She said that the black ancestry wasn't much talked about. Since he last visited the Eno River Saponi tribal office, Paul had done enough work to tie his native ancestry to the Saponi. But he was further away from tribal thinking than ever. He spared Vickie and Giselle pronouncements on his life as a renegade.

"Yeah, you could be his daughter. You look like Vaughn. He was a good-looking boy. Of course, I don't know what your mother looks like." She chuckled, apparently embarrassed by her own line of reasoning. Giselle showed her a wallet photo of her mother Bobbi and grandmother Ruth. They had copies made of Vaughn's photographs, as a boy, as a soldier.

Paul worried about how Giselle was going to handle this memorial business. He didn't want to get the children all churned up about mortality. They frequently asked him questions about how old he was and whether or not he felt he was healthy. When she was five years old, Uschi remarked that she thought it must be dangerous to be old. "You fall down and break your hips."

They found the name within minutes and Giselle moved her hand over it. Then she moved away to look at the memorial from a distance again. She said, "Beautiful."

As they walked away from the memorial Uschi complained that it wasn't fair. They only had Grandmother Bobbi and people were supposed to have four grandparents. Paul said, "It was the best we could do for you under the circumstances. You did have Grandmother Ursula too, for a while."

He had been playing his old *Platt and Deutsch* composition ever since he got back from Germany. He played it and thought about how gracious Gretchen Traub had been. He hadn't played the piece since he stopped teaching English at the Jugendgilde. Giselle liked it, but the girls did not. In general, they didn't like any of his compositions. A certain "sameness" they said. Ruth called this one "deeply troubling." She was frequently melodramatic in her criticism.

Paul was starting to feel that his world of dreams and his waking world were on convergent paths. The dream world was becoming richer and the waking world more dreamlike. He theorized that when he died it would amount to being fully delivered to the dream state. And at that juncture, he would view his life as a mere scenario.

***

After his meeting with Gretchen Traub, Paul put in one more year at the university and then retired. He was going through the motions in the classroom and his productivity as a researcher was at an end. It was the Anthropology Department where he was spending most of his time. He was embroiled in discussions of genetic anthropology and preparing to launch a DNA project in his old neighborhood on the East End.

This was also about a year after Ernest Robinson finally passed his road test and received a Pennsylvania license after having failed more times than Paul cared to count. That Thanksgiving, Paul decided to have some fun at Ernest's expense and described the first driving lesson on a Philadelphia parking lot. "I tell you girls, Uncle Ernest was wheelin' and dealin'. Yeah, boy. He was a peril to himself and others."

Everyone laughed, but no one laughed harder than Ernest himself. He was bent over the table with his face almost in his plate. Paul was going to continue but Giselle cut him off. "Ernest, I'm sure that over the years my elegant husband has had his moments. Tell us something about Paul."

Ernest grew sober and looked lost. Then he began. "Well girls, your Daddy wasn't all that funny. He did do some interesting things. But maybe I shouldn't..."

Ruth begged, "Please, Uncle Ernest. Please." So Ernest continued.

"You know your Daddy is a handsome man."

Uschi begged to differ.

"Anyway, one time I saw your Daddy get into a bad spot. He had to step in for an injured teammate at the end of the Harvard meet. By the time he got the baton on the anchor leg, Yale was behind and your Daddy was getting cinders in his face. Well, your Daddy turned into a demon. It was like watching a volcano erupt. He came down the home stretch and it was like he had put a monster mask on that good-looking face. If that Harvard guy had had a rear-view mirror, he would have fainted. You know the poor guy had to be in oxygen debt at that point anyhow. It wouldn't have taken much to put him down. Your Daddy rolled on past him and it looked like he was cussing him out as he did it."

At this point, Ernest started laughing again and choking a little bit. Ruth ran around the table and patted him on the back. Then Paul started laughing and almost choked too. Uschi did her part by trying to apply the Heimlich maneuver on her father.

Giselle called time out. "Enough stories! You two codgers can't handle it."

***

Despite what Ernest had expected, it was not AIDS that would kill him. It was a garden-variety heart attack. The girls were so distraught that Paul and Giselle kept them out of school for a week.

Paul found the strength to stand and eulogize Dr. Ernest Robinson, who had received an honorary doctorate from the University of Pittsburgh two years before he died. Paul said:

Few people have the great good fortune to have two wonderful marriages, certainly not simultaneously. From the first marriage, I am the beneficiary of constant, doting attention from my wife and two remarkable daughters. This all happened in what must be considered the twilight of my years. My second marriage was also late, and has run parallel to the first. It has made me a much finer mathematician than I could have reasonably hoped to become. Taken together, the two marriages may have been enough to make me a full human being. At least, that's what I believe.

Ernest and I are both from the East End. He went to Westinghouse. I went to Peabody. But we didn't know each other until we met our freshman year at Yale. He constantly bemoaned this fact and, in my youth, I pooh-poohed it. There was a forty-year gap and then he re-entered my life in a miraculous way. All of you in the mathematics community know of Ernest's now-famous unpublished manuscript, which was referenced in my first number-theoretic paper. In fact, that paper of mine was Ernest's manuscript with a modification. He took his name off and put my name on. As the years went by, Ernest, Arnie Landau and I had a very fruitful collaboration in the area of number theory that Ernest conceived.

When I found Ernest, more correctly, when Ernest found me, after not having seen each other for so many years, he was working as a doorman. In the meantime, he has opened so many doors for so many people and these have been doors to a higher intellectual plane. He played Ramanujan to my G. H. Hardy. I'm not saying that either of us was a genius. I'm just saying that in our relationship Ernest was the truly gifted one.

There are five people who carry the doctoral title because of Ernest's influence. Officially, two of them were my students and three were students of Arnold Landau. That was because Ernest did not carry the required credential, but any careful genealogist working the mathematics scene would have to recognize Ernest Robinson as their father. Two of them are here today, David Walters and Robert DeGiacomo. Dr. DeGiacomo, would you come forward and say a few words?

At the conclusion of the service Paul moved to the ⸱ again, this time to the piano. More than once Ernest ha⸱ said, "If I go before you, play something for me. It doesn't have to be religious." Paul offered a reprise of their first evening together in Philadelphia, playing *The Whiffenpoof Song* and *Taking a Chance on Love*.

He departed the East End Baptist Church with a daughter under each arm. Ernest's death had been a closely followed human interest story and a picture appeared in the Post-Gazette of Paul with an arm over each daughter and Giselle following closely behind. Barely discernible in the corner was Arnie Landau, his hands pressed against his forehead. The caption read: "Paul McCarahan comforts his daughters, Ursula and Ruth."

If the truth be known, he would have had great difficulty making it to the car if Ruth and Uschi had not propped him up.

***

It took Paul years to complete the project. Among other things, he had to acquire all the houses on the block where his house stood, where Ernest had breathed his last. Then he pushed through the legal morass so that he could knock them all down and start clean. By the time the landscaping was complete, Ruth was in college.

He had almost modeled it on Berzelius and then thought better of it. The girls pushed for modern architecture and he let them have their way. On the first floor were genealogy study rooms, with one room dedicated to Paul's family history research. It was actually Uschi who did most of the work on this and completed the final touches just before she left for William & Mary to begin her freshman year and, more importantly to her, join her sister Ruth. Ruth insisted on making William & Mary her first choice because her father had always told her that Virginia was their ancestral home. She said she could try for Daddy's old school in Connecticut or she could go to an old school where the family's ancestral lines coalesced.

There was a large room dedicated to the genealogy of the great East End musicians: Strayhorn, Garner, Jamal, Williams, Eckstine... A small auditorium was in its own wing. It was designed with acoustics in mind, and a grand piano stood like a piece of sculpture on the stage. The other wing housed a genealogical research room with access to every public genealogy and DNA database in the world. The second floor sat over the central section of the building and was smaller. It was one room with electronic instruments around the perimeter. There was another grand piano placed slightly off-center.

Privately, Paul called the building his "last hurrah." In fact, it was not his doing solely. He had donated four hundred thousand dollars. The remaining millions were raised through corporate donations. It was named *Sunrise*.

***

Over the years Giselle's outreach to Paul's half-sister Thelma met with mixed success. Paul got back on speaking terms with her before she died, but the connection that Giselle had hoped for with Thelma's children and grandchildren never materialized. Thelma's children were more than forty years older than his. Ruth and Uschi viewed Aunt Thelma's grandchildren as "louts." Giselle discouraged such descriptions, but the girls held firm in their view.

"We've gotten old, Thelma," Paul offered one afternoon when Giselle invited her over for lunch.

She said, "Paul, I think you mean that I'm getting old. You're looking at me."

He was afraid that it was the start of another squabble, but it was not. She simply considered it for a while and said, "We've certainly lived a long time."

Then she died and Paul saw her grandchildren for the most part only when they dropped in at Sunrise. Usually, they were with a bunch of other kids up in the music room and he would have to look at them a while to be sure it was a grandniece or grandnephew. Sometimes they would give it away by saying, "Uncle Paul, listen to me play." And he always responded by putting on a headset and tapping his toe to the beat, understanding that the family resemblance was fading fast. In another generation, Thelma's descendants and his would no longer view each other as relatives.

Paul spent many hours a week at Sunrise, helping out with genealogy projects or bumping about in the music room. Grad students from the Anthropology Department at Pitt did most of the work. He funded the East End DNA Project, which offered free testing for anyone who became a regular participant in Sunrise activities. No additional E1as surfaced. It remained a closed circle on the East End, just his McCarahan cousins and, of course, Fritzi's son Albert. One of his McCarahan cousins did not carry the E1a signature. That cousin did not seem to realize the implications and Paul did not prod him to the logical conclusion.

***

By the time Uschi graduated from college, Paul was only able to do three sets of three pull-ups in his exercise session. He said to Giselle, "I think I'm in decline."

She said, "You're eighty-four years old."

Ruth came back to Pittsburgh and plunged into teaching high school mathematics. Within a year she was pregnant and married to a photonics engineer named Peter Jessup. Paul had told her that he was not comfortable with her marrying a "nuts-and-bolts" guy. When that did not sway her, he pushed the clock back more than a half-century and said, "In case you haven't noticed, he's white." She laughed and then he laughed. Paul walked her down the aisle without further protestations.

The Jessups produced Paul and Giselle's first grandchild, Ruth Gable's 2nd great-granddaughter, Bobbi Ruth.

***

"The proof is left to the reader." In his lifetime Paul had read this sentence hundreds of times in mathematics texts and papers. The sentence usually appeared when the proof followed in a straightforward way or because proving it would be a useful exercise. Back when Ruth and Uschi became teenagers, Paul began to use this sentence on those days when either one of them questioned his wisdom.

"The proof is left to the reader, Uschi." Then he would stalk off to the piano room.

"The proof is left to the reader, Ruth." Then he might grab a piece of paper and hand it to her, saying, "Work out the details."

Of course, when he did this, they questioned more than his wisdom. Sanity was put on the table.

In his mind, there was a clear plan for Uschi. It was the 'post-William & Mary plan.' She would do volunteer work at Sunrise for one year and then enter a graduate program in genetic anthropology. She was the one who had done all the electronic archiving of the family history. She had run a good deal of Sunrise's genealogy projects virtually, all through college. Paul could no longer cope with the technology. He could barely figure out how to make one of his infrequent posts to the Haplogroup E1a forum, which he started, but Uschi now maintained.

He jumped up and down for joy when Uschi returned from William and Mary to move back in with them for at least one year. His vertical displacement was not impressive, but his enthusiasm was clear. Then lightning struck and he jumped again. Uschi revealed that she had become involved with a man from the Haplogroup E1a forum, a young man named Pell Dobbins. He had posted his photo to the forum and Uschi engaged him in friendly banter. Her senior year, Pell visited her three times in Williamsburg, flying in from Minneapolis. "He says that his grandfather knew you at Yale."

Paul said, "Yes, I knew the man. He knew me. He died of something... a fever."

When Uschi invited him to Pittsburgh to meet the family, it was already a foregone conclusion for Paul. He resolved to offer only ceremonial resistance.

Paul and Pell went for a walk after dinner and Pell asked him formally for Uschi's hand. Every sentence from Pell seemed to begin with "Sir" or "Yes, sir."

"Pell, I don't know if I want Uschi to marry such a polite young man."

"Sir?"

"I was just amusing myself. Tell me now, what makes you think that a marriage with you would be good for my daughter?"

The question seemed to confound Pell Dobbins momentarily.

"Well, sir, I guess I just believe it would be everything I want. I was assuming, or rather hoping, that Uschi feels the same way, for herself, that is."

"Do you think your grandfather would agree with the choice you're making if he were here today to speak to it."

"I think so. Yes, sir. I think so. My father says that my grandfather always claimed that you were the key to his being able to have the career in law that he did, the way you roughed him up. He said it made him see what it meant to be in judicial shape, all that sparring with you in Berzelius."

"I roughed him up?"

"Yes, sir. That's what he claimed. After talking with you this evening, I believe it more than ever."

Paul turned to him slowly and extended his hand. He said, "Welcome to the family."

They made it through their lap around the block. Paul didn't have much snap in his step anymore, so this felt somehow like a longer walk than it used to be. Pell completed his biographical sketch. Later that night, Paul remembered Pell saying that he was the only one of his Grandfather Dobbins' five children and eleven grandchildren to attend Yale. And of the sixteen members of his Berzelius delegation, Pell was the only one who carried an African haplogroup signature. The two black members of the delegation carried European signatures. He said, "It's the only genomic trace of Africa that shows up for me. I'm thankful that it does. I wouldn't have met Uschi without it."

He thought he remembered saying, "It's your divining rod, Pell." But maybe he just thought it. His attempt to push his or Pell Dobbins' ancestry further back in time and place than 18th century North Carolina had failed. Of course, a common ancestor had eluded him.

***

On an anniversary celebration of Ernest Robinson's death, the Ernest Robinson Room was dedicated at Sunrise. When Sunrise was born, Paul shied away from including a mathematics room, even though Giselle told him he should. The change of heart ended up hitting him in his wallet, but he knew that he was doing the right thing. It meant carving away a third of the McCarahan family genealogy room and restricting a passageway. He devoted what little energy he had to getting it done.

In keeping with the theme of the building, it was cast as a mathematics genealogy room with the lines of notable mathematicians traced back through their doctoral parents to the earliest nodes. The permanent exhibit on Ernest Robinson showed his line going through Paul and Arnie Landau to Gauss, Euler and ultimately to the Bernoulli family in 17th century Switzerland, among others. There were several pictures of Ernest. One taken in Philadelphia showed him in uniform: "The Doorman of Rittenhouse Square."

The main display highlighted the big questions in mathematics over the centuries, the "Open Questions of Mathematics" exhibit. The hoped-for theorem that ultimately had defied them, The Twin Prime Conjecture, was described in detail. It was a room with comfortably upholstered chairs and a small library of real (not electronic) books.

The auditorium was full for the dedication. Paul did not speak. He didn't feel up to it. But the president of the regional chapter of the Mathematics Association of America spoke and a representative of the American Mathematical Society presented a plaque to be displayed over the entrance to the room. *Ernest Robinson: Trail Blazer.* The three McCarahan grandchildren made a noisy appearance, but Paul forgave them: Bobbi Ruth Jessup, Paul McCarahan Dobbins, and the infant Ernest Robinson Jessup.

Paul made only sporadic appearances at Sunrise after the dedication. Uschi decided against graduate school and became Sunrise's full-time manager. Paul was glad to see her take over. He didn't want to think about it anymore.

Everything was right with his world. Both girls were settled in Pittsburgh. When he felt up to it, he and Giselle would spend a Saturday with one of their daughters. Uschi and Ruth lived within blocks of each other in Squirrel Hill, which was an upscale Jewish neighborhood when Paul was a boy. These days he wouldn't know what ethnic stamp to put on it.

His son-in-law Pell had a picture of his mother's great-grandmother over the mantle, a sad-faced woman of the Crow Nation. Paul would sit in an easy chair and gaze at it for long periods of time, recalling that he had meant to study what was known about the Eastern Siouan languages and never did. He thought the Crow spoke a Western Siouan tongue, but wasn't sure. He did remember that they were enemies of the Lakota, another group of Siouan speakers. Inevitably, one of the children would come careening through the room and disturb his reverie. This time it was Pell Dobbins great-grandson and Ruth Gable's 2nd great-grandson Paul wobbling into the room. They eyed each other in mutual bewilderment. Then Paul pointed at Paul and said, "Grandpa," before moving on to the next room. Paul muttered after him, "Watch out for that divining rod."

Also, on the mantle was an urn that held his mother's ashes. Ursula wanted her remains to be with her descendants in America. Uschi was her grandmother's namesake. For now, the urn would stay in Uschi's house.

Paul remembered his mother's last moments. He had held her hand as she took her leave. She rubbed his wedding ring. Earlier that day, he had thanked her and praised her for having the fortitude to live through the Third Reich. She had persevered. She had given him life. He said that for a long time they were apart, but they had found their way to each other again. It is likely that the last thing she heard him say was "Mutti," which was also the first word she heard him say, soon after he took his first step.

***

At his ninetieth birthday celebration, he blew out the candles with a hairdryer. He said, "I probably could have done it myself, but then if I missed a candle my wish wouldn't come true."

Bobbi Ruth asked, "What did you wish, Grandpa?"

Paul spoke slowly. "I wished for two things. That sounds like it's against the rules, but they're really the same wish... The proof is left to the reader. I wished that there will never come a day when my descendants forget their past. They must always know that they are free people. I wished that my descendants will always hold on to the land we own in the Virginia and North Carolina Piedmont. That's all."

***

Since they were old enough to understand, Giselle had told her daughters, "I'm not going to allow a 'shaky man' in your life. Don't waste their time or mine."

All 'flare-ups' were investigated carefully by Giselle, usually well before their distracted father ever got wind of them. She had to do an intervention just one time. It was during Ruth's freshman year in college. Giselle made a visit to the campus without Paul. After two hours of quietly observing the young man, she turned to Ruth and spoke as if the boy were not present. "We can't work with this." Her manner was chilling. It was a kind of evisceration.

Afterward, when she and her daughter were alone and Ruth was sobbing, she said, "I had to do this. You listen to me, child. I would have had to hurt that boy." Ruth's first real boyfriend had not made it over the shaky-man threshold. Then Giselle smiled and pulled her daughter close to her. She whispered in Ruth's ear. "I love you. Any man you present to me has to have the capacity to love you nearly as much as I do."

Giselle was the one who ultimately said yes to Ruth's eventual husband "the engineer," Peter Jessup. And she knew about Uschi and Pell Dobbins long before she allowed Uschi to speak to her father about it. Pell had to face both her mother and Arnie Landau's wife Zoe when they met with Uschi in Williamsburg. Giselle and Zoe had been fast friends ever since the Landaus attended the wedding. If Giselle had known the details of Paul's relationship with Pell's grandfather, it would not have mattered. Pell Dobbins was right for Uschi, just as Paul had been right for her, Paul's relationship with Giselle's grandmother notwithstanding.

***

"Giselle, I've got to tell you. My dreams are fantastic these days. I look forward to them."

Giselle sat across from him in an easy chair. Paul had just woken up and was sitting between two cats who had joined him for his nap and were still sleeping.

Paul continued. "They start off with narration, like it's a news report or something, a nice, smooth male voice. And then I'm right in the dream."

Giselle nodded her head. Paul had spent most of the morning finding the perfect spot for a special thermometer he had his son-in-law Peter buy for him. It had to be in just the right place on the shady side of the house. In his waking hours, Paul had become increasingly interested in measurement.

"These dreams are stretching out my life. They're eternal. And for a while after I wake up, the rules of logic seem to have changed for the better. I mean they're easier to use. Everything's clearer.

"Another thing. I've been wondering why the days go on forever and the weeks fly by. Time is getting strange."

Giselle said, "You stayed up too late last night and then you went scampering around the yard this morning on your Scientific-American adventure. Now you're exhausted."

Paul said, "Exhausted is good."

Paul had stayed up a little past his bedtime playing the piano for the family. It was Mother's Day. Actually, he only played two pieces. "Crazy Love" was a song that both of his daughters liked when they were little and he had introduced his grandchildren to it. His view of the piece was shaped by a duet version of the song by Ray Charles and Van Morrison that he had heard years earlier and noticed how well it lent itself to improvisation. He could even improvise lyrics. The grandchildren liked it too except for the newborn Pell, III, who slept through it. Paul's baritone voice was still surprisingly strong and he played many choruses, singing out "Help me, children!" as a cue for the grandchildren to join in. But he had to look away from his mother-in-law Bobbi, whose bobbing head was indifferent to the rhythm and threatened to throw him off.

After everyone settled down, he played "Time After Time," making a florid dedication to Giselle before he started.

...I only know what I know
The passing years will show
You made my love so young, so new.
And time after time
I tell myself that I'm
So lucky to be loving you.
Yes... And so lucky to be loved by you.

Peter recorded both songs and replayed "Crazy Love" several times for the kids. Then they all went home and Paul said, "What a relief."

Now it was the next day and Giselle was looking him over. After a while she said, "You're going to have to rein yourself in a bit." Then she went over to Paul and massaged his shoulders.

Paul said, "You know, I've been in some crazy situations. I like to think I could handle them all again. But I'm not so sure. Improbable."

Giselle bit her lower lip, and then said, "I know."

McCARAHAN'S MANUSCRIPT

*What follows is the novella that Paul described as his prize-winning literary failure. It is Paul's fiction, written during his years in the Rhineland. Decades later, thanks to Giselle's surreptitious submission to a Post-Gazette competition, **The Due Set** received a public viewing. Paul was very fond of the characters.*

Along with his mathematics papers and his concise Family History document, this fable was read by his progeny for many generations.

THE DUE SET

Jake's bed was wet. The sensation of dampness was the first outside signal admitted as his mind disentangled itself from the machinery of an already forgotten dream. It galled him that he sweated so much. Even as he sat up and pushed back the covers, it galled him. Jake hated waking up in the middle of the day wet and in the dark. But it seemed unavoidable. He felt unsettled unless covered by a sheet and bedspread. An attic bedroom was no place to sleep in the middle of summer with covers.

He didn't bother to wipe the ooze from his body. Instead, he rolled out of the bed and picked up his pants from the floor. Then he bent over in the dark again looking for the belt. Jake remembered that he had taken the belt out of his pants and put it a few feet away as a reminder to do something, but he couldn't remember what it was he was supposed to do. It would come to him before too long. He shrugged off the lapse in memory and pulled on his pants. It would come to him. He crossed the room and opened the door. The staircase was not dark. It was only in his bedroom that the drapes were always drawn. He negotiated the steps down to the second floor, squeezed around the metal linen closet and into the bathroom, closing the door behind him.

Jake stood over the toilet bowl holding his ding and daydreaming, only remotely aware of the pressure easing in his bladder. It wasn't until he was shaking off the last few drops that he caught himself counting under his breath. He was up to the thirty-ninth second.

It was a childhood habit that endured. One day in grade school when Mrs. Waring had become particularly irritated by boys asking her for the hall pass, she had launched into a lecture on the unmanliness of not being able to control the bladder and bowels. Then, as an example of manliness, she had singled out Ken. Ken hadn't needed a pass all year.

"Girls, that's the kind of guy you should keep your eye out for," she had said. "That freckled-face boy is going places." She always called Ken "that freckled-face boy." There were other boys in the class with freckles, but Ken was the only black kid who had them. Ken had grinned his stupid grin and for weeks not one boy asked for the hall pass. The pressure built steadily until finally, one afternoon during social studies, Nick Pronti wet himself and the gym suit of the girl who sat behind him.

In retrospect, Jake wasn't surprised that Nick Pronti was the one who broke. His mother had told him once that in Italy the men piss whenever and wherever they get the urge. It was probably just a matter of race memory. At any rate, Mrs. Waring had then cautioned them not to put too much pressure on themselves. "Just be men," she said.

The tension was further reduced when Ken, while diagramming a sentence at the blackboard and probably figuring it was going to be a silent one, played a tune through his asshole. To which Mrs. Waring responded that she wasn't so sure about that freckled-face boy. Jake had come out of it measuring his manliness in bladder-seconds. A habit he couldn't completely break, like sleeping in the attic, even though he had been alone in the house ever since his mother's death.

He had seen Ken the other day in the department store with his three kids and pregnant wife, grinning. Jake wasn't of the opinion that black people should grin. At least he didn't allow it for himself. If he had to be pleasant, he would smile arrogantly. Let the others, including that freckled-face boy, grin if they pleased.

He remembered why he had left the belt lying on the floor. A birthday gift for Pam. He would have to get into town before the stores closed and he would have to allow a couple of hours for looking around. And that meant he didn't have time to make waffles. He decided to get something to eat in town.

First, he put on a coat and tie because he was going to have to go on to work. There wouldn't be any time to come home and change after shopping for a gift. Then he called to make a reservation at a restaurant. He never took Pam anywhere without a reservation. It was a policy.

Walking up the street to where he had parked the car that morning, he stopped and looked off in the direction of Najo's woods. A few days earlier, in the middle of the night, he had inadvertently burned down several acres in Najo's Woods. He had been performing the Fire Ceremony. During this meditation the flames had gotten out of hand. But he felt confident that no one would find out. He hadn't been seen. And Jake Strutters had never really been caught at anything.

***

Gentlemen and Ladies:

Recently, I have been considering an idea for a new mouthwash. It has always seemed to me that the problem with ordinary mouthwashes is that they only do half of the job, at least for me. And I don't think I'm the only person with this problem. If you would make a mouthwash that could be swallowed to clean all the way down to (and including) the stomach, then you would have a top-seller, I'm sure. Thank you.

Looking forward to further
cooperation in this matter,
Pokey Mobers

Pokey had not wanted to mention money in the letter but included his address so that he could be contacted. He then copied the address of the pharmaceutical company from his bottle of mouthwash onto a spotless envelope, specifying "The Research Department."

It was a relief finally to have gotten the letter written. Each day he put off writing made it more likely that the idea would occur to someone else. Pokey figured that there must be millions of people like him, who woke up day after day with yesterday's residual brooding in their bellies. It had occurred to him that if they would just come out with a mouthwash that would cleanse the stomach as well as the mouth, its commercial success would be assured.

While he waited for his eggs to hard boil, he reread the letter for spelling mistakes because they wouldn't take him seriously if there were errors in spelling. Then he checked the value of the stamp, not wanting to prejudice the recipients against the content of the letter by having it arrive with postage due. He wished he could go to the offices and talk with the people himself, but the company was too far away. Besides, a letter was more businesslike. If they liked his idea, maybe they would let him make a visit at their expense. For now, this would have to do.

***

Roop was starving. But still, he sat there looking in his lap, waiting for the right moment to come along, so he could suggest they go get something to eat. And knowing all along that he would have to say something and the timing would not be right. Just start talking. Why not jump butt-naked into the North Atlantic in midwinter? After twenty years of living, Roop was beginning to think that there was no such thing as the proper moment.

"How about something to eat, Jake?"

Bad moment. In the middle of Roop's sentence, Jake had started typing something to that computer of his and Roop knew he wouldn't answer until he had gotten a reply from the machine. Jake sat there hunched over the console, watching the ball go back and forth. Then he stood up and changed one of the disc-drive packs. After some additional typing, he turned in his swivel chair to face Roop with that strange smile of his.

"I thought you wanted to wait for Pokey. I'd just as soon go without him. But it's up to you."

"Yea, let's wait for Pokey."

Roop wished that Jake wouldn't smile that way. Actually, it was more of a sneer than a smile. Jake was okay, though. Only hard to talk to. Not that Roop had ever found it especially easy to talk to anyone. It just seemed that with Jake there was an even greater silence to break than usual.

Pokey came through the swinging doors of the computer complex singing one of the songs he had made up just to irritate Jake. Jake pretended it didn't bother him, but you could see that it did. Pokey walked over to the console bouncing to his music. Jake kept his eyes on the bouncing ball as if his life depended on it, following its printout across the computer sheet. Pokey was leaning over Jake's back now singing and moving his head and shoulders to the rhythm.

Bird in the hand
Is worth two in the bush,
But now there's none in the hand.
They're all in the bush.
No, there's none in the hand!
Lord, they're all in the bush!
I needed her bird in the hand

But she kept her kush in the bush.
No, there's none in the hand.
It's all in the bush.
None in the hand!
All in the bush!
Gimme that kush from the bush!

0, gimme that kush from the bush!
Hush, hush, hush
Rhymes with bush, bush, bush.
Ahhh, hush, hush, hush
Kush from the bush.
Yea! Hush, hush, hush.

"My singin' make you hungry, Jake?"

"Pokey, you're vulgar." Jake only said it matter-of-factly, but Roop could tell that he was highly annoyed.

Pokey continued. "Well, Mr. Night Supervisor of Computer Services, will you have a bite to eat with us bucket boys? I mean Roop and me." Then when Jake stood up to change one of the disc drives, Pokey snapped to attention chanting, "It's the changing of the disc!"

In the restaurant, there was no conversation while they waited for their orders to be taken. Jake was occupied with ignoring Pokey and Pokey was acting as if he didn't know Jake was ignoring him. Jake had his head stuck in a newspaper. Meanwhile, Roop, who couldn't break silences anyway, had an additional problem. He didn't want to order. Ordering was usually not too hard. The waitress would come over and say, "What are you having tonight?" And Roop could respond with 'fish sandwich,' or 'omelet,' or 'grilled cheese.' But not tonight. Tonight Roop was especially hungry and wanted a large hamburger. The trouble was that in this restaurant you didn't ask for a large hamburger. You asked for a Super-Duper Beefburger and the Super-Duper Shake. Roop practiced ordering in his head. "I'll have your Super-Duper Beefburger and a Super-Duper Shake, please." It was embarrassing even in his head. If he were good looking like Jake or Pokey, then maybe he could pull it off. But an oily little nigger such as he... Roop knew how he felt when he saw old people eating. Old wrinkled people with hearty appetites. Thick, juicy steaks they would eat, with pie ala mode for dessert. And a snack before bedtime along with their medicine. Sugared grapefruit with a cherry on top for breakfast, followed by hot, buttered toast. All that to support some crusty wrinkles. And Roop could hear the waitress saying, "One Super-Duper Beefburger and Super-Duper Shake coming up for the little nigger in the corner!" Roop was spared the ordeal when Pokey ordered Super-Dupers for all three of them. All Roop had to do was specify the flavor, which he did without hesitation. Strawberry.

"See here in the paper they found a body out your way, Jake. Where that fire was in Najo's Woods." All the blood flushed from Jake's genitals, leaving his ding about a half-inch long.

Pokey went on. "Charred remains of an unidentified man found in woods. Victim of the recent fire in the southeastern section of Najo's Woods." Pokey wondered aloud if it would hurt to be burned alive if you were asleep and didn't wake up. Neither Jack nor Roop offered an opinion, both apparently occupied with their Super-Dupers.

Pokey changed the subject. "You see how stuck up that waitress is? The way to handle her is to wait until you have to take a leak. Then you just fuck her unconscious. That's what you do."

Roop never found Pokey's instructions to be of much use, although he was sure Pokey knew what he was talking about. There just were lots of gaps. They always started in the middle and ended before the end. They were incomplete.

After listening to a few more of Pokey's tips, the three went back to the building. Roop and Pokey usually didn't work after the break. The computer complex was the last stop on Roop's mopping route and it was a natural place to meet and hide. Jake was a supervisor, but he didn't supervise anyone outside of himself and the computer. There was no one in the complex but the three of them. They didn't seem to bother Jake with their dart tossing. Most of the time he would even join in.

Tonight, however, he seemed more absorbed in his work than usual. He hardly said a word the rest of the shift.

Of the three, Pokey was the only one not getting any, all that bravado about a full bladder and staying power notwithstanding. That nugget was simply something he had heard someone else spout when he was in the army. In fact, he hadn't gotten any since he was in the army in Germany. It was also true that he had not gotten any before he was in the army in Germany.

In his room he had a refrigerator that he had bought used. It started up and shut down so noisily that he usually unplugged it before he went to bed, hoping that nothing would spoil overnight. Also, he had a hotplate and a radio. He was planning to buy a small TV and a record player. He had a bean plant growing beneath the skylight, which he hadn't been able to open. The place had come furnished with a bed, a table, two chairs, a sink, and a mirror. The bathroom was in the hall. Pokey was convinced that to be black and poor, and on top of that not getting any, was about as sorry a proposition as the twentieth century had to offer.

As he lay on his bed, he penciled the words NAKED MAJA onto the wall. He couldn't remember where he had heard or seen the words, but they stuck in his memory. To him, there were no words more sensual. He wanted his own Maja to strip at will. He wanted a naked Maja of his own. Instead, he was practically walking the streets with his prick in his hand, begging. He felt like breaking right through the skylight. And it was only with great sorrow and reluctance that he read articles on the new morality. It grated on him to know for sure that he had nothing whatsoever to do with the alarming and rapid rise in the incidence of venereal disease.

Pokey guessed that the problem was that he had no understanding of intimacy. Even in Germany, he had been awkward. He had chalked that up to inadequate knowledge of the language and inexperience. But he had been back in the U.S. almost a year and felt more out of touch than ever. Getting some was important. But it was something greater that was escaping him. Intimacy. He just didn't know how people got there. Sometimes on his nights off, he would take walks. Especially now that it was summer. There was comfort in walking. He would take walks along streets lined with shade trees. In the dark it was hard to tell where the trees left off and the night began. And from the porches he could hear the whispered conversations from couples or groups of couples. See their silhouettes and the lighted tips of their cigarettes. Pokey had no idea how they came to be there. No idea... Then, in confusion, he would dismiss it. Make it simpler. One of those easygoing, white hippie girls would do. That's what he told himself. He puzzled over whether or not an easygoing, black hippie girl could exist.

Pokey didn't know how he had gotten there. But no matter, he had. Maybe it did matter, but he had never been able to piece it together. So to hell with it. You start pushing too hard, you get knocked on your ass. Like tonight. He had sprung for dinner. He had tried to make a little friendly conversation. And Jake just sat there looking like he wanted to vomit. He hadn't even thrown darts with them after the break. If you push too hard, you get knocked on your ass.

A much taller group of buildings stood directly east of where Pokey lived and so even though the sun had begun to rise, the skylight betrayed hardly a hint of its coming. Pokey fell asleep talking intimately with Maja.

***

Jake wasn't going to let himself panic. He knew that there were thousands of crimes that went unsolved every year. Not that what he did should be considered a crime. Unfortunate, yes. Criminal, no. But should it be considered a crime, it had a good chance to be counted among the unsolved ones for that year. The paper had made no mention of crime anyway. Not one word of arson or murder. It wasn't against the law to start a fire in Najo's Woods and if the fire had gotten out of hand, well, that was an accident. What was the guy doing out there anyway? Probably sleeping off a drunk. Jake just wouldn't be made responsible for a drunk sleeping through an accidental fire. Charred remains or not.

There had been times when he deserved punishment and wasn't even caught. Take the time in fifth grade when he brained the gym teacher for calling him a weakling. He had called him a weakling in front of the whole gym class. Jake hadn't been able to master an exercise on the Swedish box. The gym teacher hadn't stopped to consider that maybe it was because Jake was upset. He hadn't had the slightest suspicion that that very morning Jake had had waffles for the first time since his grandfather died. That they had used up the last of his grandfather's homemade syrup. He had only seen Jake sprawl helplessly on the Swedish box six times in a row and then called him a weakling. More precisely, he had accused Jake of not eating his Wheaties that morning, being slow on the uptake, and being generally unfit on the fourth, fifth, and sixth failures, respectively. Two days later, after school, Jake knocked him cold. Jake had forgotten his scarf and come back into the building to get it when he saw him sitting on top of his desk in the hygiene room doing one of his yoga exercises. He had seen the oil on the scalp glisten, the uneven crew cut. He laid the window opener across the gym teacher's head and then went upstairs to the locker and got his scarf. He hadn't hurried out of the building. It had been more of a float. Like in a dream. No one ever suspected him. Everyone thought it was a prowler or one of the older boys. They held an assembly for the sixth, seventh, and eighth graders but no one came forward to admit guilt. Mr. Czerniski had worn a pack of bandages on his head for three weeks.

That detective stuff you see on television is bullshit. If you were to believe half of it, you'd think they could tell you how many times you farted two weeks ago. Jake wasn't going to panic and he definitely felt no need to go to the police with a confession. They would almost certainly list the thing as accidental death, even if they did suspect the fire was of man-made origin.

That didn't alter the fact that he had killed someone. Indirectly. But you probably kill someone indirectly every day without knowing it. If what you do today doesn't kill someone in the next twenty-four hours, it might be the cause of someone being killed in the next twenty-four years or the next twenty-four hundred years. Perhaps he was stretching it too far. It was a matter of perspective. Carelessness was a matter of degree. And if he were to sit around trying to analyze the consequences of every action, he'd probably never make it out of the bedroom. Even trying to analyze at what point it didn't pay to analyze any further was a ridiculous proposition. So these charred remains they talked about in the newspaper weren't going to bother him. To keep on thinking about it would be to go crazy. He was going to dismiss the goddamn ashes. It was a setback for the Fire Ceremony, however, at a time when he was really making some breakthroughs. He would have to perform it elsewhere, find the past somewhere else.

***

No, Pokey's instructions were never complete. Roop ran it through his head once more. Wait till you have to leak. Then screw her unconscious. He hadn't said a word about contingencies. Pokey shouldn't assume that everyone is able to fill in the gaps.

Roop knew that there was more to it than Pokey allowed for. With his landlady Roop had developed a fairly involved procedure:

1. Invite her up for tea. (She doesn't drink coffee.)
2. Say as little as possible. (She likes to talk.)
3. When she asks for a massage make sure that the tea kettle has been removed from the fire. (It is embarrassing to be interrupted by a whistling teapot.)
4. Always make your initial approach from behind. (She has had one breast removed and until she reaches a high level of excitement is very shy about it.)
5. Don't forget to give her a hug and a kiss before she leaves. (She'll think you're using her unless you do that.)

Of course, Roop could give instructions in greater detail but these were the basic ones. He also realized that Pokey had been describing a general procedure, leaving some of the specifics out, maybe to save time. But he had left out too much. Like how do you time your having to take a leak with her wanting to have you? How do you know that she wants to have you at all, and if not, how do you change her mind? And above all how do you begin in the least awkward and embarrassing way?

Right now, Roop was on his way downstairs. Although it was two o'clock in the morning his landlady was still up baking. All he had to do was make the invitation and things would take care of themselves. In fact, just asking her to have tea gave him an erection.

***

Roop had always been shy. Cautious. But he hadn't always been possessed. If any one event could be singled out as being responsible for his present state it would have to be that fly ball his senior year in high school. A fly ball is not usually considered an event. But his fly ball was. Roop's fly ball.

Roop had been the best outfielder in the history of his high school or at least that's what his coach had told an assembly held to honor the team at the end of his junior year. That was the year they won the championship. Roop had thought he was pretty good, too. He felt at home in center field. He could catch them standing on his head. He could do no wrong.

It was with all this behind him that Roop had moved after that fly ball in the top of the fifth in the last home game of the season. Moved after it with two men on base and every girl he had ever cared about seated in the stands. His stride, it was silky smooth. No wasted effort. He settled under it for a basket catch, just in time to have it smack him in the balls. He stood there in agony asking himself how this could happen to him. How could this happen to him there in center field, the one place where the timing had always been correct? He hadn't dared run after the ball, which continued on toward the center field fence. He knew that any effort to move would have been interpreted by his hands as the go-ahead to clutch at his crotch. So he had just stood there, slightly bent at the waist, arms hanging loosely at either side, the ball rolling toward the center field fence, his teammates yelling for him to retrieve it, the boys rounding the bases, the other team cheering and happy, and every girl he had ever desired sitting in the stands. He felt betrayed. It was a four-base error.

After the event Roop became markedly more cautious, feeling that if something like that could happen to him in center field, then he wasn't safe anywhere. He began to do everything by prescription and if none was available, he would sit and wait for a good impulse. He became hesitant.

***

His junior year at the State University extension campus, Jake had written a paper for his course in Progressive Thinking. Strutter's title was: A Probe into the Relationship between 'Ideal' and 'I deal.' Jake had insisted in this paper that the reason the word 'ideal' maintained its linguistic vitality in the English language was an almost indiscernible, subconscious association of the definition of ideal with the sentence 'I deal.' Anyone would readily admit that to have the deal was ideal. You could either cheat or be reasonably satisfied that no one else was cheating. He had then gone on to establish a hierarchy of possible forms of deal with pronouns.

a) ideal, *b*) wedeal, *c*) youdeal, *d*) itdeal(s), *e*) hedeal(s), *f*) shedeal(s), *g*) theydeal

The ranking of ideal and we deal at the top of the list required no explanation. You deal was ranked ahead of *d*, *e*, *f*, and *g* because third-person is more likely to be an outsider, or so the argument went. The *d*, *e*, and *f* categories were ranked ahead of *g* because third-person singular plural (outsider) was considered less threatening than third-person plural (outsider). Finally, *d* ranked ahead of *e* and *f* because it was neuter gender, hence neutral party and *e* was ahead of *f* because the feminine gender qualified as being more treacherous than the masculine.

Jake received an 'A' for Progressive Thinking. But what was of much more far-reaching importance, he had received the impetus for a different kind of exploration. Progressive Thinking had taught him how to bring things forth. Everything that had been in his ancestors was in him and everything that was in him could be brought forth. He could reach all the way back to the first forms of life. The cumulative experience of life on earth was at his fingertips. Of course, the proper environment for such a regurgitation had to be produced. Jake had established that sitting before a fire in solitude produced the most conducive atmosphere for bringing things forth. He sought certification of his own worth, a historical testament to an inherent nobleness. He called it the Fire Ceremony.

***

Pokey was killing Roop in darts. Roop had always had trouble throwing darts. It was a lot different than throwing to home plate from center field. Somehow, he couldn't follow through the same way. Putting his body into it didn't seem to help. Pokey, on the other hand, had the touch. He talked and threw at the same time.

"Roop, I had this dream the other day. Dreamt I was bathing in shit." Bull's eye. "It stunk a little bit but the idea was to get it off." 50 points. "When you didn't smell shit anymore then you knew you were really clean." 50 points.

As soon as Jake finished up his work and joined them, Pokey planned to invite him and Roop to come over to his place to do some beer drinking Saturday night. He didn't want to interrupt now. Jake looked busy.

Pokey wondered if Jake might just be doing some kind of janitor work like they were, only with the computer. Maybe he was just cleaning out the computer, getting it ready for the people who worked during the day. What a laugh that would be. But he probably wasn't. He was probably doing some kind of important research. Pokey had once asked Jake to explain to Roop and him what he was telling the computer to do, but Jake said it was too complicated. That they would never understand. No, Jake was no computer janitor. He had been to college. Pokey figured that with that kind of education Jake was making the computer tell him all sorts of things. Or at least he could.

Pokey let another dart fly. 50 points.

***

Christ's sake. God's sake. Holy Ghost's sake. Trinity. Trinity. Let it flow. Let it flow, that after three hundred and fifty years we must finally emerge as the one, driving, force in America. That those newcomers, including those late-arriving, mother-fucking wops, are nowhere. Poor grease monkey Andy Graniwhat-you-may-call-it and his lube jobs, trying to be first all his hunky life, just better step back into the crowd where he belongs. No, they would never root for the home team against Notre Dame. Pretty soon all the Fightin' Irish are going to be Black. Because we are the survivors of the Africa-America transit, the descendants of the First Families of Virginia, the continuation of the Iroquois Nation. All in one. Trinity. Trinity. The fading importance of apple butter in the American diet. There was a time when apple butter... No heroes anymore. All the politicians are beginning to look like Hubert Humphrey or Sam Levinson. People laugh when you complain that animal crackers are hard to find.

It's just that people can't develop completely anymore. The cities are to blame. Overstimulation stunts you. Trying to go everywhere at once leaves you nowhere. Nowhere is where all those outsiders came from around the turn of the century. Man was made to live in small towns. Each town with one pretty girl and one good athlete. One schoolhouse and one dunce. A place where you could leave your mark because you knew what you had to do to leave it. And they weren't always changing the rules of the game. It should be like the place where you have to kill a man in battle before you are allowed to marry. You know what's required of you.

Jake had wound down. But he had brought a lot forth. He had learned more than usual for one session. Now that his primary focus was on the last two centuries, everything was falling into place. He doused the flames and opened the cellar window to vent the smoke. He almost wished he had killed that man on purpose, whoever he was. There had been no further mention of the charred remains in the paper. No doubt some transient that the world is better off without. An Irishman. All the way from the potato famine to death in the woods while in a drunken stupor. It would have been better if he had done it on purpose, stalked him, trapped him in a circle of fire. No, he wasn't really worth the trouble. It was more appropriate that he die as he did, the incidental victim of an accidental event. In survival, he received an 'F.' Nature's roundabout way of weeding. And he was a weed. The Fire Ceremony had just substantiated that. In fact, maybe he wasn't Irish, or Italian, or

Scandinavian or any of them. Maybe he was black. But then every group could stand a little weeding. Even black people.

Here Jake broke it off. He was getting himself worked up in an undisciplined fashion. There wasn't even a fire. He climbed the steps from the cellar to the kitchen. The ceremony had made him thirsty. He drank a glass of water and then went to bed.

***

There was no porch furniture, so they sat on the steps at Pokey's place. Roop sat on the bottom step. He had brought his glove along with him thinking that someone might want to play catch before it got too dark. No batted balls, just toss it around. Pokey had neither ball nor glove and Jake had given such a scornful flaring of nostrils that Roop wished that he had stayed at home, which he had been about to do. It was the first time he had been invited anywhere since the time of the fly ball. Actually, he had been avoiding invitations since it happened. His graduation, coming shortly after it occurred, had allowed him to continue this avoidance with little difficulty. His only real social activity in the last two years had centered on tea with his landlady. Anyway, he didn't mind so much, now that it was dark and no one could see the mitt. Roop was getting high, which also helped. Besides, he knew all of the people. Pokey and Jake. And Jake's girlfriend Pam... Pam had gone to his high school. Luckily, she graduated before he did and knew nothing of the fiasco in center field.

Pokey was also glad it was dark. Summer in the dark, just the right conditions. Jake had not only surprised him by showing up, but he had also brought his girlfriend along, a well-structured figure and, a constant pout. A spoiled bitch no doubt. Good-looking women couldn't help but be spoiled. Probably pouting because there hadn't been enough cinnamon on her sweet roll that morning. Or something like that. She didn't have much to say and what she did say she mumbled into Jake's ear. It could be she wanted Jake to take her home and screw her unconscious. But the main thing was they were all here. His friends.

The conversation had died. Pokey concluded that they must all be feeling mellow. He knew he was. He felt he could share something with them, something more than the case of malt liquor he had bought. Intimacy demanded more than that. People walking by could see them sitting on the porch together, four silhouettes and the lighted tip of Pam's cigarette.

Pokey decided to share a thought with them, an intimate thought. "Just think if they would come out with an X-rated version of Amos 'n' Andy." Pam burst into laughter.

"It would make a lot of money, Pam."

Pam spoke to him for the first time. "Are you going to write this, Pokey?"

"Sure. I'd write and direct. Can't you hear Sapphire saying, 'Give it to me Kingfish!' You know, with her voice crackin' a little as she says 'Kingfish.'"

Jake was ignoring him again, but Pokey didn't mind. He was high. Pam was laughing. "You're too much, Pokey."

"Maybe she'd neigh a little bit like... like a woman horse." If he had been sober, he could have thought of the word for a female horse. "And Kingfish would say, 'Whinny, you bitch! Whinny!' I'd send Amos and Andy off gangbanging!"

Pam had thrust her fingers deep into the curls of her afro and was taking a laughing fit. She leaned over to Roop. "Do you want to be Amos or Andy?"

Roop answered without hesitation that he wanted to be the lawyer, Calhoun.

***

Pokey lay on his bed and looked up through the skylight. It had been a success even though Jake and Pam had left a little earlier than he might have wished. He made Pam laugh and he was sure not just anyone could do that. Not the way she had laughed. Even Roop had loosened up. Roop, who couldn't order a sandwich half the time without stumbling over himself. He had been a lot of places, in a lot of foster homes, but he had never been around such laughter. He had never made a girl like Pam laugh. Those German girls weren't discriminating. They had laughed at anything. But a girl like Pam. A Naked Maja, like Pam. Pokey broke into a song.

Goodness sakes alive
I'm off in overdrive.
I have no fear
Of this brand-new gear.
Cause I am mean.
I'm a bad jelly bean.

***

Roop's landlady hadn't been in the mood for tea. And it was only on rare occasions that Roop's landlady wasn't in the mood for tea. The last time she wasn't in the mood was when her mother-in-law came for a visit. For the whole week of the visit, in deference to her late husband and her mother-in-law, they hadn't had tea. This time there hadn't been any apparent reason for her to decline. Roop feared her refusal might turn into a trend.

Maybe he had offended her in some way. But he couldn't remember breaking any of the rules. Last payday he had even bought a new tea service, just for the two of them. No more of those mismatched cups. Perhaps it had been a forward gesture to present it as "our tea service." But that was the way he felt about it. It was their tea service. He could just never find the right moment. That's what he got for not sticking to the script. But she had seemed so happy. There had even been tears in her eyes when he showed it to her. They skipped the massage phase. And now, when he wanted her so much, she wasn't in the mood.

It could be that age was starting to tell on her. She was almost thirty years older than him. Little by little, they would have tea less and less. It was something that Roop didn't want to face. He couldn't imagine giving her up. He wanted always to have tea with Mrs. Bragg.

***

"Pam, I would have told him to kiss my ass. You don't have to take that shit offa him."

"Girl, that was just the beginning. He started getting on me about drinking beer from the can and smoking too many cigarettes. He said only whores drink from the can."

"I woulda told him to kiss my black behind."

"First of all, I told him it wasn't beer. It was malt liquor. You know how he's always trying to be so exact."

"Uh-huh."

"Then I told him that until he puts a ring on my finger and is paying for the cigarettes, he didn't have a goddamn thing to say. I know the real reason he was acting like that. It was because I laughed at that guy's story about Amos 'n' Andy. Just before we were going to bed, he said, 'So now you want to play Sapphire.' I asked him what that was supposed to mean and he went into his silent act. He just sat there on the edge of the bed. I said, 'Hurry up and get undressed. I'm hot to whinny.'"

"What'd he say?"

"He didn't say anything. He just slapped me across the face."

"What?"

"Slapped me across the face. I have a cut on the inside of my mouth to prove it. Listen, I didn't say a word. Just put on my clothes and left. Like it really upset me. All the time we've been together he's never raised his hand to me. And then all of a sudden, he hauls off and smacks me in the face. And now he hasn't called for two days. No apology. Nothing."

"So what now?"

"I don't know. Look, Rochelle, we'd better hang up. He usually calls around this time and if the line's busy he'll just get pissed again. Okay?"

"Yea, I'll talk to you later."

***

Jake had decided to let her stew for a few days. She had brought it all on herself. If it hadn't been for Pokey, the whole mess could have been avoided. He was so goddamn lewd. And he had to go and choose Amos 'n' Andy of all the possibilities. It would have been just as funny if he had said that Abbot and Costello should be brought back as faggots. Which they probably were, anyway. But naturally, he had to climb on Amos 'n' Andy.

He picked up the telephone receiver. She had stewed enough. He wasn't going to do without because of a mistake she made. It was two in the morning. She'd come over and she better not mention what happened. And if she brought up marriage, he'd tell her they'd get married when he was good and ready. Maybe in a month. Maybe two or three. He wasn't sure yet. But it was his decision. Just like this was his house. Just like Pam was his girl. Just like that.

***

There was a fly loose in the computer complex. Pokey was destroying Roop and Jake in darts and humming *The Impossible Dream*. He had been humming it all evening, all through the mopping and the break and right into darts.

"What'll the two of you give me if I stick that fly when he flies past the target?"

He received no answer. Both Roop and Jake were poor losers.

"I bet that's happened thousands of times. Look at all the times someone has thrown a dart or shot a gun. Just think of the war. Flies probably saved a lot of lives by flying into bullets and knocking them off course. But there were probably a lot of guys who shot like the two of you throw darts and flies put their bullets on target."

Jake interrupted. "You're stupid."

Pokey let it pass. "Maybe there are smart flies and when there's a war or a gunfight they try to ram the bullets off course. If they do it, then God lets them come back as human beings. Maybe my grandfather or somebody was in a war and got saved that way. Maybe I have the soul of a fly."

"And maybe that's why you dreamed you were bathing in that tub of shit the other day," Roop added.

"Roop, you're getting as bad as him. You're both stupid."

Jake was thinking of the poem about niggers and flies, but he didn't want to tell them and add to the string of nonsense. Like last night, when Pam started crying. One thing had led to another and before he knew it, he'd told her they were getting married in three months. He'd pretty much intended to marry her in three months anyway, but he didn't want her to think she could pressure him.

Now Pokey was ad-libbing to the melody of *The Impossible Dream* and waving his arms as if he were conducting a full orchestra.

My God. I've the soul of a fly
Oh, yes. Shit, I'm yearning to smell.
Please world. Don't you dare call me filthy,
Just cause, that one scent rings my bell.

And then with a smoothness of transition that only could have been accomplished by Pokey, the tune was suddenly *With Every Beat of My Heart.*

Once I rammed my head into a bullet.
Our God he turned me into a man, a man, a man.
Now I'm the one they call Pokey, no not Skokey
No not Yokey, I was Pokey from the start.
Lordy, do I smell a fart?

Pokey picked up a dart and flung it at the target, narrowly missing a bullseye. "Now that I have your attention, Jake, I want to tell you this idea I've..."

"You've never had an idea in your life."

"Just because I mop floors for a living doesn't mean that I can't have an idea now and then. Then and now. Now and then."

"For God's sake, what's your idea?"

"That computer does what you tell it to do. Right?"

"Sort of."

"So why don't you get it to tell you what the number's going to be tomorrow?"

"I can't get it to do that. Nobody can predict what the number's going to be. You can only get it to do what people can do."

"Well, shit, what good is it then?"

"It can do it faster." Seeing that Pokey wasn't impressed Jake offered another angle. "We could even play our own little numbers game right here. In fact, I could write a program to do that right now. Anything would be better than losing to you in darts again."

Jake stared toward the terminal.

But Pokey wasn't satisfied. "It's not going to be any fun unless the machine pays us money when we win."

"We can bet instead. We'll just bet on whose number comes up first."

Now Roop wasn't satisfied. "I can't afford it. I just bought a new tea service..."

Pokey turned on him. "You just bought a what?"

Roop had blundered. He could feel the beads of sweat breaking out along his hairline. "I just bought some things for my kitchen. Silverware, tea kettle, stuff like that. It's kind of expensive."

"Come on, Roop. We're only going to bet nickels."

"Yea, Roop. Just nickels, man."

***

Roop had lost twenty-five cents. Pokey was up five cents, Jake twenty. Roop, of course, had long reconciled himself with being a loser, when gambling was to any extent involved. He was waiting for the day when he would walk into a diner, order a fish sandwich and get food poisoning. Bingo! Like being the one-millionth customer, only backward.

That was why Roop ordered fish sandwiches more than any other kind. He wanted to get food poisoning and be done with it. He wanted it behind him so that he could get on the road to recovery. He didn't want it ahead of him anymore. There was this guy he knew who got food poisoning. It didn't hit him until a few hours after he had eaten and was sitting in the stands watching a basketball game. Vomiting and diarrhea. They practically had to carry him out of the stands. Roop wanted that behind him.

Jake had written a program. He called it a random-number-generating program. Before the game started, each one of them picked a three-digit number. And the one who's number came up first was the winner. Then Jake would push the interrupt button and start the game again. It just rolled along.

```
IS YOUR LUCKY NUMBER 019?
IS YOUR LUCKY NUMBER 658?
IS YOUR LUCKY NUMBER 233?
IS YOUR LUCKY NUMBER 791?
IS YOUR LUCKY NUMBER 245?
INTERRUPT
Run
```

Like that. Except that after the first game Jake made the machine stop printing the words. With just the number and a question mark, the game went much faster.

```
515?
890?
583?
```

Like that.

They were there a half-hour past the time they usually left for home and it had surprised Roop to find Mrs. Bragg still up and waiting for him. She asked him to put the teapot on. Had said she would be up in a few minutes.

***

Only a couple of years earlier, on the train from Frankfurt to Cologne, Pokey learned a new word. Himmelfahrtskommando. In fact, he learned several while sitting in the second-class compartment, but this was the most interesting one. The other occupant of the compartment had begun the conversation, a middle-aged German who had fought on both fronts during the war. From what Pokey could understand, he had destroyed six Russian tanks. He had taken great pains to explain to Pokey why it was called the Himmelfahrtskommando. Dangerous he had said. Gefährlich. You could easily get a trip to heaven. Himmelfahrt.

Pokey was on his way to see Gabi, a girl he had met the week before. She lived in Cologne and had only been in Frankfurt visiting. They spent the night together and she had invited him to come to Cologne the following weekend for her birthday party. He had looked forward to the party, pictured a cozy gathering. What he got was two dozen Germans sloppy drunk and falling over each other. Not intimate at all. A few times, Gabi had come to him with puzzlement on her face asking him if he was enjoying himself. "Nicht froh?" Then she would kiss him on the forehead and disappear again.

He was not able to understand a word that the people around him said. And this pained him. He had worked so hard during his tour of duty to pick up as much of the language as he could. Because if there was one thing he had learned as a foster child, it was that if you pay attention and learn the people's system then they tend to be nice to you. To take an interest. But now he didn't understand a word being said. No one was taking an interest. And Gabi was only being nice to him at irregular intervals. It was not until the end of the party that he had gotten a real chance to talk with her. He told her about the beautiful word he had learned on the train. Himmelfahrtskommando. Gabi laughed and laughed. "Das ist aber zu schön," she said. "Das ist aber zu schön."

***

"I just think that I'm holding you back. You're so young. You ought to be spending your time with someone your own age. Not wasting it on me. I don't want to be selfish. Look what you've done. You spent all that money on a tea service. Just for us. It's not right for me to monopolize you..."

Roop didn't want to say anything. He sat there dipping his tea bag, waiting for any amendments she might want to make, wishing he had never, ever bought that tea service. He wondered why he hadn't recognized it as a risk. His life had been going along absolutely fine with the mismatched cups.

"I'm going to be completely honest. Lately, I've begun to think of you as my boyfriend. Me, a middle-aged woman with one breast. I don't think that's healthy. Do you?"

Roop was still dipping his tea bag.

"Are you angry, Roop? Say something."

"Don't you want a massage or anything?"

***

Sitting in his windowless room looking at the skylight that he could not open, Pokey imagined that he was a one-man Himmelfahrtskommando on an assignment in the depths of outer space. And as he drifted further into space, he was little by little losing radio contact with Earth. A suicide mission to protect all the intimate homes all over the world. He could see several stars through the skylight. Slowly he repeated to himself,

"This is Pokey to earth. Pokey to earth. Come in. Come in."

***

They were all strong and pure and beautiful. Noble. They played in the rolling hills where only grass and trees grew. No flowers. No decadence. And the land was unbounded. There were no rivers. No rivers to erode. Only lakes with hidden sources. On some of the highlands, there was golden grass that grew tall like wheat. And on one plateau there was a cottage that stood on the edge of a meadow and the periphery of a forest. It was the home of generations.

There was a tradition. That had all been good, these generations flowing into him from the beginning of time. Times in which he had not lived, but was certain he knew. Times that were his. Times that he would pass on and enrich.

Jake opened the cellar window after having doused the last remaining embers. He was satisfied. He would call her tomorrow and tell her she could start making plans for decorating the house. It was up to her. All up to her. To create her own world within his.

He climbed the cellar steps to the kitchen. It was raining outside. Not hard. Jake checked the lock on the back door. It was okay. Then he went through the dining room and the living room to check the front door. It was okay. Everything was okay. He made his way up to his attic bedroom to sleep.

***

Pam was a lucky girl. More precisely, she was a lucky woman. She was Jake's girl. She was her own woman. Pam was a lucky woman. She was going to marry Jake Strutters, a twenty-three-year-old with his own house. Already paid for. And money in the bank. Handsome. Just what she wanted. Her mother liked him, too.

And she had always wanted to be pregnant. Always. As long as she could remember. Jake said she could get pregnant as soon as they were married. He insisted that they wait until then. In a few months, she would be pregnant and in her own house.

Pam was a spoiled bitch. She didn't mind saying so herself. Actually, she would only admit to being spoiled. Her friends added the 'bitch.' Pam was well-liked. And it was her peculiar genius that allowed her to be well-liked and a spoiled bitch simultaneously. Her being a spoiled bitch would just about imply that she was well-liked during some period or periods of her life. But the thing about Pam was that she was well-liked even when she was behaving like a spoiled bitch. And that was what set her apart from the rest of her class.

How she managed it was not at all clear. It seemed to be some sort of sleight of hand. Because it was when it appeared, she was behaving her worst and should be condemned, that she was most likable. Instead of a negative trait, it was suddenly a positive trait. Suddenly being a spoiled bitch was the way to be. All the world should love a spoiled bitch, all spoiled bitches. She was a credit to her type.

Except that with Jake it didn't work because as far as he was concerned, she was his, and what was his didn't go topsy-turvy. That's how he was able to slap her when no one else had ever dared to. That was why she had decided to be more careful. Jake had some of the bitch in him too. With him, sleight of hand didn't work.

***

Roop didn't like department stores in the first place. Crowded department stores were a few rungs further down the ladder. This time, it had been an old woman with two shopping bags. Roop had nothing against old women, in and of themselves. Old women had always been good to him. Only in department stores with shopping bags, they were something else again.

He had been behind her in a narrow aisle in the cosmetics department and he had tried to pass her five different times. He would have made it each time if it hadn't been for her bags. What he should have done was crack her one behind the ear. That would have been better than letting her frustrate and embarrass him that way. When she fell to the ground, he would have come to her aid, a concerned bystander willing to get involved. As crowded as that store had been, no one would have noticed that quick jab to the back of the head, just the collapse and the gallant young man bending over her.

Maybe there is even a reporter nearby who takes his name and writes a human-interest story about how the world isn't really sick, how some people still care. All the world needs is a little cooperation among groups, old and young for example. When Mrs. Bragg reads the article, she realizes that her worries about not being a fit companion aren't justified. They could go on having tea together and cooperating without her pangs of conscience.

Instead, here he was sitting in a movie theater alone because she insisted that he go out at least once a week. This was a horror movie that was guaranteed to make you vomit. The management took no responsibility if you didn't use the bag provided. At least that's the way the ad ran. So far, no one had screamed. Roop was never sure if a movie deserved to be rated as frightening unless someone screamed. Maybe the movie was scary, but there was no screamer in the audience. Unfortunately, Roop was not a screamer.

After the show, he sat at a counter and played with a strawberry shake, when what he wanted was tea. A strawberry shake and a fish sandwich. When he finished, he would go to the cashier and, with his left hand, place the exact amount of money for his food and a box of chocolates in the cashier's hand and with his right hand take the candy from the display. It was always nice to eat in a restaurant you knew well. He didn't want to wait for a bus. He walked home.

***

Yea, I'm ready to show you
That I ain't no runt
I'm fixing to sock you
Right dead in your cunt.
Yea, now is the time
For making some sparks.
Cause Pokey needs pussy
Like Noahs need arks.

"Are you finished, Pokey? Are you really finished?"
"I guess so. At least for the time being."

"Then what's your number going to be?"

"I'll put a nickel on triple fours."

"Four, four, four." Jake wrote it down on a pad. "You still holding on one ninety-two, Roop?"

"Yep."

"I'm going to play five eighty-four. Everybody set."

"Jake, I think you're pulling a fast one. Taking nickels from us poor bucket boys."

"Fuck you, Pokey. Do you want to play or don't you?"

"Shit, you don't have to get all offended and everything. Start the computer. Goddamn! You can't even joke around here."

```
run
444,192,584
1 515
2 239
3 079
4 981
5 694
6 211
7 438
8 753
9 391
10 624
11 802
12 444
GAME IS OVER. WINNER IS 444.
WINNER COLLECTS BONUS FROM EACH PLAYER.
```

"Alright! That'll be a nickel plus a quarter bonus from both of you. Thirty cents apiece."

"No, Pokey. We said a quarter if it comes in the first ten. A fifteen-cent bonus for the next ten and a nickel bonus for the next thirty after that."

"Then how come when you hit the bonus the other night in the second ten, Roop and I had to give you a quarter bonus?"

"That wasn't the second ten. It was the first ten. Am I right, Roop?"

"He's right. It was the eighth one up."

"Twenty cents apiece then. Pay up."

They paid up and then Jake started the next round. Pokey took zero seventy-three. Roop stuck with one ninety-two. Jake took nine hundred.

***

Ashes! Ashes!
We all fall down.
That wasn't it.
Ashes! Ashes!
They all fall down.

What a joke. Charred remains. If he was going to be honest, he'd have to admit that it had given him a scare. But now, a few weeks later, it seemed nothing more than a funny little dream. He was even tempted to tell Pam about it. Tempted only. Yielding to temptations like that was what turned funny little dreams into nightmares. And he wasn't about to have any nightmares. Not any. Take Pokey's suggestion that he try to use the computer to beat the numbers racket. He could have announced right then and there that he was working on a scheme to do just that. But no, he waited. Don't talk until you're sure you have something going for you. In the case of the burnt corpse, he wasn't ever going to talk. But the numbers were another story. He figured he had about as good a scheme as anyone was ever going to come up with.

Actually, statistics had been Jake's worst subject in college. He had just about failed it. He hadn't done much better in probability. In the final analysis, he wasn't really sure what the difference was between the two. What he was sure of was that with a little of his intuition and common sense he could make his scheme work. Probability was nothing more than intuition and common sense anyway. All you needed to know how to do was count and do a little multiplication and division just to speed things up. From that, you could build up the whole system. Your only limiting factor was ingenuity.

Jake had compiled the results of all the nightly competitions with Roop and Pokey, listing every single number that had been generated by the computer and the order in which it had appeared. From Pokey, he had gotten a tip-sheet that contained the winning numbers for the past year. He decided that the best approach was to bet on a set of numbers which he called 'the due set.' At first, Jake wanted to determine the due set in the following fashion:

The due set consists of all those numbers that end with the digit that has appeared least recently on the end of a winning number. But this was so simple that he decided that it could not possibly be right. Furthermore, someone taking the bets would easily get onto the idea. So Jake reformulated. He had noticed that the winning number, generated from the action of the stock market, was taken from the last digits of 'advances', 'declines' and 'unchanged.'

The due set consists of all those numbers whose digits add to a number whose last digit has least recently been the last digit of the sum of the digits of a winning number.

This was not only the correct due set in Jake's view, but it was also non-transparent and allowed for a compact representation of the one hundred possibilities. He only had to bet on an easily constructed set of twenty-two numbers that yielded the due digit and specify that the bet also cover all their permutations. Jake had determined that the due digit was presently eight. This yielded a due set of:

008, 017, 026, 035, 044, 099, 116, 125, 134, 189, 224, 233, 279, 288, 369, 378, 459, 468, 477, 558, 567, 666

Those mathematicians were always overanalyzing things, trying to make situations completely rational, talking about independent events and the like. Jake didn't believe in the independence of events. Pokey once said that watching the numbers coming in from the computer was like going to the horse races except that you only saw the winner cross the finish line.

According to Jake's way of thinking, where there was a winner there was also a loser, and usually not too far behind. The due set represented this loser. But if you started at the right point on the circle it was a winner.

Jake had pored over both lists. The list from their private game and the list furnished by the tip-sheet. In not one case had a due digit stayed due for more than fourteen draws. How many times could a loser be lapped on the track in all probability? Usually not fourteen times. Usually quite a bit fewer. If he were to put a penny on each permutation in the due set, that would be a dollar. Increasing the bet by fifty percent each time, the most he would lose if the due set stayed due for fifteen rounds would be eight-hundred and seventy-five dollars.

The cost for the fifteen rounds represented his entire take-home pay for a month, but he didn't believe he would lose, and if he won on any of the bets along the way, he would make a tidy profit. Anyway, he wasn't exactly embarrassed for cash. In the last couple of years, he had been putting anywhere from three to six hundred dollars a month in the bank. The house was paid for and so was the car. And he had not even touched the insurance money he received at his mother's death. He might even let Pokey and Roop in on the deal.

***

Pokey figured he was either going to have to break the world's record in the marathon or get himself a woman quick. One way or the other. He wondered how Rufus M. would handle it. Rufus M. was his hero and had been since childhood. Rufus M. was magnificent. He had a way of seizing the time. Unfortunately, Rufus M. was eternally eight years old. He never had to look for a Naked Maja. He didn't feel the need.

But still, he wondered how Rufus would handle it. Maybe the same way he had handled the invisible piano player. But in the case of the invisible piano player, Rufus had at least been able to see the piano keys going up and down. Pokey could discern no such evidence of the existence of his Naked Maja. If he just had some sign, a sign like the moving keys, then he would be just as bold as Rufus was. When Rufus felt for the invisible piano player and felt nothing there, he hadn't given up, only assumed that the invisible man could not be felt. He hadn't given up until he discovered it was a player piano. Maybe he would reach out and find that Naked Maja didn't exist. In that case, he would rather not know.

Earlier in the evening on the radio, Pokey had heard a bizarre news report. A man claimed he stabbed his best friend to death because he refused to give him a bite of his devil's food cake. Pokey was sure there was more to it than that, even though the summer had been extraordinarily warm. He was willing to bet that one of the two went reaching for the other's Maja. You had to be careful.

The analogy with Rufus' invisible man was by no means complete. He would never reach for Pam, for example. Even though he thought she might be what he wanted. Jake was the kind of guy who would kill him and then pretend he was crazy, that he had lost his mind. He'd probably claim he killed him because he wouldn't give him a bite from his super-duper. Or some such nonsense.

***

Roop had never pinched Mrs. Bragg before. But tonight, for some reason unknown to him, he had pinched her right before the massage. An impromptu pinch on her very firm right buttock. Immediately he had questioned the prudence of his action. He feared she might find herself thinking that she was his girlfriend again and pull away from him. Roop didn't want any more flare-ups. But she hadn't said anything. She hadn't said anything about anything in the last few days. She hadn't even insisted that he go out more. Everything seemed to be back to normal.

***

"Goddamn it, Pokey. You're the one who wanted me to figure out a way to beat the numbers and now that I'm giving you a chance to do it, you're whining like a two-year-old. I don't need to ask for money from you and Roop. You know that. But I thought you two would jump at a chance like this."

"I didn't ask you to figure out a way. I asked you to get the computer to do it."

"You don't need the computer to do it. Let me explain it to you once more in simple terms. Are you listening, Roop?"

"Yea."

"Okay, the twenty-two numbers on the sheet are due. They could hit any time now. Our first bet is a dollar, which is a penny on each number we're playing since we're playing all the permutations."

"Tell me once more what a permutation is."

"Jesus Christ, Roop! I've only told you a million times. It just means when Pokey gives the guy the slip, he tells him to box all the numbers. You guys kill me. Do you think I'd be risking seven hundred of my own money on something shaky? This is a great chance. Pokey, you might even win enough eventually to make that Abbot and Costello film you were talking about."

"It wasn't Abbot and Costello. It was Amos 'n' Andy."

"Well, whatever. How about it?"

"Okay."

"What if we don't win?" Roop was still squirming.

"Then we lose. But we're not going to lose. These numbers aren't going to stay due for more than fourteen rounds. I've tested it. Just no way. And we're betting fifteen rounds for insurance. Come on, Roop."

"Okay, I'm in too."

***

At first, Pokey had taken it as a bad omen. He had ripped open the palm of his right hand trying to get the skylight in his ceiling open. After thinking it over, he decided that it probably wasn't a sign. Like Jake had said, they couldn't lose. Besides, the cut was in a way not such a bad thing. He would have an excuse for not using the buffing machine for a couple of weeks, which meant he would have time to play darts before the break as well as after. That is, if he could talk Roop into neglecting his buffing too. No one ever checked their work anyhow. And in so far as it was not the hand that he threw darts with or masturbated with, it was a good omen. He could have been in trouble. Masturbation with his other hand didn't work. Several years earlier he had his left hand in a cast and he had nearly lost his mind for the lack of sex.

It hadn't been the good hand, but there was another worry. The last time he masturbated he had experienced a disturbing aftereffect. At least he thought it was an aftereffect. He had gone into a trance-like state for a minute or two, during which the rhythms of his refrigerator and alarm clock took on lives of their own. He had the feeling that everything in the room, including him, had shrunk by some enormous factor. The spell had lasted until the thermostat switched off the refrigerator motor, deadened the reverberation.

Pokey didn't know what to make of it. He thought that maybe he had fallen asleep for a few minutes and only dreamt that he had been in a trance. One thing, though, that he hadn't dreamt was the trembling that followed. Maybe he was coming down with something, possibly a mild infection from the cut.

They lost their first bet. Pokey would tell them tonight at work if they didn't already know. The winner on the old stock was 301, which wasn't among the numbers they played. But in the other house, the new stock, which they weren't playing, one of their numbers had come out. 828. So maybe Jake was right. Those numbers were due. He hadn't really understood much of Jake's explanation, but he was going to try to ride it out. Jake wouldn't let you down. He was solid.

***

Jake wasn't greatly impressed with what he had brought forth in his latest fire ceremony. For one thing, his intention during any Fire Ceremony was to bring forth from his ancestral past and not his personal past. Second, if something from his personal past forced its way into his meditation, it should at least be demonstrative of the kind of nobility that he was certain typified his ancestral past. But somehow, whenever his personal past invaded the ceremony, it was the kind of memory he could do without.

This time it was the picture of his grandfather on a winter night, coming up the hill past the gas station. Drunk. A dry, cold night and his grandfather fifty yards or so away talking loudly to himself. The four-year-old Jake and his mother stood on the corner at the bus stop. Maybe his grandfather's crazy. And that had been all. Except for the red light blinking on and off on the horizon. Jake wasn't sure why they were standing at the bus stop. He knew that his grandfather had withdrawn his mother's car privileges from time to time. He had meted out such punishments, trying to force her to tell him who Jake's father was. Jake eventually learned that his grandfather thought it was one of the dagos in the neighborhood. His mother never told. She never even told Jake.

If he hadn't been thinking about the numbers so much, he would never have allowed his thoughts to drift during the ceremony. He was glad they hadn't won on the first bet. He was hoping they wouldn't win until the fifth or sixth bet at least. That way they could get a little working capital. If the set would just stay due that long. It could hit any time.

***

"I'm pregnant, Roop."

He sat on his bed alone in the dark and asked himself how she could be. It was the straightforward statement of a condition, but it had the ring of a fairy tale. A scary fairy tale for Roop. How could she be? A woman her age didn't get pregnant. With one breast? She was pushing fifty.

"I'm pregnant, Roop," she had said.

Tears welled up in his eyes and without even stopping to consider he said, "I'm scared." She nestled him against her and Roop realized she had two babies, him and his.

"We're a good team, Roop. You and me."

Roop tried to picture his son playing center field. It could only be hoped that there would be no recurrence of the humiliation. Humiliation. The whole thing would be a humiliation.

"I want to have this child. I don't care about the personal risks. You'll see. It's going to be good. It's going to be okay with us and our baby."

It could come out deformed. She was too old to have a baby. It might look like him. If it looked like Mrs. Bragg it'd be okay. Mrs. Bragg was pretty. She didn't really look the forty-seven years or whatever she was. Maybe the baby would come out okay.

She wanted him to start sleeping with her in her bedroom. She wanted a family life. Her late husband had been infertile. This was a second chance. They could turn Roop's room into a nursery, and the money Roop had been giving her for rent could be put aside for whatever the child might need.

Roop had no idea how he was going to tell his mother and father about it. He could tell his sister and let her tell them like he used to do when he was little. But now she was twenty-five years old and she and her husband were expecting their own family. And he was almost twenty-one.

He'd tell them himself. It wouldn't be too difficult. Anyway, his parents had a way of making him feel good after he had done something bad. All he had to do was confess.

***

Memphis had been Pokey's only real friend while he was in Germany. He was also one of the most physically unattractive people Pokey had ever known. Exempting the fungus-like material that grew on the very crown of his head, Memphis had no hair. The rest of his scalp was scar tissue, out of which wispy sideburns began and then faded on either side of his face. His complexion did not have a healthy appearance. It was not brown. It was the color of wet cardboard. Memphis was overweight

After his hitch in the army was up, Memphis had decided to stay on in Germany. At the time Pokey got acquainted with him, Memphis had already been there five years as a civilian. Pokey was never able to discover what Memphis did for money. It wasn't that Pokey was nosy. It was just that he had considered staying on for a while himself and wondered how Memphis managed it. He thought that maybe he could do whatever Memphis was doing. But all that Memphis had ever said about money was that it didn't cost that much to get along.

Memphis had two children who lived in Mannheim with their mothers, a girl six and a boy three. About a month before Pokey was to return to the States, Memphis invited him to go along with them on a picnic. It surprised Pokey that both of the women were coming. Memphis simply packed both of his families into a Volkswagen bus and headed for the woods.

On the way to the picnic site, Pokey talked mainly with the children. The two women and Memphis talked too fast for him to understand much. The little girl seemed to understand that German was difficult for him and took her time, pausing at the end of each sentence and making gestures with her hands, when the words themselves were insufficient. The little boy was more difficult to understand. He was still a baby. His sister would tell Pokey not to pay any attention to him.

The two women clearly enjoyed each other's company. From what Pokey could tell, Memphis took them on outings like this all the time. They went to work preparing the picnic site for the meal, each apparently knowing what her share of the task was. They had divided the responsibility for the food in a complementary way. It was all very organized. Pokey and Memphis sat under a tree waiting for them to finish preparations and playing with the children. Memphis tried to give his daughter an English lesson. Every time he asked her to repeat something she started laughing. She thought it sounded funny. Memphis was trying to get her to say, "I'm a little nigger."

When the food was ready, Pokey was served first because he was their guest. They waited momentarily before they served themselves and the children. Barbara asked Pokey if he liked Germany and if he had found a girlfriend. Pokey had only answered the second question, saying that he had a girlfriend in Cologne. He figured he had a right to say this because he had been to bed with her twice. He was sure, though, that she didn't consider him her boyfriend and he had not seen her since her birthday party. Barbara maintained that Pokey would stay in Germany. When she said that Pokey's girlfriend would make him stay just as the two of them had made Memphis stay, the two women laughed as if they shared some secret.

Pokey and Memphis played hide-and-seek in the woods with the children, while Barbara and Helga cleaned up. Then they sat around drinking beer until it began to get dark and the kids became irritable.

That was the only time that Pokey saw either of Memphis' families and the last time he saw Memphis. He could remember vividly the good-byes, as Memphis delivered each pair to its respective home. A kiss on the cheek for Barbara and a hug for the daughter. Waving. Then a few streets later a kiss on the cheek for Helga and a handshake for the boy. More waving. Auf Wiedersehen in the gray streets of Mannheim.

***

Nothing relaxed Jake more than watching a baseball game on television. Pam snuggled up against him and they played find-Pam's-ear-underneath-her-afro. Jake was allowed to forage with his nose and mouth. No hands allowed. The game could last as long as an hour. It all depended on how long Pam wanted to resist. She was allowed to use one hand.

The television spewed forth the Star-Spangled Banner as Jake narrowed in on a lobe. Just as Pam successfully forced Jake to retreat, there was a sudden drop in volume, which was undoubtedly due to a technical failure somewhere along the relay. But it had the same apparent effect as if ninety percent of the crowd had forgotten the words.

"Listen to the goddamn hunkies. Can't even remember the words to the national anthem."

"Why don't you leave the poor hunkies alone, Jake?"

"If that were 'My Wild Irish Rose' or 'O, My Papa,' I bet they could get it straight. Mumbling the national anthem."

"Have you forgotten about my ear?"

"I mean all of them trying to be more American than us. I mean even Uncle Sam isn't more American than Aunt Jemima. That fucking wop up the street hangs out the flag every time Nixon farts."

"Maybe he wants to see if he's downwind."

"You get smart with me and I'll bust your cute little ass."

"Temper, temper."

Jake surprised her with an assault on her ear.

***

They were back to throwing darts full time. None of them had any interest in the computer game now that they were playing the real thing. Tomorrow they were going to place their seventh bet. Eleven dollars and fifty cents or eleven and a half cents on each permutation. The way Jake had originally calculated it, the bet would have been eleven dollars and thirty-nine cents, but they were forced to round up to comply with the rules of the house. The rules only allowed bets down to the half-cent.

Jake and Pokey had been giving each other the silent treatment for most of the evening. It all started when Pokey asked Jake if he was sure the numbers were due. "Cause if they were due six bets ago, they're mighty late now. That's all I can say." Jake had told Pokey to stop his whining. Pokey responded with two fifty pointers and a bull's eye, all thrown in rapid succession.

Including the upcoming bet, they were down about thirty-three dollars, most of which was Jake's money since he put up about eighty percent of each bet. He had opened an account, in which he deposited the total amount of money necessary for the fifteen rounds, should it go that far. Pokey and Roop contributed ninety dollars apiece. Jake had effectively locked them in for the duration. He was the only one who could make withdrawals. Since it was mostly his money, he thought it only fair. Anyway, if Pokey really wanted out, he could remove his money when he placed the bet. He was the one who carried the thing out. He was the one who made the contact.

**

Roop knew that the best thing he could do was say as little as possible. Just let his father talk himself out. Even though Roop knew beforehand everything he was going to say. Even though his father talked so slowly it took him a year to say it.

"I bought you your first glove when you were five years old. Not any old glove either. It was a Wilson. You didn't know that it was a good glove, but I did. Kept it oiled for you, too. Then there was little league. You were the best that league ever had. That home run you hit, two hundred and sixty-five feet. Over the fence and into the swimming pool. What other twelve-year-old could have done that? Wasn't because you were big. You've never been all that big. You take after my side of the family. Small-boned."

Roop's father stopped to get his bearings.

"Then there was high school. You were a starter as a freshman. All-Conference, sophomore, junior, and senior years. A four seventy-three batting average over the last two years. You were making headlines. Roop Moore!"

The number four seventy-three had hit two days earlier. Roop hadn't even remembered that this was his batting average. All the wrong numbers were coming out. Like Pokey said, Jake's numbers were overdue.

"You deserved to be team captain your senior year. Best batting average, best glove, best arm. The fastest by far. But it doesn't matter. They always like to pick the catcher or the shortstop for captain. No matter if they deserve it or not. Well, the scouts don't really care who the captain is. They want to know where the talent is. If you had played legion ball after graduation, you would have gotten a contract for sure. And once you started in the minors, the majors were only a few years away. But you didn't want to play anymore. You traded in your bat for a mop handle."

He seemed winded. Roop was about to stand up and go talk to his mother, who was sobbing in the kitchen.

"Now this. With a fifty-year-old woman."

"She's forty-seven." There was that four and seven again. Roop thought he might mention this to Jake tomorrow. Maybe he had miscalculated.

"She's almost as old as your mother. I could choke that woman to death! She ought to know better. You're not even twenty-one yet. Won't be for another five months. Instead of being out playing ball where the scouts can see you, you're playing house with a fifty-year-old widow. What could you see in her? What could you possibly see?"

Roop wasn't expected to answer. His father was wearing him down. He wanted to go into the kitchen and tell his mother to stop crying. He wished he had asked his sister to tell them.

"I think you ought to move back home. I don't know why you moved out in the first place. You had the whole second floor to yourself after your sister got married."

"Mrs. Bragg thinks we should get married. Even if we don't, I want to stay with her. Can I go talk to Mom now?"

"Yea, go on into the kitchen. But first let me tell you one more thing. I know you have a lot on your mind. You're going to have to work some things out. But try to keep it all in perspective. You're young and strong. You could still play ball and you could still make it to the majors."

Roop went into the kitchen. To his mother.

***

Most of the other books had frightened Pokey. They were all so bizarre, a woman taking stars from gingerbread bars standing on a ladder and pasting them to the sky. The ladder had rested on nothing. It had defied the law of gravity and all else. And with her funny, high-top buckled shoes. Or the book about the babies in the water; the Water Babies and that chimney sweep. These were all too macabre for Pokey. He had read Rufus M. instead. Over and over. Better Rufus M. than little girls lost in labyrinths.

The Raymonds let him keep the book when he left their foster care. But he lost it somewhere along the line in one of the other homes. Since he had been on his own, he had often thought of getting his own copy. He had even gone to the library to see if they had it. They didn't. He was sure that the book would give him as much pleasure now as it had when he was little.

Pokey could remember all the good parts, like the time when Rufus found the money under the ice. Rufus had bought kindling wood and potatoes, eggs and fruit for the whole family, plus some good coal. And good coal was hard to get during the war. Or the time he thought he had seen the eyes of a wild creature in the drainage pipes and it turned out to be just Catherine-the-cat.

He wouldn't have had the bean plant growing in his room if it hadn't been for the chapter "Rufus' Beans." He had always kept a bean plant with him without exception. Every spring, wherever he lived, he planted a single bean seed in a pot and watched it grow. If human beings could have flowers like states do, Pokey would have chosen the bean plant. This year's bean plant was among the best Pokey had ever grown. The only one that he could think of that was better was the one he grew for his science project his freshman year in high school. But that one had been grown under special conditions, so it wasn't fair to put it up against this one. He would say "Grow beans" to his plant because Rufus did, not because he had heard that talking to your plants helps. There was no other book that could touch Rufus M. All he had to do was to think about it to achieve inner peace.

***

Pokey was enjoying it but it couldn't go on. He was flattered, but it couldn't go on. He drank the last of his instant breakfast and ran some cold water into the glass. To his dismay, he discovered a lump of instant breakfast powder still remained in the bottom of the glass. Who could say what that meant? It was only a small lump, but who could say. It might be his entire vitamin C and half of his vitamin B_1. There was no way of telling. He could only be sure that he had missed out on part of his nourishment.

He would explain to her that she couldn't be his girlfriend. But he didn't want to hurt her feelings. She was such a cute little thing. You had to be careful with little kids. If you weren't, you could warp them for life. Pokey knew that much about psychology. A gift and his permission to call him 'Uncle Pokey' might do. That solution had worked pretty well with him when he had a crush on the older daughter of his foster parents.

Pokey wondered if she went to school. She had the prettiest copper skin and her hair grew in shining curls on top of curls. She reminded him of Pam. If he could remember, he would ask Jake if Pam had any relatives in the neighborhood.

But it would have to stop. The dandelions at the bus stop couldn't continue. Her flattery: "You're cute. You're my boyfriend." Her prancing.

***

Don't it feel bad,
When you been had?
It sure feels bad
When you been...

"Okay, Pokey, what's your point? You don't think we're going to hit tomorrow or what?"

"I don't know anything about math and I guess that's why I don't understand why the numbers are due. I mean, what makes them due? What's pushing them?"

"Look, I can't reason with you. You don't seem to be able to get with it. This is our last bet. Two hundred and ninety-two dollars. Of the two hundred and ninety-two dollars, roughly thirty are yours. You have the money there in the envelope. Take your part out if you want. I still win or lose the same amount."

"You're rich. You can afford it."

"I'm not rich. I'm comfortable. Listen, Pokey. You've already invested sixty bucks. Thirty more isn't going to kill you."

"Why don't you throw in a kiss from Pam as incentive, as a consolation prize if I lose. I'm just kidding, Jake."

Roop had run out of patience. He started for the exit. "I've got to go."

"Wait up, Roop. I'll give you a lift. Pokey, whether you play or not is up to you. You're the one who places the bet. Just make sure you put in the money for Roop and me."

"I've been edgy lately. When we started out, I was okay."

Roop and Jake went through the swinging doors, but Pokey continued as if they were still there. "I just want to know how you know they're due. And if they were due then, are they more due now?"

***

It was only the second time that Pokey had wrapped a gift. The first time was the gift he had taken along with him to Cologne for Gabi. He wished that he had more excuses to give gifts. The whole process excited him. He had pored over the offerings in the children's section of the bookstore for most of the morning before he made the selection. No Rufus M. but, all in all, pretty good books. He had read several passages from each one.

Pokey picked up the package again and felt the heft of it. Packages were good he decided. Even if she couldn't read yet, she could feel the weight of the package. He would ask her mother to read them to her, whenever she got a chance. He would have enjoyed doing it himself but didn't think it was his place to volunteer. They might think he was trying to force his way into the family. But he had taken the liberty of writing 'From Uncle Pokey' on each title page.

He had only planned to buy one book, but then the number came in and he was able to splurge. One hundred and fifty dollars. Pokey and Roop each got three fifty-dollar bills. Of course, money had already been put in. Still, it was a windfall that he had not expected.

He had delivered the money to Jake. Almost fifteen hundred dollars. It was one thing to see that they had won, but to hold all that money... Jake had to be a magician. 314. It was on the slip and Jake said that they were coming, but Pokey had almost lost heart. Almost had pulled his thirty out. But it arrived. And now he was able to splurge.

He took the package and descended the stairs from his room, past the closed doors of people he hardly knew. He had seen all of them at one time or another. There seemed to be something wrong with every one of them. Either lame or obese. Scarred or blind.

There was no sight of her in the yard when he reached the house, so he went up to the door and knocked. He wanted to talk to her mother anyway.

She turned out to be a stout woman, not as pretty as her daughter but there was a clear resemblance. She had the same smile. The same glow.

"Yes?"

"Are you Emily's mother?"

She furrowed her brow in anticipation. "Yes."

"My name is Mobers. Pokey Mobers."

"What is it?"

"For the last couple of weeks, Emily's been giving me dandelions at the bus stop. I happened to be in the bookstore today and I bought her a few books."

"That's so nice of you. It's a shame she's not home now. You just missed her. Her father always takes Emily to her grandmother's on Saturdays. She'll be thrilled."

"I just wanted to give her something for the flowers. Four of them are just regular storybooks and the other one is a book that teaches kids how to grow their own gardens."

"That's so thoughtful of you. I really do appreciate it. What's your name again?"

"Pokey Mobers. Just tell her the man at the bus stop."

Pokey left the house and walked back up the street to his place. He felt drained. Drained and disappointed. Emily had not been there. He had missed her, and maybe she wouldn't know who the books were from. Maybe he wasn't the only man she gave flowers at the bus stop. In front of his building, he stopped and considered going across the street to the bar. He thought that maybe he might meet someone like Memphis, someone who would take him on a picnic. But then he remembered that Memphis had not answered any of his letters and that he didn't get along with people in bars. He wasn't even convinced that Memphis really existed.

He continued into the building and up the stairs to his room. There were no lights or windows in the stairwell, so it was always dark. There was light from the doorway only if someone else happened to be coming or going. No sense in complaining to the landlord.

Pokey sat on the side of the bed looking at the alarm clock, trying to determine if he should cook dinner and take a nap afterward or take a nap first. He had bought a steak in celebration of hitting the number. There were foods he liked more but he didn't know how to prepare them, so he had settled for steak. The refrigerator switched on with its usual racket and that same feeling came over him, that everything had shrunk. That he and his entire environment had been miniaturized. Then he grew drowsy and slept. And there was the dream of a room with unexpected depth, unexpected space. A sanctuary rarely used, with the magical quality of only being there when summoned by a sincere wish.

***

He and his would be the eternal winners. Jake Strutters. Every foe must succumb to the burning heat of the infinite savannah. Again, his ability to win had been demonstrated. 314. They had again been shown. Every last whisper would be silenced. Every last one. Who cares who my father was? Every goddamn, gossiping mouth would be shut. Frozen like the winter-orange reflection of the January sun. Numb. Lifeless. Dead.

***

When Pokey woke up Sunday morning, he had still not eaten his steak. All he had done was sleep fifteen hours like a man unconscious. After establishing that it was really Sunday, he began his Sunday routine. First, he tidied up his room and mopped the floor. Then he bathed. It was in the bathtub that he remembered why he felt so depressed. Emily.

He remembered the reason for his depression while studying the ring in the bathtub, a ring that had grown darker and wider with every week that he had lived there. It seemed to be an unwritten law that no one apply cleanser to the ring. Somewhere within the ring, there was a particle of dirt for every boarder that had ever lived on the floor. None of the present occupants was likely to wash such a comprehensive history away. But once in a while Pokey weighed buying some cleanser, some cleanser to wipe it all away.

It was the thought of buying that reminded Pokey of the day before and his failure to deliver the books to Emily personally. He didn't know why this depressed him and he didn't try to figure it out either. She couldn't be his girlfriend. He kept the water level well below the ring and washed himself clean. Then he went to the drugstore and bought a Sunday paper.

On his way back to his room, he realized that he had not checked his mailbox on Saturday. He didn't know why he bothered. He didn't have any bills. And that was the only kind of mail that he was a candidate for. But he didn't want to give up hope. Someone could have written him and there was always the chance of getting some interesting junk mail or some unsolicited pornography.

He reached into the mailbox and pulled out a letter. It was addressed to him, and not junk mail either. It was from the pharmaceutical company. He fought off the urge to open it right there on the porch and bounded up the steps two at a time. It was too good to be true. First they hit the number and now he gets a letter from the pharmaceutical company. He threw the newspaper on the bed. In his haste to open the envelope, he tore into the letter itself. But no matter. It was still readable.

Dear Mr. Mobers:

We appreciate very much your sharing an idea with our company. Unfortunately, we do not foresee an application of this idea to our line of mouthwash. We remain, of course, open to any ideas you may care to offer in the future.

Sincerely,

If Pokey had had anything to burn the letter with, he would have. He thought of using the hot plate, but the hot plate would produce no flame. He chucked the letter into the wastebasket and used the hot plate to cook his steak.

Half of the steak also found its way into the wastebasket. Pokey's depression deepened. He was hopeless. It was the same feeling that he had had when he was a little kid and inextricably tangled the strings of his marionette. There were other ideas running around in his head, the idea for a loaf of heels for people who liked that particular slice of bread. But it was no use. No use at all. At twenty-two, he had achieved all that fate was going to allow, a janitor with a bean plant. All there was left to do now was get old.

***

"You can put the money aside for when the baby comes. But I wish you would stop playing the numbers. Even if you did win this time. Gambling is a bad habit to get into…" Mrs. Bragg showed just the slightest hint of a pout.

Roop responded with a rare display of annoyance. "You're not my mother, you know." Then he smoothed it over. "The numbers man says he can't take our kind of a bet anymore. He says it's too much trouble. Jake says it's because they're afraid."

"It's just as well." She began pinching him under the covers. Their relationship had grown increasing relaxed since she had gotten pregnant and Roop agreed to share her bedroom.

"I'm hungry. What do we have down in the kitchen?"

"Marble cake. It's store-bought, but it tastes pretty good."

Roop climbed out of bed and started for the door. "Bring me some too, with some milk."

Roop didn't turn around as she spoke. He went right through the bedroom door into the hall and down the stairs. He was deeper in love with her than ever. Down in the kitchen, he cut her slice into little chunks so he could feed it to her. If only she could stay her present age until he could catch up. That would make everything perfect.

***

Himmelfahrtskommando to Earth, please come in, please. Himmelfahrtskommando to Earth. Do you read? Do you read? Himmelfahrtskommando. Pokey Mobers. Come in. This is Pokey Mobers. Come in.

***

Roop was nibbling his way through a super-duper while Jake and Pokey discussed ways of placing their bets without the numbers man knowing that they were using their system. Roop had already told them that he wasn't interested anymore and Pokey wasn't too eager either.

"Look, Jake, the only way we can get around it is to have a lot of different people placing bets and then they would have to be in on it. That would be messy. Why don't you come up with an idea that doesn't involve playing so many numbers at once?"

"Let's just forget it then. I've come up with a way to win. You'd think you could come up with a way of placing a bet. Shit, let's just forget it."

Roop became aware of the noise his eating made and switched to sipping on the strawberry shake until Jake and Pokey resumed conversation.

"Anyway, I made my point and have a nice piece of money to show for it. That'll buy Pam a fitting wedding present."

"You and Pam getting married?"

"Pokey, I must've told you."

"No, you didn't. Did he tell us, Roop?"

"Uh-uh. What's the matter, Jake? Why didn't you tell us before?"

"Well, it must have slipped my mind, that's all. I thought I'd told you two."

"When's it going to be."

"In a couple of months."

"And I, Pokey Mobers, will be right there in the front row."

"We're not going to have that kind of wedding. Pam wants to keep it small and intimate. Just relatives and some of her closest friends. I'm not even telling most of my relatives about it until it's over."

"But I've never been to a wedding before."

"It'd just bore you, Pokey. Pam's going to give a big party after we've settled in and she gets the house fixed up. You're both invited."

Pokey sat back and drummed his fingers on the table. Then he stood up. He felt lightheaded. "I got to get back and wax those floors."

"No darts?"

"No, just waxing and buffing."

Pokey went back to the building and lost himself in buffing and waxing. Lost himself in the moan of the buffer and his song.

Not all the king's horses
Not all the king's men
They couldn't put Humpty
Together again.
Now you couldn't blame Humpty
For being down in the dumps.
Cause dearest old Humpty's
Been taking some lumps.
Been taking some lumps
He's down in the dumps.

And then the Kingfish said, "She buffed me and then she buffed me again. I was rebuffed." He was going to have to make that film someday.

***

The supervisor of maintenance knew as soon as he entered the building that something was wrong. It occurred to him as his feet went out from under him on the floor of the lobby. Someone had waxed it and the lobby floor was never, ever to be waxed.

The supervisor was not slow in getting to the root of the matter. After getting up and promising himself to stop wearing shoes with smooth soles, he found Pokey standing casually in a nearby corridor with one hand on his hip and the other hand pulling at his hair. His ear was cocked to the electric clock on the wall. The buffer was still running.

What the supervisor demanded to know was why Pokey was still in the building and if he was the one who waxed the lobby floor. Pokey asked him to be quiet. He told the supervisor that he could hear Maja coming.

One of the attendants from the ambulance also slipped on the lobby floor and the supervisor improvised a few caution signs until he could get the wax stripped. He had a lot to do before the other employees started arriving. Pokey had waxed, buffed and polished everything in sight. The attendants avoided the lobby on the way out, escorting Pokey through a side exit.

***

Pokey sat somewhere in space trying to make radio contact. "This is HFK1. Come in. Come in. Himmefahrtskommando One to Earth. Come in. Tell Rufus I'm doing my best. Think I got it licked. Think I got it licked, Rufus!"

Then Pokey picked up a Walter Cronkite news broadcast on his receiver.

"Nothing has been heard from Himmelfahrtskommando One and crew of one since radio contact was lost three days ago. The Pope has requested that people of all faiths join in praying that Pokey Mobers might somehow do the impossible and return."

Pokey Mobers was released from the hospital after five weeks. He had lost his job and was on the verge of losing his room. There was almost no money. It didn't take him long to reach the decision to reenlist in the army.

He had an awkward moment or two when he stopped by the computer complex to see Jake and Roop. He felt ashamed that he had broken down and found it hard to look them in the eye. Jake was incredulous. "You know there's a war going on and you reenlist? Vietnam is just a setup for killing black people anyway. This doesn't make a damn bit of sense. You just got out of the hospital."

"I'm okay. I'll do fine. The service really isn't that bad."

"You'll do fine! Pokey, they are killing people over there. If you need some money... I think I can help out. And I have a vacant rental property. It needs some work, but it would probably meet your needs. Just don't do this."

Pokey lifted his head and met Jake's eyes. "Don't worry. We all have our outs. Roop's got a high lottery number. You have high blood pressure. Me, it's not my time to die. With all the bad luck I've had lately, no way. I'm not due."

***

He poured her and then himself another cup of tea. She asked if he had thought of a name yet. "I was thinking that maybe a baseball name would be good. It might cheer my father up. He's a real baseball fan."

"Baseball! What's baseball have to do with my baby? Did he name you after a baseball player?"

"No, he named me after a friend of his. But it might be a nice thing to do."

"I'm not giving any baby of mine one of those ugly baseball names. We don't need any more Willies. I'm just not going to do it and that's that."

"Who said anything about Willie? Vada's a pretty name."

"What if it's a girl?"

***

It was a matter of policy that the pockets of enemy personnel killed in firefights be searched. At least a half dozen times Pokey had squatted over a body after an encounter and carried out this policy, a man he or someone else had killed. He was usually not sure who had hit whom. These searches were to be the closest thing to intimacy he would ever know. Pokey Mobers was killed with his hand in the pocket of a Vietnamese soldier. In all that time, this was the only man he was certain he had killed. He knew it as he walked out to the body. He had seen the man go down under his fire. It was as sure as he had ever been of anything.

3.1415926...

ABOUT MEL CURRIE

A native of Pittsburgh, Mel Currie earned a BA in Mathematics and Economics from Yale University and MA and PhD degrees in Mathematics from the University of Pittsburgh. He taught mathematics in the Düsseldorf public schools for several years and has held professorships in mathematics at Auburn University and the University of Richmond. His career at the National Security Agency (NSA) spanned twenty-five years. Among several positions that the author held at NSA, he was Chief of the Cryptographic Research and Design Division (The Codemakers) for a decade. Mel Currie is a recipient of the NSA Director's Distinguished Service Medal. In 2019 he received a Lifetime Achievement Award from the National Association of Mathematicians.

He is the author of the book *Mathematics: Rhyme and Reason*, which was published in 2018 jointly by the American Mathematical Society and the Mathematical Sciences Research Institute.

Made in the USA
Middletown, DE
12 December 2020